# MAN'S-EYE-VIEW
### vs.
## WOMAN'S-EYE-VIEW

Take a strong science-fiction theme and ask two well-known sf writers—one male and one female—to tackle it. That's the idea Yarbro and Scortia postulated for this anthology of all original stories, and the results are fantastic. These paired writers may have started at the same launching pad, but their stories are light-years apart. Who says men and women think alike? You can't prove it by this book!

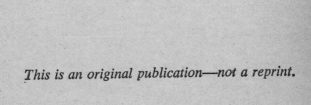

# TWO VIEWS
# OF WONDER

*Edited by*
**Thomas N. Scortia**
*and*
**Chelsea Quinn Yarbro**

BALLANTINE BOOKS • NEW YORK

SBN 345-23713-7-125

First Printing: December 1973

Printed in the United States of America

Cover art by Mati Klarwein

BALLANTINE BOOKS, INC.
201 East 50th Street, New York, N.Y. 10022

# CONTENTS

# INTRODUCTION

## "Vive laquelle difference?"

In these days of Everybody's Lib, unisex, and assaults on real and imagined sexual chauvinism, one issue has been largely ignored: that there are qualities, cultural and biological, that are uniquely "male" and uniquely "female," and these qualities affect our modes of thinking, often quite subtly. (The fundamental equality of men and women in intelligence and ability is not in question here, nor do we pose any question of differences in talent or individuality.)

But—and it is a sizeable but—we suggest that if there is some inherent difference of whatever origin, it should be reflected in the approach to storytelling. Writing is, after all, an intensely personal craft. So this is the *raison d'être* of this collection. The idea developed (as so many good writing ideas do) in extended bull/cow sessions late at night over coffee and good wine at Quinn Yarbro's opera-and-cat-infested house in Albany. This is the result.

What you have here is an experiment, testing the contrasting approaches to science fiction to see if any male/female difference can be demonstrated. The mechanics were elaborated by Scortia, Yarbro, and a third collaborator, Ma Bell, to the point where it seemed like a viable idea.

The mechanics seemed simple enough: pair a group of writers, male and female, assign them the same general story theme, and publish the results. To do this, of course, we had to develop a list of themes from which the pair could select one which appealed to both of the partners. This meant that the editors had to dip into their own idea files, a singular feat of self-cannibalization when you think about it. Done. A list of twenty-five themes, general enough to allow artistic variations and elastic enough to encourage strong development, was finally compiled.

There was some concern about the possible temptations of writers to compare notes. Our first concern was to pair writers using a certain loose rationale; for example, Joe Gores and Miriam Allen de Ford are known for their mystery fiction, and at the same time they have a wide difference of background and experience. Beyond that, we were familiar with all the writers in the anthology, and we liked and respected their work. Once this was done, and the pairing completed, we made a point of keeping the partners unknown to each other until after their stories were in our hands.

This created a new problem, since the two authors on a team could not compare preferences with each other in selecting a theme. We felt, however, that the working professional writer could respond to an assignment in which the theme was explicitly stated. Therefore, quite arbitrarily, we let either the man or the woman of the team select the theme and went to the other teammate for agreement. In some instances this process was repeated three times before a theme satisfactory to both was selected.

We tried in our selection of authors to introduce a further contrast for reader interest. We asked contributions from a number of well-established writers such as Reginald Bretnor, Miriam Allen de Ford, Harlan Ellison, etc., whose works had drawn extensive followings over the years, and where possible we paired them with relatively unknown writers.

Betty Ballantine, whose creative editorship is responsible for more than one bright new career in science fiction, heartily encouraged us in this decision. The story by Tamsin Ashe in this anthology, for instance, is only her second published story, while Michael Kurland's story marks one of his rare excursions into the short story form.

We also made an effort to develop a wide stylistic base. This explains the presence of such writers as Willo Davis Roberts, who is primarily a gothic writer, and of Joe Gores, who excels in mystery fiction.

For the reader's benefit the bare themes are presented in the back of the book. The aspiring writer may well wish to test his own creative imagination by asking how he/she would have approached the theme. The student who is interested in the creative process can follow the story from gestation to finished product. For once there is an answer to that perennial question, "Where do you get your ideas?"

Finally, our thanks to the grandest group of writers we have known. Their patience with the arbitrariness of not one but two editorial minds deserves a special mark from whoever is keeping the records of writerly virtues. Yes, even a kind word for Ma Bell, who may in the end have reaped a greater financial return from this venture than any other participant in it.

And no "thank you" is complete, of course, without a special bravo to the reader who is willing to give us his/her time and attention. We would be hard-pressed to justify our existence without this final step in this very special collaboration.

THOMAS N. SCORTIA
CHELSEA QUINN YARBRO

*San Francisco and
Albany, California
March, 1973*

# TWO VIEWS
## of
# WONDER

# JOE GORES
## and
# MIRIAM ALLEN deFORD

# FAULTY REGISTER

## Joe Gores

**Joe Gores** is a short man with steel-grey hair and the build of a Sherman tank. That he was once a weightlifting instructor is no particular surprise. He was for many years a private eye specializing in skip-tracing and automobile repossession. He writes primarily mystery or crime fiction, although he has done a number of noteworthy science fiction stories, mostly for the men's magazines. He is the author of the Edgar-winning novel **A Time of Predators** (Random House and Ballantine) and the definitive **Marine Salvage** (Doubleday). His past private-investigator activities formed the basis for the latest Random House mysteries, **Dead Skip** and **Final Notice.**

Joe, now transplanted from the bustle of San Francisco to the calm of nearby Mill Valley, has, to the regret of Mystery Writers of America members in Northern California, finally stepped down from the local chapter presidency and editorship of the chapter **Lineup.** During his period of service, he brought the Northern California Chapter of MWA national recognition for its professionalism and creativity.

Gores is referred to as "the professional's professional."

His ability to take a simple theme statement and elaborate it into the following brutal tale of a black astronaut stranded in an alternate world is ample evidence of this quality.

•

UP FROM THE GHETTO TO THE STARS. No shit, that was one of the headlines when I was picked for the mission by NASA. The first spade on Mars, from rats in the cradle to my black ass lighting up the firmaments. Something else entirely.

But we missed.

Dig it, man, whatever you look like who's reading this, in whatever millennium of whatever crazy universe you inhabit: we missed Mars. Which makes it a hell of a drive to the next off-ramp.

"Honey. Wake up."

"Huh?"

"Wake up." Clemmie's voice. "You're having that dream again."

I sat up in bed, nude and sweating. Moonlight through the open window silvered Clemmie's dark and lovely breasts. Of course I'm talking about *this* Clemmie. Here. This not-quite-Clemmie in this not-quite California in this not-quite. . . .

"It isn't any dream, lady. I'm *not* the Zeke Dooley you think I am."

She put a hand on me. I reacted—hell, I'm only human. She giggled. "You *act* like Zeke, honey."

I spent half an hour acting like Zeke, while she acted like Clemmie. *My* Clemmie, back in *my* California, same flashing dark eyes full of bawdy promise, same smooth brown hide turning feverish under my caresses. So why *not* Clemmie?

Because, goddammit, we missed Mars.

Three of us on the flight: Major Long, USAF, mission captain; Jackson, USN, astronaut; Dooley, civilian, computer engineer, token black. Long and Jackson are dead; I'm alive because I was back checking out the reentry vehicle. No memorable last words; they'd never incise on a tombstone what was said back and forth over the intercom—even if there were anything left to put under it.

"Son of a bitch, anyway." Long, big sandy-haired cat with an Indiana twang with, then, only irritation in his voice. "We've lost contact with Houston Control."

"We've also lost Mars," said Jackson. Concern in his voice.

I thought they were putting me on because I wasn't a regular astronaut, merely an election-year token. But there was a sudden frightened awe in Jackson's voice.

"Mars is just ... gone. As if a cloud has drifted between us and it. But ... there can't be any clouds where there isn't any atmosphere. Can there?"

"Everything's dead," said Long in a terribly conversational voice. "Everything's just gone—"

Tremendous slam of naked force, a rending of metals, the reentry vehicle with me encapsulated inside was ripped out of the womb of the mothership like a foetus aborted in a high-speed crash. I was staring at the deformed remains a dozen feet, three hundred yards, a mile away as we moved on divergent courses. The spaceship became a silver pencil, stretched to a thread like molten glass, was a ray of light, then was rammed down into zero volume, into infinite density. Gone, through the black hole into the time-space singularity which I had somehow escaped.

"I just don't *understand*!" cried Clemmie doggedly over post-coital coffee. She wanted me to be *her* Ezechiel Dooley. "If you're not him, then—"

"Then he's a pinhead of crushed matter somewhere else, or has taken my place in *my* universe—"

She burst out, "Oh, Zeke, see the medics! *Please*! You *are* Zeke, *my* Zeke, and—"

I was shaking my head.

"For one millisecond in time, Clemmie, our alternate universes brushed wings. And two spaceships, at the rims of their respective universes—"

"But how can two universes coexist without ... without—"

"A universe is a vast closed system. So vast that no light can escape. So until they actually touched, neither would know that the other was there."

"Oh, Zeke!" she wailed.

Coffee cups dumped on the floor, hands all over each other. Only when our bodies were mated could she totally believe in me.

But she couldn't *disbelieve*, either. Clemmie's point was that *if* our universes were identical even if coexistent, then how did I know I was in a different world from my own in the first place? I tried to explain it as faulty register.

"See this picture?" I picked up the *TV Guide* from the coffee table and pointed to the cover. "This required four separate color runs. One of them was just a little bit off, see? The color isn't just exactly where it's supposed to be in relation to the other three. In printing that's known as *faulty register*. Just a little blurred. Like this universe is to me ..."

She was the only one I ever tried to convince. I'd learned something was wrong almost immediately, right after the press conference when they'd finished the reentry vehicle with me in it from the ocean. Until then, dig, I'd thought I'd somehow made it back to earth in some sort of amnesiac blackout which prevented me from remembering the solitary months of the return voyage.

It was General Harginson, Chief of Mission, who started it when I was back in the debriefing area.

"You made some remarkable statements out there, Dooley."

"I've had a remarkable experience."

He turned from the window of the small cell-like room. "Why did you refer to yourself as a black man, Dooley?"

Was this dude trying to put me on? I didn't have to take his sass, I was *civilian,* man.

"We can use Negro if you prefer, general. Colored if you're old-fashioned. Darkie if you're a Mormon. Maybe even spade, if you smile when you say it. But—"

He was shaking his head. "You know that all racial differences were ended by decree over a century ago."

I put my black arm up next to his white one. I also mentally rehearsed where the door was, just in case. He was into his sixties but he was big. If he got violent...

"Black ... white. See, general? Simon Legree chasing little Liza across the ice floe?" I did a minstrel buck-and-wing, ended up on a knee with my hand out in the Jolson manner. "Mammy?"

"Men with different colored skins, Dooley?" It was the general who had edged toward the safety of the door. "Unthinkable. Absolutely unthinkable."

Two extra weeks of medical tests looking for the loose screws. If it hadn't been that I was able to talk to Clemmie by intercom from the isolation trailer, see her through the thick glass seal, I'd have thought it was some sort of Rip Van Winkle jazz. You know, man, waking up twenty years later and all that. But the newspapers confirmed what the Harginson episode had already suggested. This *was* a world different from the one I'd left. No stories of international tensions. No race riots or prison breaks. No unemployment figures. No crime news.

And yet there was Clemmie, finally come to pick me up from the medical isolation and take me home. Goddammit, *my* Clemmie, you dig? Voice, face, eyes, *everything.* But *not* Clemmie. Couldn't be, because I was in the wrong place. After we'd embraced and kissed, I said, just to test the theory I'd started developing, "Let's drive through the ghetto on the way home."

She burst out laughing.

"I swear, Zeke, they should have kept you locked up for *another* two weeks. Ghetto! You know very well the decree against poverty is nearly a hundred years old—ever since they abolished capitalism—"

"Not a time warp," I said sadly. "Another universe."

Shot through a goddam wormhole from one universe to another. Coexisting, similar, but not mine. Clemmie stopped the car in front of a double for my own familiar house. Her big black eyes looked at me in sudden solemnity.

"Zeke, you been having fun with me, and from what those space agency people said you had fun with them, too. But ... Zeke ... not when we're alone, honey. It ... gives me a scary feeling."

"What color are we, Clemmie? You and me?"

"Color?" She started to giggle. "*People* color."

A honky woman was wheeling a baby carriage by on the sidewalk. It was getting on toward dusk, but there was enough light to see *that*.

"Are we the same color she is?"

Clemmie looked. She nodded, sort of solemn-like. I sighed.

"Then there's no difference between her and us."

"There's no difference between anybody and anybody, Zeke. Why ... why, if differences between people were allowed, that would mean there were *inequalities* between people. And that would be—"

"Yeah." I'd been hearing the word a good deal during my debriefing, so I used it. "Unthinkable."

So here I was, man, where they'd just about solved 'em all. Racism. Poverty. The Protestant work-ethic. Crime.

No racism, because it was unthinkable that men could be born with any inequalities between them. Dig? No poverty, because there was no private property. No unemployment, because everybody who worked, worked for the state. But you didn't really have to work. You could do your own thing. No pigs, of course, because there were no jails to put people in and nobody to arrest anyway, because there weren't any criminals.

"What if I went next door and zonked old what's-his-face—Jennings—on toppa his bald pate?"

"*That* wouldn't be a crime!" Clemmie laughed. "That would be the unvolitional action of a clinically disturbed man. You'd need help—"

"So would Jennings."

Not the point, dig? The state would take care of *both* of us—or Jennings' widow if it came to that. He would be succored, I would be cured of my anti-social illness.

"Cured how?" I asked cautiously.

"Therapy, of course." She giggled at me. "Sometimes I almost believe you *are* from a different universe. . . ."

Clinically disturbed. If you did anything criminal you were ill, not evil—because where there is no personal responsibility there can be no morality. Or immorality.

The perfect society, man. Racism, crime, guilt, all unthinkable. Heaven on earth.

Except for the Hour of Release.

It was the night after we'd had that discussion about whapping old man Jennings next door on the head. I suppose that was what got her thinking about it, but anyway Clemmie turned on the big color TV. I'd had it on a time or two in the afternoon, but it'd been what you could expect when a creative enterprise is being run by state bureaucrats. This was different.

"Hey! Cops and robbers!" I sat down on the couch beside Clemmie and put an arm around her shoulders. It was a chase sequence, with the heroine being threatened by . . .

"It's the Hour of Release," she said in a hushed voice. She had sweat on her upper lip. "They're going to get her."

"If they do, it'll be the first time in the history of TV."

"Get her," Clemmie repeated.

The girl was a slender fox in her twenties, the baddies were like out of an old Nazi movie, big and blond and hard-faced and wearing trenchcoats. Industrial sort of streets, but then I realized it was inside a deserted factory. The chick was a good actress, really terrified-seeming, throwing these wide-eyed looks over her shoulders. But the baddies knew their business. I settled down for the hero to show up.

"Get her get her get her." Clemmie was almost chanting it.

Man, they got her. I mean, they really *got* her. One of them finally trapped her, and then suddenly came up with this long thin knife and slashed her right across the face with it. She went down, yelling. Suddenly the second one was tearing her panties off.

I tried to keep the shock out of my face. The one with the knife was *banging* her, right there on the TV screen! Banging her in fifty million homes!

"Do it do it do it," chanted Clemmie.

He not only did it, he held her so the other one could do it, too. Finally the second cat started moaning and thrashing around on her and then, through clenched teeth, got out a single word you could hear even through the noise she was making.

"Now!" he said.

The knife plunged into her throat. Her screams cut off into wet gurgles. Blood sprayed over the two rapists, so realistically that it made me feel sick. I looked over at Clemmie, mouth open to say something unbelieving, and then I *really* felt sick. She was making it, too, right along with the guy mounted on the fox in the movie.

She caught my eyes on her, suddenly put her head down and the tears came, a real case of hysterics.

"They murdered her!" she screamed. "Oh, I'm so ashamed!"

I finally caught it. Hour of Release.

That's right, man, it had to come out somewhere. Nobody responsible, nobody guilty—they'd been able to *logically* convince people that nothing was forbidden, nothing was wrong, but something inside the people still didn't believe it.

Hitler tried the same thing with the Master Race. Just a matter of logistics, transport X units here, dispose of Y units there. The Nazis really *believed,* man. But when the Allies were coming in, they tried to obliterate the camps. It was more than just fear. It was guilt. Shame.

Here, the Hour of Release. Revel in innocence destroyed. Enjoy vicarious rape, murder, torture through the actors. Come out cleansed, released, purged.

Get an orgasm out of it, on the house.

To my shame, Clemmie got a second orgasm out of me, on the floor in front of the now-dark TV twenty minutes after her hysterics had stopped. It was the closest to rape I've ever had done to me.

"I'm just sleepy," she said in a sweet sated voice against the hollow of my throat when I mentioned my shame afterwards.

I sat up on the rug. "How ... often do they run that damned thing?"

"Eleven to midnight seven nights a week."

"Is it the same every—"

"Of course not, silly."

"Ah ... How often do you watch it, Clemmie?"

"Whenever I feel ... oh, *you* know!" She giggled. "I watched it a lot while you were gone on the Mars-shot."

My trouble was, once the shock value had passed, I couldn't get caught up in the Hour of Release. I could be disgusted, or nauseated, but rationally I knew it was just actors and bladders of chicken blood and special effects, and there was no dramatic illusion to carry me beyond that knowledge to emotional involvement. For one thing, nobody ever defended himself. For another, no plots, just unvarying awful destruction: blood and death and torture. Screams, groans, shrieks.

The illusion was even less compelling when I started to recognize actors. I hadn't again caught the big-eyed fox who'd "died" that first night, but the knife-wielder of that show was finally written into a script as a victim. He and three others had just started torturing a woman in lace scanties when she stepped out of her bonds and pointed at him.

"Take him!" she commanded the others.

"No!" he said. He was holding out his hands in sudden supplication, backing away from the camera. "You must not! I am one of you! I—"

"Random selection," intoned the girl.

"The computer never lies," said one of the other baddies.

They crushed his thighs under a truck wheel. While he was screaming, they castrated him.

"Doesn't anyone *ever* object to these things?"

Clemmie was wiping her eyes after a nice cathartic cry while the cat bled to death. "Who ... who could ... object? It makes you feel so ... cleansed."


At the Space Center, I'd been able casually to get a look at the Mission Blueprint for the flight *this* earth's Zeke Dooley had gone out on. Same day, hour, second as my flight from *my* earth. Same crew, Long and Jackson and Dooley. So who would ever believe I was from an alternate universe? Not even Clemmie, the only one I'd tried my theory out on.

So here I was, and never going to get back, so why not lean back and enjoy it? Accept *this* Clemmie as *my* Clemmie, learn to swallow the Hour of Release as a cathartic, and try to overlook the differences from my own universe.

Right on, man. But when I got home from work that night, just as dusk was switching the streetlights on, a young dude in mod clothes ran into me on the sidewalk in front of the house.

"We know," he said quickly, helping me up. "We will try to contact you again when your . . . grief has subsided. Remember my face."

Then he was gone, down the sidewalk with a rather swishy walk that was very distinctive from the rear. I went up the front walk with my head in a whirl. *We know. Who* knew? What did they know? That I was from another universe? *When your grief has subsided.* What grief?

"How's your wife, Mr. Dooley?"

It was old man Jennings, out in his yard looking over his roses for aphids.

"Fine, I guess. Why?"

"The ambulance took her away about four o'clock. I thought . . . I'd hoped . . ." He had a stiff embarrassed look on his face. "I'm sorry. I'm truly sorry . . ."

It was like getting socked in the gut, entering the empty house. What could have happened? A fall? A sudden illness? Then who had called for help? Why hadn't I been notified at the Space Center? I went over and banged on Jennings' door, but he'd either gone out or wouldn't answer it.

Emergency services, that was it. Police rescue units. Private ambulance companies. Hospitals.

No police. No private ambulances. Neither one existed in this society. But there were hospitals, government ambulance dispatch centers, fire department emergency units.

An hour later I had nothing. Nobody had dispatched any ambulance to our address. Nobody had admitted a patient with Clemmie's name. Describing her when I got down to calling about unidentified accident victims didn't do any good, either. Young black women since four o'clock, sir? There aren't any black women, sir. There aren't any blacks.

Of course there *were,* but everyone in this idiot society

had been so conditioned to believe that everybody was the same that they couldn't see the difference. Differences of race, for everyone but me, had ceased to exist.

I started in on the neighbors, ringing doorbells. Did you see an ambulance pull up at the Dooley house? *That* house. Right over there. You did? Did the ambulance have a name, a number, any . . .

Nothing to identify it at all. But everyone very sympathetic, almost solicitous. "I'm sorry. I'm truly sorry . . ."

As if they'd done it themselves.

The swishy young man returned to my mind. *We know. We will try to contact you again when your grief has subsided. Remember my face . . .*

Clemmie must have been *really* sick, taken bad. Something highly contagious, maybe, so they'd had to isolate her? Take her to a special medical facility that wasn't publicly listed?

That reminded me of my own medical isolation under the space program, so I called the duty officer to get Harginson's home phone.

—The general is unavailable, sir.

—This is an emergency, damn you.

—Sorry, sir.

But an hour later Harginson called me. "Duty officer's been through on the blower, Dooley," he barked. "Something about an emergency . . ."

I poured out the whole story for him. When I'd finished he was strangely silent. Then he gave a long sigh.

"Unmarked ambulance, interns without insignia on their hospital whites to show what institution they were from . . ." Another pause. "What damned rotten luck, man. After everything you've been through! But . . . well . . . We both know it's just random, don't we? And . . . well . . . I can only say I'm sorry, Dooley. Truly sorry . . ."

I killed a bottle and slept on the couch.

I was brushing my teeth and wondering if four aspirin

would help my head, and wondering what in God's name I could do to find Clemmie, when the doorbell rang. He was an early thirties type with crisp wavy hair cut almost painfully tight to his skull and sideburns that damned near cleared the tops of his ears. The eyes of a shark.

"Mr. Dooley? I'm Doctor Mauvais—"

I was dragging him in by the arm. "How is she, doc? *Where* is she? What's the matter? What happened—"

"I don't have anything to do with that." He gently disengaged his arm and led me into my own living room. "I know how you feel, I really do. Believe me, it's my job to understand what tension and pressure can do to a man. But you must understand that in this case there's nothing I can do. Nothing *anyone* can do. As you know, the computer never lies."

I could have squeezed the bastard's neck until his eyes popped out—*wanted* to, in fact—but he was the first person I'd talked to who would even admit knowing that Clemmie existed.

"When can I see her?" I said.

He gave me an odd look; then a speculative, almost feverish look came into his eyes. He said almost lasciviously, "Tonight." Then he was suddenly all business. "But right now, we want to know about the disturbed individual who contacted you last night. Young, slender person, with a slightly feminine way of walking. We would like very much to know what he said to you."

Who the hell was *we*? But I didn't ask. I didn't want to antagonize him; he knew something about Clemmie. Even so, I was careful to make my voice thoughtful, and screwed up my face as if in remembering. This cat Mauvais was starting to smell like pig to me, whatever he called himself.

"Ah . . . He said something like, 'We know. We'll . . . ah . . . get in touch with you after your grief is over.' Something like that."

Mauvais was leaning forward with an intense look on his face.

"Are you *sure* that's all he said?"

I put on my act again. "Oh. Yeah. He told me to remember what he looked like."

"As if you would be seeing him again?"

"Something like that."

He stood up, all smiles, looking very satisfied as if he had confirmed something. He told me I'd been very cooperative and started for the door. When he was there, I called to him.

"Doc, about my wife—"

"It will be tonight, Mr. Dooley." Again that simper on the face. "Enjoy yourself."

It was the longest day I've lived. What do you do, man? Clemmie ... *somewhere*. Sick with ... *something*. Supposed to see her tonight ... *sometime*.

They'd probably come and take me to her, I decided. Probably after six o'clock—Mauvais had said *tonight*. I wanted to call Harginson to find out if he knew anything about Doctor Mauvais, but was afraid to tie up the phone that long in case they tried to reach me with the news where I might see my wife.

Sure, okay, my almost-wife on this almost-earth, but I was beyond that sort of distinction with Clemmie now. She was *my* Clemmie.

Six o'clock. Nothing. By seven I'd been on the front porch twice to ring my own bell, making sure it was working. By eight, I'd started calling the weather bureau, just to hear the first words of the taped message and hang up. It confirmed that the phone was working. By nine, I'd had my topcoat on and off a dozen times.

Ten-thirty. Those rotten bastards weren't going to call. I was walking around the living room actually wringing my hands. I stopped dead. What if she was ... What if ... if Mauvais was on his way right now to tell me she'd died,

his young earnest face long with lightly-felt sorrow? What
if . . .

I made myself switch on the TV, sit down on the couch,
crouched forward on the front edge of the cushion. I had
to get hold of myself. Lights and colors blared. Shit.
Eleven-twenty, right in the middle of The Hour of Release. Just what I needed right then.

It was a trial scene, ending hurriedly so they could get
down to the chemical blood. The camera looked past the
black defendant up at the three judges behind their massive polished desk. They wore powdered wigs and red
satin-lined capes and were pulling on domino masks. Their
movements were stylized, so they had the cadenced
formality of ritual.

"YOU ARE GUILTY!" The one in the middle had a
fine rolling voice to which I listened despite myself. "THE
SENTENCE IS DEATH." The voice got almost arch.
"BY WHATEVER MEANS THE EXECUTIONERS
CAN DEVISE."

I went to the front door, opened it on a street lying
quiet and serene under the lamps. Where in God's name
*were* they? If nobody had come by midnight, I'd start
tearing things apart to get hold of that nasty little bastard
Mauvais.

On TV, the scene had shifted to a medieval-style dungeon. Black-clad torturers fluttered around the condemned
fox like evil moths, stripping her and fondling her crudely
exposed private parts. Taken with available light in long
shot, the scene had a formalized nightmare quality like
Doré etchings of Dante's hell.

I ran my little weather-check on the phone. Still live. I
tested the front bell. Still live.

They had fastened the nude victim to the rack. The
camera moved in to caress her body from breasts to knees
as she was strapped down. One of the torturers, nude under his robe, began enjoying her sexually. It aroused me,
sending me to the front porch sick and shaken at my own

reaction. With Clemmie missing, sick in God-knows-what institution . . .

Cool air swept over me, laden with the delicate fragrances of Jennings' roses. The bald-headed old bastard probably was glued to the Hour of Release like damned near everyone else on the block.

As if on cue, behind me sudden harsh shrieks of agony started. They drew me back to the living room. I could almost smell the burned flesh as the branding iron bit into her flat smooth belly. She yelled again, her body jerking and writhing as if from an electrical charge.

The man who'd sexually pleasured himself upon her now was bending over her breasts, seizing one in his left hand. He held a knife in his right hand. His body hid the hand as it began making sawing motions. Her screams filled my ears. The man with the poker had gotten another glowing red.

The camera panned across him as he lunged forward with it between her spraddled legs, across the second man as he came erect waving something bloody aloft in his left hand, to zoom in on her dying face. Her mouth was strained impossibly wide, emitting an unformed animal sound of agony. My own mouth gaped with hers, my own formless screams echoed hers. Bloody froth bubbled up from between her gaping jaws. I fell forward to my knees on the rug. I began gently beating the floor with my fists. Someone had the conscience to be crying uncontrollably. I felt the tears on my face.

Mauvais. *Tonight you can see your wife. Enjoy yourself.* Knowing, he had assumed that I knew also, and wanted to watch Clemmie die.

Without moving my face, I was sick on the rug.

Hatred is a clean emotion, it burns as bright as thermite. Especially when it is mixed with a terror almost atavistic. But how do you get at them when a whole world has deluded itself into thinking that man is only a shaped charge fashioned by environment, and is never responsible if the nitro is joggled too hard and explodes?

A whole world knowing that nightly it witnesses real deaths, real agonies, real tortures, real perversions of mind and spirit. And approving, under the delusion that man cannot choose evil. Only Zeke Dooley, interstellar interloper farted by his universe through a black hole, had been in ignorance. Only Zeke Dooley had disapproved.

But wait a minute. *We will try to contact you again when your grief has subsided. Remember my face.*

The words took on new meaning. He had known Clemmie had been taken. Had been seeking to recruit me into ... what? Some underground opposition which recoiled from the stench of roasting flesh and the howls of the victims? I could only wait until I saw him again.

I saw him the night after Clemmie's death. I saw him die on The Hour of Release. I had tuned in because that broadcast was the enemy, naked and exposed. His hypocrisies, his thought processes, the guts of what made him work. So I was watching when my only contact with the underground died. Horribly. I remembered his face, all right, even though he had no eyes left to see the ruin his body had become before he finally expired.

I knew despair. How had they found him? From what I had told them? But Mauvais had acted as if he already knew what we had said in the brief exchange. But that would mean "Doctor" Mauvais was really ... Sure, of course, someone in security police under a more palatable disguise. As medical men, those supposed to succor mankind. That was when the hatred took direction. Mauvais. And his masters.

So they'd already had the fruiter revolutionary under surveillance. Then why hadn't they picked him up before? And how had they known what we had said when ...

Wait a minute. Maybe there was routine surveillance of *everyone*. Visual and audio sensors to monitor *everything*. That was it. I had only to look, with an engineer's eye, and I saw them everywhere: every lightpost carried its scanners, almost every light socket. Inside the houses and out. I wondered if the average citizen knew—or cared.

Somewhere there were men who *did* care. But how to reach them? How to communicate without being observed and ruthlessly destroyed? You're a computer engineer, Zeke baby. Be logical. *Analyse.* I dig it, daddy. First step: *identify* your potential allies. Second: figure out a way to contact them.

Step one was easy. Four days after Clemmie's death, I was standing before an anonymous desk in an anonymous government office. Behind the desk was Mauvais.

"You aren't going to be difficult, are you, Mr. Dooley, because your wife was one of those chosen by the computer for The Hour of Release? I assure you I regret the fact deeply, but ... it *is* a random selection which no man can change."

A random selection like the revolutionary who died a couple of nights ago? I put on my quizzical look. In the world I had come from, brother, spades learned early how to dissimulate.

"Difficult, Dr. Mauvais?"

"Blaming me or my department for your wife's unfortunate demise." He swung a languid hand at a file on his desk. "Nothing in your *dossier* suggests such emotional illness, but ..."

Nothing in my *dossier,* baby, because I ain't in it. I ain't in *anybody's* personnel file in this horror of a world, baby. I leaned forward, sincerity gleaming in my eyes. Old Bojangles, dancin' for them nickels.

"Nothing like that, Dr. Mauvais. I want to join your department."

It shook him. It really did. He cleared his throat. "That is ... an unusual request, Mr. Dooley. The first we've had from a survivor of one of the ... selectees. Might I ask why?"

"I watched that night, when Clemmie got it," I said.

Avidity entered his face. "And?"

"I realized I'd enjoyed it."

It was there in his face. He was going to explore it. Triumph sang in my temples like hypertension. I was going to end up a security agent, because he was going to find me the most apt pupil he'd ever had.

Security. The people with the power, because they had the *files*. The files of those who opposed the state's designs. The people I needed to contact.

Once I knew *who*, I still had to think of *how*. How, when the state's electronic ears and eyes were everywhere listening, watching, probing? There might be a way. It would depend on getting in good with Mauvais first, convincing him I was as sick as he was. It would mean zestfully spiriting away and killing the innocent. But once I had access to those files, once I was on the *other* side of those scanners . . .

I might just have figured out the blind spot.

Exactly six months ago tonight, Clemmie died. Tonight the first test of the blind spot will take place. I am sitting beside Mauvais right now, in his office. Waiting. He doesn't know that, of course. He thinks I am here merely to sip his brandy and listen to his tales of torture. He is head of security, he is the one who chooses who will die while passing it off to his superiors as computer selection. He saw Clemmie on the street one day, and coveted her. His joy is in destroying whatever his aesthetic sense finds beautiful. And so she died.

Oh, yes, we have talked about it. Often. I have become much more than underling and apt pupil. I have become a friend. I would like to sink my teeth into his jugular. He is describing his reactions when he dressed up as a torturer (complete with domino mask to disguise his features) so he could disembowel a twelve-year-old boy on television.

"When I plunged my hand into his intestines, I felt so

much empathy that I dirtied my pants. Isn't that interesting?"

"Fascinating," I say. Practice has made me able to say it with no tinge of sarcasm, with utter sincerity. He sighs with contentment.

"You have a brilliant future with this department, Zeke."

"Thank you, Doctor."

My eye is on one of a dozen monitors banked across his office wall. *The* monitor. The one on which the test will appear. Twelve men involved, all of them now dead. Three blacks, three yellows, three whites, three browns, hoarded carefully by me from the victims that *had* been computer-chosen. Doing what I told them for the camera, mistakenly believing it would save their lives.

It hadn't. My secret had died with them. I hope.

"Don't you ever regret leaving the Space Agency, Zeke?" he asked.

"Not for a single moment," I reply.

So many things unthinkable on this planet. Races, for one. No blacks or browns or yellows or whites here to anyone's eye but mine. Unthinkable. So I'd shot the little strip of film, developed it myself, trading outrageously on my favored status with Mauvais, the all-powerful Director of Health Services. Had fed the cartridge of film into the live coverage coming over this scanner. Seeing it, Mauvais would believe it was actually taking place on the rapid transit station platform that scanner covered.

"Why not?" he probes, wallowing in it. I look at him with limpid sincerity, thinking that his hide would make a wonderful lamp shade.

I begin, "Well . . ."

I pause. On the monitor, my film is starting. My twelve doomed players, acting as if their lives depend on their performance. Sorry, boys.

"Well, what?" he asks pleasantly, reaching for his brandy snifter.

"What's happening on monitor seven?" I ask.

Mauvais, soulless bastard, looks up sharply. I cast an eye toward him. He is staring, unbelieving. My actors have begun milling around at the door of one of the rapid transit units.

"They're fighting!" Mauvais exclaims. No one fights here. They've been conditioned out of belief in their aggressions.

Mauvais half-rises from his chair to contact security agents. I turn up the sound of monitor seven very loud, so we can hear the voices.

"Watch where you're going, nigger!"

"You goddam slant, who do you think—"

The epithets fill our ears. I look over at Mauvais. He is settling back, his placid, contemplative look returning.

"Kike!"

"Jig!"

"Honky!"

"Wop!"

Fists are thudding on faces. Mauvais is sniffing his brandy, swirling it in the cupped crystal to release its aroma most fully.

"You were saying you don't regret leaving the Space Agency—"

Freud, with his usual genius for misnomers, called it *negative hallucinations*. Another Viennese, Breuer, didn't do much better with *hysterical conversion*. Misleading, both terms. Nothing hallucinatory or hysterical about it. Moebius used *vacancy in consciousness*. Better. Better yet, *deliberate amnesia of defense*.

"Hebe!"

"Chink!"

Thud thud thud.

Today it's called *denial*.

Denial. A defense mechanism by which the conscious mind refuses to accept something the subconscious tells it is true. So the subconscious obligingly buries it. As if it had never happened. It was happening right in front of Mauvais, but he wasn't seeing it. For him it wasn't hap-

pening. While it was going on, anybody could say anything
to anyone, could plan anything—and he wouldn't see it.
*No* one would, not one of those over-conditioned security
guards manning the scanners. Meets could be set up, actions planned, right in front of the scanners, as long as
something this society had been conditioned to think was
unthinkable occurred around the meet so the observers
would go into a psychological state of denial.

"Spade!"

"Dago!"

"Greaser!"

"Coolie!"

Everyone trained by the state to believe there are no
races, cannot be any, cannot be any difference between
men, either. No poverty, no prejudice, no aggression, no
personal responsibility, no moral guilt.

So you cannot afford to admit it, even when you see it.
You refuse to admit you saw it. It isn't there. You refuse
to accept—*denial*—the situation, the fact, the sight, which
upsets your preconceptions. Because to admit that situation or fact or sight would cause you grief, humiliate you,
bring you extreme emotional pain.

"You were saying, Zeke?" repeats Mauvais courteously.

I swirl the brandy in my own snifter. Next week I will
contact the underground. I already know them, their
names, their haunts, their descriptions. And now I know
*how* to go about it. Through the prejudices of this preju-
dice-free society we outlaws will destroy them all.

And among the first to go . . .

"I was going to say," I tell Mauvais, "that I can't con-
ceive of enjoying anything more than I will these next
months. . . ."

Among the first, Mauvais. He's dead, that mother-
fucker, he just doesn't know it yet. Doesn't know that the
computer—now serviced by bad-ass Zeke Dooley—is
going to randomly select Doctor Anton Mauvais as the
subject of an evening's sport on The Hour of Release.

# LONE WARRIOR

### Miriam Allen deFord

The incredible **Miriam Allen deFord** began her writing career before the First World War and hasn't stopped since that time. Now in her eighties, she bids fair to be going strong when the next century rolls around.

An independent and strong-willed woman from the beginning, Miriam worked at jobs that were considered tabu for most women till the present day. She has been a labor reporter and an insurance claims adjuster, and in the heyday of the pulps in the thirties she provided material for almost every title on the stand, be it horror, science fiction, detective, or romance. She is noted today as much for her mystery writing as for her science fiction, and is a respected member of both MWA and SFWA. Her books on Bonnie and Clyde and on Ma Barker were stringent tonics to those people influenced by the romanticized versions of those grisly lives.

But then, horror and tight situations have never thrown Miriam—as witness the following.

•

So this was to be her punishment: not a dungeon for life, like Nick; not a fatal electric bolt, like Esther or a double dose of strychnine, like Matt; not even a lobotomy, like poor Gerald; but to be chained to this chair facing the screen, her hands and feet bound, her eyes fixed open with adhesive tape, forced to watch the three-dimnsional colored action while They tortured Hal until at last he could die. They were as ingenious as They were cruel; each of them was alloted the least endurable penalty.

Ellen sat grimly silent, her whole being concentrated on not letting a cry or a tear escape her, not giving in one inch while Their agents watched avidly for her to collapse, to beg for mercy for her lover. Never!—any more than Hal would let out a single name or word. The raid had broken up the underground cell forever, but there were still comrades somewhere, though the somewhere was unknown, and she would join them and keep on fighting. Her jaws ached as she ground her teeth to keep the horror, the agony, the fury inside.

There were three of them against Hal. He was naked; there were bruises and scabs from the beating during the raid. They threw him down, kicked him in the face with heavy boots till blood spurted from his nose. They dragged him up again and bent him backward over the table, tormented him with electric charges up his anus and against his scrotum. They kept yelling deafeningly at him: "Confess, you swine! Confess! Who gives you your orders? Who are your leaders?" Hal, dead white and streaked with blood, never opened his mouth. They opened it for him and knocked his front teeth out one by one.

It went on for hours. When he fainted they revived him and began again. One of Them took hold of his right arm and broke it against the table edge; Ellen could hear the bones crack.

The lovely body she had felt so often on and in hers. The body she had kissed so many times. They pulled his hair out in bunches with tweezers where it would hurt the worst; one eye—oh, Hal's beautiful dark blue eyes—lay like a gob of jelly on a cheek slippery with blood.

They themselves tired and called in fresh torturers to keep it up. Every time Hal fell to the floor unconscious Ellen prayed frantically to anything—any god, any devil, any element of compassion anywhere—that this would be the end. It went on and on.

It seemed an eternity. But at last it was over. Hal lay in a crushed heap on the floor and could not be aroused again. One of them bent over the broken body, felt the pulse, the heart. He shrugged. Hal had escaped them. He was dead.

The screen went dark. The tape was ripped savagely from her eyes, the chains unfastened, leaving open wounds where they had bound her so tightly. She was pulled to her numb feet, hardly able to stand on her shaky legs.

What next? Nothing. They thrust her through the unlocked door into the silent street. She was free. But only through communication with another of the secret cells of the Movement could she fight back against the enemy.

Not one of her own group had given in. Except for Nick in his dungeon, the mindless vegetable that used to be Gerald, and herself cast out with nowhere to go, they were all dead. She alone was left to seek for vengeance. But vengeance was impossible for a solitary guerilla fighter; only an underground group—a cell—could plan and execute it. So the immediate objective must be to find and join another cell.

How? She was not a trained evader of the universal electronic surveillance; Gerald had been their expert for that. But she had a good mind: she could learn—technically untrained though she was, she *must* learn.

She had had courses in elementary chemistry and physics, like everybody else, but now she must go far beyond them. She had the incentive; she must acquire the power. She could of course deactivate a simple bug or tap or viewer, but They were more devious and complicated than that.

First, however, she must find a place to hide in. Cell headquarters, disguised as a commune pad, had been a good cover, but the building had belonged to Nick, so she dared not approach it under its new owner.

It took four days, hiding under an assumed name in a cheap hotel, snatching hurried furtive meals in its coffee shop, before she found a crummy room where the landlady did not seem to recognize her. Even so, it was dangerous—she had been seen and heard so often in vids of demonstrations and protests—but she had to sleep somewhere.

She holed up there and searched night and day for a plan.

It was obvious that most of the female tenants in the house were prostitutes; the walls were thin and Ellen could hear. For a while she toyed with fantasy—she would join them (what did it matter about her body now that Hal was horribly dead?), and perhaps a few cautious words dropped to a customer would reveal him as "one of ours." But that was silly: she had no notion of how to pick up a trick or exactly how to act afterwards. Besides, Movement men didn't go to prostitutes; they slept with comrades, female or male according to their bent. Gerald and Esther had been lovers as she and Hal had been. Everybody knew Nick and Matt had a thing between them. (Nick must be going through agonies now trying not to think of the dreadful convulsions of strychnine poisoning. Knowing Them, she wouldn't put it past Them to infest his dungeon with rats and then feed them strychnine before his eyes.)

It was like a problem in algebra: Let A represent the listen-bugs, B the random beam intrusions, C the enormous file of details in everybody's dossier. Then X would be the present whereabouts of somebody, anybody, in one of the hidden, secret cells. The trouble was that no feasible way seemed to add up to proof of X.

Sometimes when they were planning a project they had given it an alias to conceal its nature. Procuring arms against a rumored raid would be known as "preventing a hydrofoil accident." Ellen wasn't sure whether the same vocabulary was employed throughout the Movement, or whether each phrase was peculiar to one cell alone. Suppose she inserted a 'personal' in the daily newstapes, asking for any witnesses of a hydrofoil accident on the date of the raid? No, They would know there had been no such accident, and They would be alerted and hunt for her and find her. There was nothing worse They could do to her than what she had endured, which was why They had set her free to brood upon it as long as she lived, but if she got a response from the advertisement They could nab whomever responded.

She ought to kill herself, Ellen thought; it would be a blessed relief. But she couldn't; she was a dedicated member of the Movement, and as long as there was the faintest possibility of becoming enmeshed in its activities again she had no right to destroy a life that might be of use and value.

If the members had some secret means of identification on their persons, then she could post herself somewhere beside a street corner and watch every passer-by. But of course they hadn't; it would be too hazardous. Nonsensically she began wishing they *looked* alike. They didn't—they were old and young, tall and short, white and black and brown and yellow. Even They had never been able to spot a Movement member by looks alone.

If only ESP were real! Then she could have communicated, so to speak, by remote control. But even if there were truth in it, Ellen did not have the gift; she could not even receive, and certainly could not send. In any case, Movement members were apt to be purely logical, pragmatic people. That way was out—far out.

How, then? She racked her brain. She had never been a creative thinker, just a steady devoted, intelligent one.

For this very reason wasn't she, Ellen pondered, best adapted to approach the problem in terms of fundamentals? Specialists become too specialized, generalized forms evolve.

But there was another avenue to success. The enemy contemptuously failed to plant spies in the Movement, but Ellen knew that at other times in other places there had been infiltration by their own side, and it had been a highly successful maneuver. She was not afraid: nothing They could do to her would be worse than what They had done already. Slowly she worked out a possible plan.

First of all she must become someone else, an impenetrable stranger to Them. She faced the immediate task with the boldness of separation.

No plastic surgeon, no beauty operator, would help her; they too were under constant omnipresent surveillance. She must do the best she could by herself. Furtively darting into and out of widely scattered stores at their most crowded, unobserving hours, she changed the color of her hair and skin, got tinted contact lenses to turn her greenish eyes to hazel, learned a new walk, a new posture, a new tone of voice. Her mirror image startled even herself.

It was infinitely harder to produce the necessary identity papers and cards that must always be shown on demand. Hal—oh, God! Dear Hal!—had been their expert in forged printing and photography, not she.

For the first time she felt grateful to the grandfather whose hoarded wealth had trickled down by legacy to her. She was in need of neither employment nor welfare aid—fortunately, since one would have been unobtainable now and the other denied. Quietly she walked out of the rooming house, leaving all her belongings behind her, bought here and there a complete new wardrobe from the skin out, changed in a public restroom, threw the clothes she had been wearing into the nearest trash receiver, and moved temporarily into another hotel—a better one this time, to support her new persona—under a new name.

So far as she could, she had ended one existence and begun another. The needed documents were next. She scarcely dared leave the hotel (where she had been lucky with a negligent registration clerk) without them, but she must trust to fate.

The obstacle seemed insuperable. But, as the old-time writer Ray Bradbury had once said, "If something can't be handled it must be handled."

In her double-locked, carefully debugged hotel room, Ellen got out her old legal papers—the passbook, the coded identification card, the intercity passport, the registered certificates—and studied them intensively.

Could she learn, unaided, to forge a new set of papers which would deceive Them? For if she could not, the one possible way she could devise to communicate with the comrades in other cells was unthinkable. She must, and therefore she could.

And so, hour after hour, day after day and late into the night, Ellen taught herself patiently to be a master forger.

The actual materials, the paper and plastic, she need not worry about; she had only to obliterate her old record and substitute a new one. The violet printing ink was another matter; it was a peculiar shade confined to government documents. She must analyze and duplicate it, something that the government itself loudly boasted could not be done.

Earned gratitude to the public library! Nervously visiting branches she had never entered before, Ellen pored over works on chemistry and color manuals for art students. Her bathroom became a laboratory, its equipment locked in a closet when the chambermaid was due. She slept when she had to, she ate when necessary: the rest of her time was divided between study and practice in the expertise of forgery.

It took two solid years. She was only twenty-five by then, but the grey streak she left in her dyed hair was natural, and she had become painfully thin. All the better:

the new Ellen, when she was prepared to emerge, would resemble only slightly the photographs of the old one.

When she felt she was ready, she went on to the next stage. In her new handwriting she filled out the application form for the next civil service examination. Her new false identity number was the big stumbling block; half the figures were the old ones, half random substitutes. She scaled the hurdle without incident. Didn't They check? Apparently not: audacity like hers was beyond Their thinking. It was encouraging to find that she had not over-estimated Their arrogant security.

She told herself she felt no fear. But as she entered the examination room a thrill of pure terror shot through her. Was this a trap, had they accepted her application only to expose her? Then she remembered how Hal had died, and didn't care any more. She was cool and collected as she took the examination questions to the desk assigned to her. Nothing happened to suggest any suspicion.

When the results were announced Ellen was Number Four among 283 applicants. She was practically sure to be summoned to fill a vacancy soon.

The department to which she was called had nothing to do with communication surveillance. That didn't matter: she was in.

But each morning as she entered the office two things assailed her, a shiver of apprehension as eyes turned on her (was this it? was she about to be accused?) and a growing discouragement. Her original idea had been to obtain access to records, to the files in which all known members of the Movement (including her old self) were listed. But soon she found that no one in the lower echelons had the slightest chance of even entering the place where they were kept. Her own department dealt with the upkeep of highways and bridges, subjects of not the least use to her.

Was all the risk, all the labor of two years to come to nothing? No, she *must* find a way; she owed it to Hal.

She began to cultivate acquaintance with even the humblest employee who had any connection with the "sedition file," as it was openly referred to. The men were easier to attach herself to; they were susceptible to the wiles of a pretty woman and not suspicious of an ambitious rival as the entrenched woman employees were. During the long purgatory she had neglected her appearance; now she bought the right kind of clothes, used make-up again, practiced before her mirror an engaging smile, a flirtatious eyebrow-raising. Many a secret was leaked into ears side by side on a pillow; she was quite prepared for that expedient too.

She studied the men in the file department—doubly valuable because it adjoined the electronic center—as she had studied chemistry. Not the executives: no mere general office assistant, the social equivalent of a typist in the days when typing was done by hand could come within miles of companionship with them. But the young men, the bureaucrats on the lower rungs of the ladder preparing to climb it to the top, were open to flattery and had not yet hardened into adjuncts to the mechanical surveillance system they served. Alone in her room at night she carried on one-sided conversations that could lead to information without arousing suspicion and she listened to her own voice to make it warm and interesting. She knew that her colleagues laughed at her, thought her a sexpot on the make. What did she care? To avert any inkling of the truth she courted a few men quite outside the only place with which she was concerned. Ellen became known as Hot Pants and Little Roundheels. Fine!

Carefully she developed her closest affiliation with a young man named Barry, who had access to and minor duties in Central Control itself. Oddly enough, Barry wasn't bed-ward bound; his interest was not in her body but in her mind. Intensive study had given her a command of subjects most pretty girls knew nothing about or hid their knowledge of, and Barry in another era not so fanatically technological would have been a philosopher—generalized thought was his passion. Poor innocent! He would probably have to be sacrificed in the end. Ellen hardened her heart and invited him to her room, not for wine and kisses but for long animated talks.

Subtly, with seeming casualness, she brought the talks gradually around to the official surveillance operation. Barry had no power in the vital center, but he had eyes and ears and an eager mind—and the lack of suspicion of the dreamy idealist. How he had ever been accepted and assigned to his department Ellen could not imagine. He was just the sort of person she herself as recruiter for the Movement, would have turned down on the ground that he was too naive to be safe. Why hadn't the Establishment realized that? Another proof of Their smug, arrogant self-assurance. Unless They could with Their gadgets catch a man or woman making statements They would consider subversive, They rested complacently on Their ingrown belief in Their utter control of society.

Such innocent little revelations as Ellen gleaned from Barry as the months went on by!

"A funny thing happened in our office today. The woman who dusts the vault came out with a little cog and asked the boss what that had fallen out of. You should have seen him turn white and rush in! We were all going to be put through the wringer as suspected saboteurs when he discovered it had fallen out of somebody's chrono timepiece."

Ellen would join him in derisive laughter at the gullibility of bosses with watchful bosses above them.

Or, "Franklin's done for, poor devil. He was feeding the main computer. He must have had a hard night; he fell sound asleep. Lind found him and told the boss. It was his duty," Barry added hastily.

"Of course."

"So now Franklin's back with us in the outer office, and Lind's in the vault at about 100 percent bigger salary.

Lord! Do you realize, Ellen, that while Franklin dozed off the whole city's surveillance system was suspended?"

"Oh, how awful . . . and nobody knew."

There. That was it. Now how to get into the vault? Barry was speaking again—he spoke too much.

"You know I sometimes wonder—what would it matter if we *didn't* watch and listen, twenty-four hours a day? In other countries they—"

"Don't say it!" she cried sharply. Poor Barry, I may have to destroy you yet. Don't give me more ammunition than I need. Barry subsided, looking snubbed and a little alarmed. Ellen almost smiled: was he thinking that *she* might be a spy?—not an Establishment spy, just an anti-Establishment one.

Yet she *should* encourage him, put him helplessly in her power. She would need someone to hold the fort, to institute a delaying action, afterwards, while she took advantage of the dormant period—someone who though he might guess from her unexplained absence that she must be responsible wouldn't be shocked into betrayal, who would owe allegiance to her above allegiance to Them. Barry was her only hope.

With no surveillance operating, even for only an hour or so, she was confident of getting word (by freed vidphone, even by post-express) to one or more of the comrades she had known in the past. There were many, they were here in the city. But with surveillance alive, to have approached them would have been to notify their murderers.

She smiled at Barry. The time was almost ripe.

A week later, when the office closed, Ellen shut herself in the women's restroom. The cleaners would come soon; this was no safe hiding-place, but it would do until she could flit back to her own room after they had finished with it.

Voluntarily working late (on a deliberately uncompleted task), Ellen had cased the terrain like a professional bank robber. The night crew was smaller than the day shift, no general workers except messengers, just the night computer operator and those who serviced the mechanism.

In her office was a cupboard for stationery and supplies. When the last voices and footsteps vanished from that direction, she scurried back, her shoes in her hand, a soundless, shadowy figure behind the backs stopped over mops and buckets. She could just fit into the cupboard, and enough air for breathing came under the door. The cleaners would be through and leave that floor by half-past twenty at the latest. She would wait till then.

She found herself shaking uncontrollably. Her mind fixed on her timetable, she willed herself to be calm.

She heard the night shift people walking past her office to their own. She heard Lind bid goodbye to the night operator and leave.

Nearly three years now since she had been fettered and forced to watch Hal being tortured to death. "Vengeance is mine, saith the Lord," she murmured with no blasphemy. For good or ill, this was it. In a few more minutes she would have succeeded or she would have been caught.

Ellen fingered the pocketed belt around her waist under her loose tunic. The snicker was there, waiting to be drawn.

Before the raid, all of her cell had had clandestinely manufactured snickers. Not one of them had been able to pull his or hers out before they were overpowered and all their defensive weapons confiscated. She had not had a notion of how the things were constructed, only how to load and use them. But her private course in chemistry had carried her far beyond the blending of violet ink. The snicker she had made for herself was crude, but it would work. Having no other laboratory animal, she had tried it out on herself. The blast of the frozen gas compound released when she squeezed the trigger had put her out for seventy minutes, and all that time she had been completely paralyzed. Reloaded, her homemade snicker would do.

To reach the vault directly, she would have had to go through its outer office, where the night workers were, and some of them might know her. She had found another way.

The entrance to the vault itself was strongly guarded. Leaving her shoes outside the cupboard door, Ellen tiptoed through the hall to the ramp leading to the heliport on the roof. Even the building's architect could not have known its every detail better than her concentrated observation enabled her to do.

The night shift's commute-copters were parked across the roof. Ellen chose the one standing nearest to the edge of the roof and hence over the windows of the surveillance office. Deftly she reached inside (nobody ever bothered to lock his copter there) and started its warning signal. The siren wail would penetrate even closed window panes. Then she darted back to the deep shadow by the port's hatchway.

Within three minutes she heard hasty footsteps and a man scrambled up the ramp. Was an airborne thief swooping down trying to loot a copter? Alerted, one of the workers was running to the rescue.

Ellen aimed the snicker. The man dropped in a heap and lay still without a sound except his muffled fall. She turned off the siren.

Quickly she pulled his pass badge off him and pinned it on her tunic. She hurried back down the ramp.

Carrying a pile of papers that concealed her face she darted busily through the outer office. Good so far—no one observing her knew her, and she would be taken for a new messenger with data for the operator. There was plenty of fuel left in the snicker for him.

It worked so smoothly that Ellen felt as if she were moving in a dream. The guards at the vault eyed her badge and let her pass; one of them whistled and she waved at him. The computer operator had his back turned. He looked around and said, "Oh, messenger, just leave the papers there."

She squeezed the trigger.

With the operator paralyzed and unconscious, the computer suddenly went dead. Ellen walked back through the outer office calmly, minus the papers, and this time no one even glanced at her. In her own office she retrieved her shoes, went quietly down to the entrance ... and opened the front door to be grasped by two waiting arms.

It was too late to struggle. Ellen stood as motionless as the two paralyzed men upstairs.

And Barry's voice said, "You little fool. I guessed right, didn't I?"

She clamped her lips shut and took deep breaths to still her pounding heart.

"Come on, let's get away from here," he said brusquely.

He pulled her roughly after him, and she had to run or fall. They raced through the dark streets and she saw they were heading for her room. Well, there was nothing evidential there; she had disposed of all the material when she had finished with it.

Dully, bitterly, she realized that it had all been in vain. Naive, trusting, idealistic Barry, who had all the time been a spy for Them. The provocative remarks he had made, goading her to respond.

He pushed her inside, then bolted and chained the door. She fell into a chair and he stood threateningly in front of it. She was a prisoner again. A backflash of Hal's last hours seared through her mind. Now she would be sharing it in more than empathy, or undergoing still worse, if worse there were.

"Why?" Barry said hoarsely. She shook her head.

"I hinted and hinted!" he cried. "I kept bringing up all kinds of subjects that should have enlightened you. I wasn't even certain this evening when I saw you hide and then sneak to your office. But when you went up the ramp, I was convinced and I waited outside for you.

"By then I knew for sure that you were one of us."

"Us?" she said bewildered.

Barry gave the secret password of the Movement.

A miraculous week later, when not a hint of alarm had been detected and the Establishment had given up its search for the culprit—after all, nothing had happened; the two men had recovered without memory of the attack, Central Surveillance had been dead for over an hour but not a sign of revolt had been demonstrated, above all They had not lost face publicly—Ellen was received into Barry's cell. She was home again.

"Oh, Barry," she said on one of their long evenings together, "what an imbecile I was. I had you all wrong and put us both in such dreadful jeopardy! When I think what you risked for the Movement—"

"Not just for the Movement, little idiot. Don't you know I'm in love with you?"

"Oh!"

Something warm she had almost forgotten moved within her. Then the terrible memories chilled it. For the first time since it had happened, she talked about Hal and the others.

He listened soberly. "So that's what They did to all of you," he said. "We tried to find out but we never could."

"It can happen again, to any one of us."

"I know. We take in that knowledge before we join. But we've weakened Them. They know now They are vulnerable. A few more such daring exploits as yours and we may win out yet while you and I are still alive and free. In the end we *must* win—and They must pay for such horrors as you experienced.

"But there I was, already in that very department, and not one of us had the brains to think of an act like yours. The most we hoped for was that in my position I might sometimes catch an unwary useful word. You are our heroine."

"I had reasons no one else had, that's all."

"And strength and courage and patience and inventiveness. Don't downgrade your triumph, darling ... Ellen, it's true we live in danger always. But for what time we may have, could we share everything together? I know I'd never take Hal's place, but could you give me a little place of my own?"

She felt tears rising in her eyes—the first tears she had shed for so long. Her lips trembled in a smile.

"You know our slogan in the Movement, don't you?" she whispered shakily.

"To die resisting Them, to live in love with our own," he quoted, his eyes shining.

Ellen held out her arms.

# PAMELA SARGENT
## and
# MICHAEL KURLAND

# IMT

||||||||||||||||||||||||||||||||||||||||||||||||||||||||||||||||||||||||||||||||||||||||||||||||||||||||||||||

## Pamela Sargent

New York-based **Pamela Sargent** has been producing fine, tough-minded short science fiction stories for such magazines as **The Magazine of Fantasy and Science Fiction** and **New Worlds** over the past four years, appearing in science fiction anthologies as well. This year marks the sale of her first novel, **Cloned Lives,** to Gold Medal.

Holding a master's degree in philosophy from Harpur College, State University of New York, Pamela Sargent brings not only this academic background but her great concern for the role of women in the next generation to this tale of bureaucratic hassle.

•

Lisa Fernandez closed the folder containing the IMT report, stared at it for a few seconds, then swiftly opened a desk drawer and shoved it inside. She shut the drawer and began to scratch her desk top with her fingernails. I can't handle this, she thought; it's too much.

Lisa turned in her chair and faced the wall screen in back of her desk. She leaned toward the console on her left and pressed a button. An image of the Westchester arcology appeared on the screen, a multi-leveled pyramid of houses surrounded by trees and hills. She pressed another button and the camera panned in for a close-up. The levels of the arcology were beginning to show signs of age. Paint was peeling from the houses and the streets running along each level were cluttered with old newsfax sheets, empty bottles, and abandoned toys.

She pressed another button. NO GO, the red letters seemed to shriek at her. They had been painted on an abandoned truck along 110th Street. She watched the screen and saw the abandoned buildings, glass windows shattered. This area was in such disrepair that there had once been talk of walling it in and moving the inhabitants to another part of the city. But there had been no other place for them to go and finally the people had built their own barricades, blocking the streets with abandoned buses, cinder blocks and whatever they could find. 110th Street was the boundary. NO GO. Lisa had grown up there, determined to get out.

The city was a prison and a trap. Lisa had made it only as far as upper Manhattan. She could not live any further from her office and be sure of getting to work every day. The subways were rarely on schedule and a hovercab was almost impossible to get. Cars, of course, had been banned from the streets years ago and it was not safe to walk in many areas. Some people had managed to leave the city altogether, but in recent years many of them had returned, unable to find a way to earn a living outside of the urban clusters that dotted the country like cancers. So they huddled together, unable even to move around the city freely. Her thoughts reminded her again of the report sitting inside her desk drawer. That damn transportation committee, Lisa thought, I ask it to help solve things and it only compounds my problems.

Lisa's picturephone buzzed at her. She picked up the receiver and saw the face of her receptionist, Linda Marat, on the small screen attached to the phone.

"Mr. Gorton is here," said Linda. Her green eyes stared expressionlessly at Lisa from the screen, and her characteristically empty smile seemed plastered on her lovely face.

"Send him in," Lisa muttered.

"Certainly, Ms. Fernandez," said Linda, still smiling. Lisa hung up the phone, then pushed a button on her console. 110th Street vanished from the screen.

Her door opened and Dan Gorton strode in, slamming the door behind him. "Hello, Lisa," he said in his low voice. He walked quickly to her side of the desk, kissed her on the forehead, and smiled. She smiled back at the stocky, white-haired man. Ten years before, she had fallen in love with Dan. It had almost been a fever and she had passed through those days intoxicated by it, unable to sleep well, her senses heightened to everything around her. His lovemaking had not satisfied her but had only increased her desire. Gradually the passion had burnt itself out but it had been replaced by friendship and a quieter love. Occasionally the passion would flare again, but it took the form of arguments and fights. We're both too stubborn, thought Lisa, if we had any kind of a life together, it wouldn't be peaceful. She was reminded of Ramon at that point, and tendrils of guilt brushed at her mind.

Dan leaned against the desk and folded his arms. "I have to admit," he said, "that Linda looks as beautiful as ever. And as stupid."

"Don't make fun of her, Dan, she does her job." Linda did. She greeted everyone courteously, let in those who had passes or appointment cards and turned away anyone else. Linda, being retarded, did not listen to excuses or explanations. She couldn't understand them. She saved Lisa and her security guards some time and kept out unwelcome visitors. Besides, hiring Linda had set an example for the other city workers most of whom were reluctant to hire any of the thousands of retarded people in the city. Lisa had no idea where all the retarded people had come from, although there were theories about the effects of pollution on various parts of the populace. She said quietly, "You'd be surprised at how many of the men around here come in just to see Linda. She's beautiful and she doesn't say much, I guess they think she's the ideal woman."

"Joe Taglia's mad," said Dan, "about something called an IMT report that he gave you."

Lisa was startled. "How the hell did you know about that, Dan?"

"Taglia was talking and I have ears. I know he was the head of that transportation study group you appointed four years ago, and I know he saw you this morning, so I grabbed him out in the hall and asked how things were going. He mumbled something about an IMT report, then he clammed up and wouldn't tell me what it meant, and after that he said it would solve everything. So I got curious."

"Taglia should keep his goddamn beak buttoned," Lisa said angrily. "I'm putting a lid on that report, I told that committee to shut up about it. If that report's publicized, it'll raise a lot of false hopes."

"Didn't they come up with anything?" Dan asked.

"I'll tell you what they came up with." Lisa glared at her desk top. "They hired a bunch of experts to study various means for improving our transportation facilities, a lot of technocrats, you know, the usual crowd for stuff like this, and then somebody on that committee had the bright idea of hiring a couple of nutcrackers named Goldfarb and Leonov. The way Taglia put it to me was that the experts didn't seem to know what to do, or else their schemes were too expensive, so it wouldn't hurt to throw a little money into some crank research. Apparently Taglia was persuaded that Goldfarb with his crazy theories might come up with something. Well, it was Goldfarb and Leonov who invented the IMT."

"Well what is it?"

"An instantaneous matter transmitter," said Lisa, "and apparently these two characters put it together out of nuts and bolts. Taglia said it would be cheap."

"Almost anything would be cheaper than that excuse for a transit system we have now." He reached over and brushed a hair from her face. "I don't know why you're looking so dubious. That committee actually came through with something."

"I don't like it." She watched Dan's face for his reactions. "I know," she went on, "I'm not much of a technician and I don't really understand the theory for this thing, but I don't exactly relish the thought of having my atoms beamed from here to there. I could wind up with my head on my ass. Christ, the IMT hasn't even been tested properly."

"So they'll test it and work out the problems. If it works this could be really incredible, Lisa. Our problems would be solved."

Lisa looked down at her desk top and scratched at a coffee stain. What am I doing here, she thought suddenly, why am I supposed to handle things like this? She began to wonder if her position had been achieved by luck and not ability. She had started working for the city as a programmer at the age of nineteen. She had been efficient, but not outstanding, and then her superiors had discovered her real talents. She could make decisions and get things done. She learned quickly and whatever she didn't know she could usually find out. She could gain the respect of others and get them to work harder than they normally would. She understood the problems of the city from first-hand experience, having grown up in one of the roughest areas of New York. By the age of twenty-five, she had become an administrative assistant to Dan Gorton, the city manager.

A couple of years after Lisa began working for Dan, Amanda Greeley had been elected mayor. She had immediately appointed Dan as one of her assistants, and Dan had recommended Lisa for his old position of city manager. Amanda Greeley was primarily a politician, unconcerned about Lisa's administrative talents; there were others who could have done about as well. She had given Lisa the job on political grounds, knowing that it would look good to the poor of the city to see one of their own in such a position. It had. Amanda Greeley had managed to win a second term on the basis of Lisa's appointment and other similar maneuvers, even though there had been no improvement in the city. Now Lisa was stuck with the IMT report and Amanda Greeley was lusting after a third term. Mandy would love this damn thing, Lisa thought; she could use it as a ladder to the governorship at least.

"Dan," she said softly, "are you sure you want to see something like the IMT here? Do you really think it's going to make things much better? It could make them worse, you know. Oh, people could get around easily, but—"

"For God's sake, Lisa." Dan's face was growing red. "Do you know how much the city loses every year just from people being late to work because they can't get to the job on time? If it solved nothing else, it would be worth it."

Oh, Dan, she thought sadly, are you that shortsighted? Can't you understand what I see? She felt disappointed, and yet she really had no right to be. Dan was intelligent but he had never been imaginative. She sighed. She would have to go ahead without his help.

"I've made up my mind," she said at last. She stared into his grey eyes. "I'm sitting on it; I have the authority."

"Jesus Christ, Lisa!" He pounded the desk with his fist. "I really can't believe it. You have some vague feeling about this thing and you're going to act on that with no regard for the facts. You're a fool. I never thought I'd see the day you'd do something like this. If that's female intuition, the hell with it."

"I've made up my mind."

"You don't feel right about it, so you're saying the hell with it. Well, I'm not going to let you do it, Lisa. I'll go to Mandy with it myself." Dan began to walk around to the other side of her desk.

"I've got the authority to suppress this thing," she answered. "You try getting to Mandy. Even if you can get through that crowd of courtiers she's surrounded herself with, she is still going to have to dump it back in my lap. And you know goddamn well I can convince her that she could destroy herself politically by letting it out too soon."

"We'll see," said Dan. "We'll see." He stared at Lisa across the barrier of her desk. Her hands began to tremble and she quickly removed them from his sight, hiding them in her lap. He turned quickly and walked out the door.

Lisa looked across the living room at Ramon and repressed the words that rose unbidden to her lips. He buckled his knife belt around his still-slender hips and checked himself in the mirror, then adjusted the red cape draped over his shoulders.

"Muhammed asked me today," she said at last, "when you were going to file your report."

"Muhammed's a *mierda*," said Ramon. "All he knows is paper pushing. I talked to him already."

"I know," said Lisa. She was using her gentlest tone. "And that was very helpful, but he wants you to write out your suggestions so he can circulate a report—"

"I talked to him. Let him write them down."

"Where are you going?"

"Must you check on me like a mother?" He turned and faced her. "I'm going downtown. There are people to see. I must gather more material for my reports." He grinned at her. His eyes were cool.

"Go," she said. Ramon was already unlocking the door.

He vanished into the hallway, leaving the door open behind him. Lisa got up and closed it quickly, replacing all the bolts and resetting the alarm system.

She sat down again. Her husband was gone once more, maybe for the night, maybe for three days.

*She is Lisa Ramirez and she is sixteen. She sneaks out of the room crowded with the bodies of her sleeping sisters and climbs down the fire escape to Ramon. He waits in the street for her, his tall lean body resting against a broken street light. She is always a bit self-conscious around Ramon Fernandez, grateful for the darkness of the night which hides her acne-scarred face, her oversized nose, the teeth which have never seen a dentist.*

*"You are beautiful, Lisa. Your eyes reveal your soul." Ramon speaks in Spanish now, holding her tightly. They lie along the floor of an abandoned building, hidden from others.*

*"I love you, Ramon."*

*They hold each other and spin their dreams and their hopes. They will leave the streets. Their children will pick flowers and play among trees.*

Ramon's love was dead now and their daughter Ada did not play among trees. She had died at the age of twelve beneath the collapsing walls of an old subway tunnel with a hundred other people. Lisa had been thirty then, city manager for only two years. She had wept and cursed the city for Ada's death, and then appointed her transportation study group. *"Do something,"* she had said: *"this must never happen again."*

The city had not been content with her daughter. Now it wanted the soul of Ramon Fernandez, had made him a purposeless shell, wandering the streets with his old friends. She had made him a consultant in her office after Ada's death, hoping that the work might heal him, remembering all the times she had cried on his shoulder in despair at the decisions she was called upon to make. Ramon would leave her soon. He had left her already. He would embrace the streets, hating them, yet knowing nothing else. Lisa walked over to her window and stared through the iron bars at the street below. A group of boys were standing near an overturned garbage pail. One of them was painting something on the lid with a spray can.

*Lisa sprays her name in small letters, swirling the can of green paint in her hand. Ramon is using red paint, and he covers the old white tiles with it, blotting out other names and splattering Lisa's.*

*RAMON. And at least a million people would see it as they rode by on the subways. RAMON. They couldn't miss it.*

"You see my problem," Lisa said into the phone. The image of Shigeo Nishimoto nodded gravely on the picturephone screen. "I have to sit on this IMT thing, and I'm being crowded."

"With whom have you conversed?" Shigeo asked.

"Almost no one. Gene Woodruff in Los Angeles and Myron Eason in Denver; I can trust them."

"No one in New York?"

Lisa thought sadly of Dan. "No," she said finally. "Look, Shig, I need your help and you owe me a favor, a big one."

Shigeo looked slightly pained. "I am in your debt of course, Lisa, and I have often offered you my services in the past years." Shigeo, as one of the directors of the World Picturephone Service, had tried to sell phone service on a large scale to the United States several years earlier. Lisa, realizing that the Japanese phones, satellite relays, and service were both cheaper and more reliable than the archaic system then in use, had ordered installation of the Japanese phones in all city offices under her control. Soon others had done the same and now World Picturephone controlled most of the service in the United States. Shigeo had felt indebted to Lisa ever since, itching, she knew, to pay off his debt to her.

"I need to talk to your contacts in Africa and Mongolia," Lisa said. "And anyone else you think will help."

"Of course," Shigeo said. He sipped at his tea. "This IMT device is most interesting. It would have an enormous effect on Japan."

"No doubt," said Lisa. Japan, for the most part, was one huge arcology, levels of Japanese homes surrounded by carefully tended forests and gardens. The building of the arcologies had coincided with a resurgence of traditional Japanese culture, might even have encouraged those traditions.

"Things will change here," Shigeo went on. "I do not know if I like the idea."

Lisa was becoming aware of shouts outside her office. "At least," she said, "if we do things right, we may be able to handle this thing properly." Lisa suddenly felt tired. "I'd better ring off."

"I look forward to hearing—" The office door opened abruptly. Linda Marat stood there, wringing her hands.

"I tried, Ms. Fernandez," Linda said. Her beautiful green eyes were filled with tears. "I said, Ms. Fernandez is busy and you can't . . ." Linda's voice trailed off and large tears began to flow down her smooth cheeks. Lisa hung up the phone.

Joe Taglia stood in the doorway, his arms held in back of him by the security guard posted at Lisa's office door. "It's not your fault, Linda," Lisa said. She stood up behind her desk. "Don't cry. Just go back to your desk, I'll take care of it."

Linda rubbed her eyes, smearing her makeup, and left. "You want I should throw this bozo out?" asked the guard.

"No, I'll talk to him." The guard released Taglia and closed the door behind him. "What the hell are you trying to do?"

"I want to ask you about that report," said Taglia. He

ambled toward her desk and sat in one of the chairs. His lanky frame slouched. Lisa quickly sat down again.

"There's nothing to ask," she said. "I commissioned it; I found the results inconclusive."

"I didn't spend four years working on that commission so that you could just throw the work away. You don't know how hard it was to deal with Goldfarb and Leonov. I had to practically beg them. Leonov's a raving paranoid, you have to cajole him to get anything done, tell him what a great guy he is. And Goldfarb, my God! He sits around staring into space thinking all the time. And eating. He's the fattest guy I ever saw. We had to hire a caterer to get him to do anything. I had to sit there with those two, and you're going to suppress the report."

"That's right."

Taglia leaned forward, brushing some disorderly grey curls from his forehead. "I won't let you do it, Lisa. I won't let you deny this city the transportation it needs. I can't believe it. Don't you care any more?"

"I don't trust it, Joe. You admit yourself that the two fellows who invented it aren't the most stable people in the world. We could have problems we don't know about yet. What if somebody's atoms are lost in transit or something? Or we wind up with two of the same person? I don't see how we could set it up now unless we used wires or something to connect the stations and beam people through the wires, at least that would be safer. And that would cost us a fortune which we haven't got."

"I see," said Taglia. The skin on his lean face was tight. "So because you're a little squeamish, you're going to suppress the IMT. Leonov's been beaming himself around in it quite safely, he's having a great time with it. Sometimes he does nothing for hours but beam himself from one side of the lab to the other, laughing like a fool."

"A lab. That's a small enclosed area. What about going from one end of the city to the other?"

"Goldfarb says distance doesn't matter according to his

theories, but he won't get into the thing himself." Taglia
had blurted it out. He looked as if he regretted it.

"Well," said Lisa. "The theorist doesn't trust his own invention." She looked across the desk at Taglia. "And you
expect me to trust it."

"All right, Lisa, I might as well tell you. It does work
over distances, quite large ones too. Three thousand miles,
to be exact."

"How," she said, "do you know that?" She began to
scratch at her desk top with her nails.

"Goldfarb," said Taglia, looking down at the floor, "had
Leonov fly out to San Francisco about six months ago,
with some of their equipment. It took us a while to find
out about it." Taglia wiped his brow with the back of his
sleeve. "It turned out that Leonov had built one of the
IMT booths in the back of a Chinese restaurant there.
Goldfarb was ordering meals and sending Leonov through
the IMT to pick up the food. Naturally, we didn't want to
put it in the report, but maybe we should have, it proved
the thing is safe." He glanced at Lisa. "Naturally, we removed the booth and I'm afraid we had to exert some
pressure on the kitchen help to keep quiet. We told them
we'd have them committed to a mental hospital if they
said anything, Dr. Myers said he'd sign the papers." Taglia
was sweating profusely. He pulled out a handkerchief and
wiped his face.

"Bunglers," said Lisa. "I can't believe it." She watched
Joe Taglia squirm in the chair.

"You can't just suppress this report," said Taglia. His
voice quavered. "I'll go to Mayor Greeley. I won't let you
do this."

"You go to Greeley," said Lisa. "Even if you get
through to her, you know what she'll have to do. She'll ap-
point another committee to study the feasibility of your
recommendation, and they'll take at least a year to figure
out what to do. You go ahead, Joe. There's really not a
thing you can do; I can block you at every turn. Now get

your ass out of that chair and move it out of here; I've got work to do."

Taglia stood up and leaned over the desk. "You think I don't know," he said softly, "that you're up to something." She suddenly wondered if Taglia knew of her plans. But that's ridiculous, she thought, he couldn't or he'd be helping me, not arguing. "You want to use this for your own ends, you're not stupid enough to block it out of fear and ignorance. I won't let you do it, Lisa. I'm sick of seeing you in this office. A gutter rat."

She stood up, clenching her fists.

"That's what you are."

"If you don't leave right now, I'll throw you out myself, Taglia; I'll break your fucking back."

He turned and left the room, slamming the door behind him. She sank into the chair, hands shaking. That goddamn Taglia, she thought, and I probably just confirmed his opinion of me. She knew he had never really liked her but she hadn't realized that the animosity was so deep. She had another problem now.

But Joe Taglia couldn't do anything; there was no way. Was there?

The Manhattan Landing had once seemed like a monster. It was actually a city in itself, built on platforms above the East River bordering Lower Manhattan. Its inhabitants rarely left the area of the Landing. Most of them worked there and didn't need to travel through the rest of New York.

The people of the Landing had become independent, thinking of themselves as somehow different from the rest of the city. They preferred to take care of their own problems, relying on the city government as little as possible. Maybe they're right, thought Lisa as she strolled along Javits Avenue with the Manhattan Landing Commissioner, Brant Dunlap. Six security guards trailed the two, but this was one area where they weren't really needed. I suppose,

Lisa thought, if the rest of the city wasn't so dependent on our bureaucracy ... but even the Landing was having trouble. Brant had already complained to her about elevator breakdowns and on a structure like the Landing, elevators were crucial.

"Here's an example," said Dunlap. He gestured at a playground in front of them. Dunlap was a short, wiry man becoming prematurely bald. He was bored and so was Lisa, but Mandy insisted that Lisa make tours of various parts of the city in the interest of public relations. It was, after all, a way of showing the people that even those at the top of the city governmental structure were interested in their problems. I could learn more, she thought, if I just talked to people over the phone and looked at things through my screen.

She looked at the playground. It seemed sterile to her, all concrete and metal and rubber. Groups of children climbed what looked like metal vines twining upward toward the sky and crawled through metal pipes. A few were on trampolines, others turned somersaults on the rubber mats which covered the ground.

"Each parent in the area donates two hours a week, and we let them pick the hours," said Dunlap. "We can keep each of these areas open for most of the day. Frankly, I think these small localized areas are better than those huge recreational places your office wanted to shove down our throats."

Two little girls looked over and waved at them. "And how," said Lisa, "do you force the parents to donate the time?"

"We don't *force* anyone," said Dunlap. "But there is considerable social pressure involved. I don't think the rest of you people actually realize how much pride we take in the Landing. You always seem so puzzled by it." Dunlap smiled.

Lisa turned away and looked down the clean street. Javits Avenue, like the rest of the Landing, was always neat. A crowd was beginning to gather on the sidewalk near them, and she noticed a few newsmen in the group. She motioned to Dunlap. "We'd better give them some time," she said, "or they'll retaliate with a few nasty editorials." The two began to walk toward the crowd and she saw that there were several cameras among the newspeople. Strange, she thought, my little tours don't usually rate this kind of coverage; they must be doing a special about the Landing. It was one way to convince people that New York wasn't so bad. She gestured at one of the reporters.

"How you doing, Bernie?" she said. Several electronic wands suddenly appeared under her nose.

"Joe Taglia held a press conference just an hour ago," shouted a male voice. She couldn't tell who was speaking. "He said you were suppressing a report he submitted on behalf of a transportation study group he chaired. Is that true?"

Lisa stared at the wands. That son of a bitch, she thought, I'll have his hide for this. "He said," the voice went on, "that you were denying the city a cheap and efficient transportation system for your own hidden reasons." She had found the speaker at last. It was Jon Ortega and his moustache seemed to bristle with anger. She knew he wouldn't let her off easily; his muckraking editorials were too popular for that.

Lisa tried to look calm. "As a matter of fact," she said, "I decided to suppress a report about a system that hasn't even been tested thoroughly, a system which would only complicate the problems we already have." Her mouth was dry and she tried to swallow. "I have the legal right to do so, and Joe Taglia is violating both city and federal laws governing the implementation of new discoveries."

"But Taglia claimed that this IMT, he called it, was foolproof, that it could move people anywhere in the city almost instantly." Ortega wasn't going to drop it. The crowd had grown ominously silent. She began to feel nauseous.

"I think," Lisa said, trying to smile, "that Joe Taglia and I have a different idea of what 'foolproof' means. He's willing to take a chance on something that's only been tried a few times under controlled conditions." I hope, she thought, he didn't mention that goddamn Chinese restaurant. "Are any of you willing to step into something that'll take you apart, molecule by molecule, and reconstruct you out in the Bronx? You might lose all your memories. You might wind up with an extra head." Someone in the crowd began to chuckle. "And criminals would love it. They could rob any of you standing there and be in Forest Hills a second later. It would be a nightmare for the police. All I want to do is sit on this thing and study it. I don't think Joe Taglia has done any of us a favor by talking about an untested device in such misleading terms. You all remember what has happened in the past when things were released for public use with little testing or regard for the consequences."

The crowd seemed to have grown more sympathetic. She glanced at Ortega and saw him getting ready for another question. "I'll have a statement for you later on all of this," she said. "Right now I have to get back to my office." She turned from the wands and grabbed Dunlap's arm. "Come on, Brant."

"What is all this?" asked Dunlap. He looked bewildered.

"You'll find out," she muttered. "Just get me out of here."

Lisa didn't know how well she had come off in her formal statement. Oh, she had looked sincere enough and in control of things, sitting behind a desk in front of the cameras. But she didn't have the demagogic talents of Joe Taglia. I didn't know, she thought, that a scrawny runt like Taglia could look that good on a screen.

She finished rerunning Taglia's press conference on her wall screen, then turned it off. The bastard. She couldn't believe he had the balls for this stunt. The thought circled the edges of her mind. Unless . . .

Someone put him up to it. And there was only one person in the city who could have talked him into it.

She leaned forward and rested her head on her hands. Oh, Dan, she thought, why, why, do you have so little faith in me? I wish I could still cry about it.

She started to scratch at the desk top. At least Shig had come through; he had even contacted a man named Dolohov at the Moon Base. The Russians were interested in the IMT. They were very close to unlocking the secret of fusion power; it would be the perfect power source for the device. The Russians were willing to dicker. Lisa remembered how excited she had become. "Unlimited power," she had shouted to the startled Shigeo, "and the ability to go anywhere. We'll be gods!" The vision had intoxicated her. The face of the earth would change; humanity would escape its prison, might even find its way to the stars.

She needed time. Dan and Taglia had forced her hand. They were ready to force the IMT on the world still unprepared for it. The result would be chaos. What happens when you break out of a prison, unprepared for the sudden freedom? She could see it now, the masses of people leaving the cities, invading whoever was at the other end of the IMT. The resulting carnage might be so horrible that the device would at last be completely suppressed, and the fearful survivors would once again huddle in their concrete caves.

Mary, help me, Lisa prayed. She caught herself, startled. She hadn't prayed in years. I can't handle this, she thought, it's beyond me. She felt the knife of hysteria cutting through her body.

The office door swung open. "Mr. Gorton just arrived," the night guard said. "Do you want . . . ?"

"Send him in," she said. She was suddenly calm. The guard gestured toward the waiting room and Dan strode into the office and closed the door.

"Congratulations, Lisa," he said. He moved past her and over to the wall. "You did a brilliant job of raising all kinds of irrelevant objections to the IMT today. You probably scared the shit out of the ignorant, which of course includes a large segment of the citizenry."

"Did you put Joe Taglia up to his stunt, Dan?"

He glared at her. "Yes, I did. I'm proud of it. Somebody had to do it. I suppose you think you can convince Mandy of the wisdom of your course of action. Maybe you really believe all that shit you were shoveling on the news tonight. Ignorance strikes again."

"Dan—"

"You're not going to get away with it, Lisa. I have some influence with Mandy. If I have to, I'll screw her; it might be more rewarding than your bed turned out to be."

"Are you finished?"

"Lisa, I—"

"Are you *finished*? At least listen to what I have to say."

"Shovel away."

She slouched in her chair. "I know that the IMT is probably safe and I know that nothing in the report seemed to indicate any serious problems with it. But think of the social consequences, Dan. You think people will just get aboard and use it like a subway, but they won't. You'll have the equivalent of mass invasions. People will be able to go anywhere. Do you think they won't? And they won't be too concerned about who's at the receiving end."

He considered. "Then what the hell do you suggest?"

"Dan," she said softly, "the cities are dying; there's no sense even trying to preserve them. Maybe the people on the Landing or in the arcologies are happy but a lot of others are trapped. We can change that, but we need time, time to prepare people for this." She looked away from him. "Consider what we could do. We can move anywhere on the earth; we won't have to stay in one location because that's where the work is. A person could live anywhere and work anywhere. Food and materials could be taken anywhere they're needed. If a place like India needed skilled people for a job, they could come from anywhere immediately, and in an emergency like a flood or cyclone, volunteers could be on the spot right away. You might even have a new kind of migrant laborer, a person who would work construction here for a while, then go to Africa to help build a dike, and yet still have a home. And that isn't all, Dan. The entire solar system, even other systems will be open to us. The possibilities are endless." She paused and looked at him. His hands hung awkwardly at his sides. He seemed lost suddenly.

"We're trying to build a new human society, Dan. I've been contacting people who want the same thing. But we need time. We can't rush it. We need time to set things up, and then to prepare people. It'll be gradual at first, negotiating with people in sparsely populated areas so that others can migrate, building new homes for them, getting them where they're needed and where they want to go. Don't stop it, Dan. I *want* the city to die; all cities have to die. And the only way is to delay the IMT. If it is used now, IMT will needlessly prolong the life of this and all cities."

He was silent, looking at the floor. For a moment she thought he didn't understand, that he would see only grandiose fantasies. Then he looked up.

"I'll help you, Lisa." He seemed to force the words out. "I'll help you." His body straightened and his eyes became alive. "I know just what to say to Mandy; I know I can get her to hold back on this thing and she'll know just how to do it. I'll appeal to her maternal instincts; she always thought of everybody as her children." He was watching her with awe.

So Dan would play a role in this, and an essential one, but minor. He could conciliate and carry things out, but he would not be one of the real planners; she knew that now.

He came to her, held her hands in his. "Forgive me, honey," he said. "I guess I didn't trust you enough."

No, she thought, you didn't. The memory of his distrust would be a barrier for a long time between them. He had been too ready, like Joe Taglia, to assume that she would work only for her own ends, that she could succumb to fear and ignorance. She would remember that. She looked at the big hands holding her small ones.

She would remember. She felt tired.

"I want to go home," she whispered.


"I'm leaving."

Lisa took off her coat and looked at Ramon. He twisted a ring on his finger.

"That's nothing new."

"I won't be back." His dark eyes looked away from her. "Ever. There's nothing for me here, Lisa."

"Go, then." She stifled a yawn. Ramon moved to the door and began to unlock it. "Ramon," she said suddenly, "I'm sorry." Somehow it sounded inadequate. "Really I am."

He was gone. She replaced the bolts and sat on the sofa.

*Ramon smiles at Ada as she sleeps in her crib. "I want another place for her, another world." He grasps Lisa's hand. "I want sunshine and flowers in her hair."*

I hope you find what you want, Ramon, she thought; I hope that you find what you're looking for. It'll be a new world, Ramon; be ready for it, embrace it.

Lisa got up and turned out the lights. Below her, in the streets she heard the sound of a siren racing through the dying city.

# SMALL WORLD

## Michael Kurland

**Michael Kurland** is an adventurous young man who has proved as adept at blackjack as he is at writing fiction, which is to say a winner all the way. He served as an army radar technician and in Intelligence in Germany—undoubtedly the background for his American-based organization of technical military advisors called, appropriately, Weapons Analysis and Research, Inc., in his series of books about WAR, Inc. One of the series, **Plague of Spies**, won a Mystery Writers of America Special Award in 1971.

He is currently at work on several novels, and has recently directed a production of that classic Prohibition play, **Ten Nights in a Barroom.**

He is one of the few writers alive who can claim the distinction of having been the hero of a book (Chester Anderson's **The Butterfly Kid**). He reciprocated Anderson's creative favor in his own **The Unicorn Girl.**

Living alone in Berkeley, Michael Kurland cultivates his taste for good wine at odd hours between bouts with the typewriter, which may account for the unique flavor of this story.

•

It was supposed to solve all our problems, remember? That's what they told us the day the City Manager of Earth stood there and cut the ribbon.

It was twelve years in the making: a symbolic twelve years to the day after Professor Vanspeepe dropped his braunschweiger sandwich between the charged plates at the east end of his highly-experimental, six-kilometer long gravity-wave discriminator, and noted with mild astonishment that the sandwich had disappeared. Twelve years less one day since Vanspeepe's research assistant, a zoftic young dedicated physicist named Lena Bright, noted the thick smear of organic matter coating the west end plates, and called the professor.

"Well, what is it?" the professor had asked in his annoyed, don't-bother-me-with-trivia voice.

"It smells like mustard," little Lena said. "You know, German mustard—like the stuff you use." It was clear that she suspected him of sneaking over in the middle of the night and sabotaging her end of the experiment. "With maybe a hint of spoiled liverwurst," she continued accusingly.

"Ha!" Vanspeepe said. "Listen Lena, turn that thing off at your end and get over here." He hung up to do some hard thinking. Humbleness, he decided, was the tack: humbleness, modest enthusiasm, and carefully unassumed surprise when the Nobel committee called to inform him.

Once the thing was done its theory became immediately obvious to anyone with more than a smattering of matrix algebra and a thorough topological understanding of $n$-dimensional space (where $n > 6$), and the only wonder was that no one had thought of it before. The first six years were spent working out some minor velocity transfer problems. "Engineering details," Professor Vanspeepe explained to anyone who asked—and everyone did—while he tried to figure out how to prevent the braunschweiger sandwich from becoming a smear of spoiled liverwurst at the other end.

The next six years were spent in constructing the giant concrete-to-bedrock foundations in all major cities and the connecting supercooled waveguides with their attendant liquid-helium pumping stations and power supplies. It was a tremendous drain of money and resources, but we set to work with a will: the Vanspeepe Matter Transporter Gate Web was supposed to solve all our problems, remember?

"City Manager of Earth" was the honorary title of the United Nations Secretary for Urban Affairs, but on that Saturday when she cut the ribbon it was suddenly no longer exaggeration. One four-inch-wide red silk ribbon, no more than four hundred yards long; it circled the world. New York was where the major ceremony was held; because of its historic association with the United Nations, because its enormous problems exemplified every other major urban area, and because Mayor D'Annunciato won the toss.

One snip of the golden scissors and the red silk parted. Pulled through the rings atop the brass posts and into the Transgate, it slid out of New York; it fell in loops in Bangkok; it sagged loosely in Tokyo; it drooped in Paris; it noticeably slackened in Sydney. Then, before the lenses of the world television networks, seen live by an estimated eighty percent of humanity, the mayors of the Earth's major cities stepped through the Transgates and collected in New York's Central Park Gate to declare One World; *de facto,* if not *de jure.*

It would have been the heads of state—it was originally supposed to be the presidents, prime ministers, kings, generals-in-power-only-until-a-free-election-can-be-held, and the like—but the Secret Service wouldn't allow the President of the United States to attend (even if he didn't have to step through a Gate); and the President of France wouldn't go if the Prime Minister of Great Britain was going; and the Prime Minister of India wouldn't step through a Transgate for philosophical reasons; and the leaders of all nations not included in this first Web vacillated between boycotting the preceedings entirely and insisting that they would all be present if one of them was present. So it was the mayors, headed by the "City Manager of Earth," Ms. Edith X, who presided over the creation of the World City.

"We are all of us sisters," she told the assembled mayors and the watching world. "And now we are all neighbors: women and men, black and white and yellow and brown and ... and ... and we must strive together to keep our neighborhood—which used to be Paris and Rome and New York, Bangkok and Hanoi; but is now—what?—oh yes, and Tokyo too; and all the other little places I haven't mentioned—now all together unified as Earth City. We must strive to keep our global neighborhood clean and sanitary, with adequate mass transit for all except to achieve racial balance, and a pollution-free environment where we can all work in peace, breathe clean air and control our own bodies.

"We will have problems, we must have problems, but if we, the administrators, work together in good faith to solve them, with an equal day's pay for an equal day's work, and my door is always open to any of you. Remember the motto done in needlepoint over my desk: *Nothing Urban Is Alien to Me.*"

The Transporter Gate Web brought people, countries, cities, closer together, providing instantaneous transportation at amazingly low cost as promised by the promoters when they were selling the bond issues. It was now cheaper to go to Sydney than to talk for more than eight minutes on the telephone (station to station, direct dialing, standard daytime rates). But proximity, it was soon discovered, was not love:

NOTISE * * * * * NOTISE * * * * * NOTISE
THE BUMS, BEING AN AMALGAMA-

TION OF ALL THE BROOKLYN
GANGS, DO HEREBY AND FORTH-
WITH DECLARE A STATE OF WAR
BETWEEN US AND EL FATAHA,
BEING MERELY A COLLECTION OF
STREET ARABIANS AND WHO DE-
SERVES TO BE TAUGHT A LESSON
AND FIND OUT WHOSE BOSS.

R    U    L    E    S    :
IT HAS BEEN AGREED THAT THE
HOME TERRITORIES OF BOTH
GANGS ARE OFF LIMITS TO
RUMBLE.
IT HAS BEEN AGREED THAT
NEITHER PARTY SHALL PERMIT
ANY OF ITS ASSOCIATES OVER THE
AGES OF 21 TO PARTICIPATE.
IT HAS BEEN AGREED THAT
WOMENS RIGHTS SHALL BE
OBSERVED BUT THIS INCLUDES
WOMEN OF THE OGRANISATIONS
EXCLUSIVELY.
IT HAS BEEN AGREED THAT NO
WEAPONS BUT STRICTLY ANTI
PERSONNEL TYPES ARE TO BE
EMPLOYED. THIS RULES OUT
BAZOOKAS FOR EXAMPLE, BUT
DOES NOT CONSTRAIN THOMAS
GUNS.
IT HAS BEEN AGREED THAT THE
SCENE OF THE BATTLE IS TO BE
ISTAMBUL, WHICH IS #12 ON THE
WEB LOCATER.
IT HAS BEEN AGREED THAT THE

GATE IS NEUTRAL TERRITORY AND
WE ARE NORTH AND THE ARABIANS
ARE SOUTH.
IT HAS BEEN AGREED THAT THE
RUMBLE WILL TAKE PLACE FRIDAY
AT 7 PM BROOKLYN TIME, WHICH
COMES OUT TO 2 IN THE MORNING
IN ISTAMBUL DUE TO THE TIME
DIFFERENCE. GROUPS WILL
ASSEMBLE AT 5
              MEL

"Abdul, I swear to you as a brother, it's the most wonderful thing in the world. Nothing can go wrong."

"That's what you swore to me, Ali, the last two times.
The last, if it comes to that, dozen times. Always you have
a scheme and always you fall on your nose. Except when
you fall on my nose."

"But this time, Abdul . . ."

"Ali, a poor man should not be a promoter. Beg a little,
steal a little, but please, stop trying to go into business!"

"Abdul, this is begging; this is stealing."

"Ah!"

"It is merely a different place to beg; a unique way to
steal."

"Better. A man should stick to what he knows. Tell me,
Ali."

"It needs investment capital. Twelve drachma it needs."

"It takes money to steal money. What does one do with
this twelve drachma?"

"One buys a token, Abdul, and enters the Transgate."

"Ah?"

"In the blink of a houri's eye, one is in Paradise."

"It is deadly then, this device?"

"This paradise is called San Francisco."

"San Francisco? Forgive me for sounding dubious,

Cousin Ali, but what do you know about San Francisco? Do you speak United States of American? How can you beg without speaking? This is beginning to sound like one of your former schemes. The seventh, or was it the eighth, which, as I remember, involved . . ."

"Abdul, dear Cousin, hear me out! This is not a second-hand scheme that I heard in the back room of the cafe; nor is it an idly remembered daydream; nor the restated plot of one of those ancient adventure shows which our beloved government has purchased from abroad for our amusement where the hero's lips move one way and this voice moves another. This actually happened to my wife's second cousin, once removed. In his case it was an accident, a misunderstanding; and he failed to see the potential in it. So I went and tried it myself which is where I've been for the last two weeks. It works. It is sure. You have my word as a relative."

"I hardly trust myself, Ali; why should I trust my cousin? But continue!"

"The scam is simple, dear cousin: one merely walks away from the Gate in San Francisco in a random direction until one reaches a restaurant. Then one examines it. If it seems sufficiently qualitative, one enters; if it is lacking in quality, one continues the search. It should not take long; San Francisco is as full of fine restaurants as a seedcake is full of seeds."

"Ah?"

"Then one enters and seats oneself at the table. Shortly one is handed a menu."

"One is not merely removed from the premises at the end of a boot-clad foot?"

"Abdul, realize this: here at home our dress immediately places us at the bottom of the social scale, on the lowest rung of the economic ladder; in San Francisco a burnoose is a burnoose. I suspect a clean, not-too-many-times-mended garment might be desirable, but beyond that . . ." he finished the sentence with an expressive shrug.

"And then—when one is sitting in this fine restaurant and holding this menu that one cannot read?"

"One can read the prices. I suggest one merely orders the most expensive item."

"Reasonable. It is highly unlikely that the most expensive item would be pork. Or camel. I assume that one then eats this most expensive item? Then one is expected to, somehow, pay for this most expensive item?"

"They bring a *check*, a piece of paper upon which is written the price and the government tithe."

"Ah. And then?"

"And then one merely repeats *Ay Kan-nód Pai*, which is American for 'I have insufficient funds to meet this obligation.' "

"And the proprietor merely nods and smiles and wishes one good day and hopes for the quick return of one?"

"On the contrary—an official is rapidly called, one is taken away to jail until the next day, when one sees the magistrate, who sentences one to serve two weeks further in jail."

"Aha! So your proposal is that one should pay for one good meal in a fancy restaurant in San Francisco by spending two weeks and one day in jail. Somehow . . ."

"Abdul, if you will show the patience for which you are truly famous for a few more seconds . . . The meal in the restaurant, you must understand, is merely the device. Food cooked in the fancy manner of another culture is not necessarily appealing. But, Abdul, the food in that jail—the wonderful food in that jail!"

SELECTED EXCERPTS FROM THE TRANSCRIPT OF THE TRIAL IN THE CASE OF DOLLIVAN (plaintiff) VS. THE VANSPEEPE TRANSPORTER GATE WEB CORPORATION (WORLDWIDE) AND THE CITIES OF ATHENS, BANGKOK, BERLIN, BIRMINGHAM, BOMBAY, BOSTON, BUDAPEST, BUENOS AIRES, CAIRO, CALCUTTA, CANTON, CHICAGO, CHUNGKING, DELHI, DETROIT, DJAKARTA, ESSEN, HAMBURG, KARACHI, LENINGRAD, LOS

ANGELES, LONDON, MADRAS, MADRID, MANCHESTER, MANILA, MELBOURNE, MEXICO CITY, MONTREAL, MOSCOW, NEW YORK, OSAKA, PARIS, PEKING, PHILADELPHIA, RIO DE JA- NEIRO, ROME, SAN FRANCISCO, SANTIAGO, SAO PAULO, SEOUL, SHANGHAI, SHENYANG, SYDNEY, TEHERAN, TIENTSIN, TOKYO, TORONTO, AND VICTORIA (hereinafter collectively called the defendant):

JUDGE: (the Honorable Milton B. Langworth) Is the plaintiff ready?

PLAINTIFF: I am an attorney in the State of New York, United States of America, licensed to appear before the bar of the World Court, your honor. I am appearing for Mrs. Samuel Breathwaite Dollivan. We are ready, your honor.

JUDGE: And the defense?

DEFENDANT: Geoffrey Vaspution, your honor, of the firm of Vaspution, Shirly, Dogeness, and Murphy, represent- ing the collective defendant except the cities of Essen, Hamburg, and Berlin, which have their own attorney, who is present, the city of Cairo, which claims that the present dispute is outside the jurisdiction of the Court, and the city of Delhi, which refuses to defend for phil- osophical reasons. We are ready, your honor.

JUDGE: You may proceed.

DEFEN: Before we continue, your honor, I would like to introduce a motion to have this case dismissed. With prejudice.

JUDGE: On what grounds? It seems a bit premature.

DEFEN: Your honor, the defendant is charged with, if I may read, "causing the instant death of the plaintiff's husband, Samuel Breathwaite Dollivan, by enticing him into and permitting him to enter a device known as a Vanspeepe Transporter Gate in the City of New York under the belief that it would somehow miraculously and instantaneously transport him to one of the forty- seven other cities in the so-called 'Web'; whereupon his body was deliberatcly, and with intent, immediately reduced to its constituent atoms, and the atoms changed from their material state into the form of energy, much as in an atomic bomb or other advanced infernal device, this causing and inducing his immediate death."

PLAIN: It seems very clear to me, your honor. A simple tort, real and punitive damages.

JUDGE: Yes. It sounds like a valid complaint. What is wrong with it?

DEFEN: Your honor, for the record, ask the attorney for the plaintiff to state his name.

JUDGE: Oh, wasn't it given? No, I don't remember. Sir, your name, please.

PLAIN: Dollivan, your honor: Samuel Breathwaite Dollivan.

JUDGE: I'm afraid I don't understand. Are you, in fact, this woman's husband?

PLAIN: In life I was, your honor.

[more]

"Doctor, I assure you, I am not crazy!"

"Fair enough, Mr. Goodale. Let me assure you, I am not a psychiatrist. A psychological dysfunction such as you are experiencing may have many direct physical causes. I'm merely going to give you a series of tests to see if we can isolate one of those causes. I'm a neurologist."

Mr. Goodale visibly relaxed. "I thought I was going to be, you know, laughed at," he said. "I almost didn't come, but my wife said I'd better. I never heard of anything like it: a forty-seven-year-old man waking up in the morning and suddenly he can't read. Nothing. I didn't think of it like it was a, you know, medical problem. All I could think of was Kafka. Everything felt strange. Kind of backward. And I couldn't read except in a mirror. You know, at first I was afraid to look in the mirror, like maybe I *had* turned into a, you know, giant cockroach. I haven't thought of that story in maybe twenty-five years and first thing when I woke up and everything was backwards I thought I was a cockroach. You *sure* you're not a shrink?"

"I'm not laughing at you, Mr. Goodale."

"Well, you feel kind of funny walking into a hospital and telling them you can't read anymore. I see fine, but I just can't read any more. Except in a mirror. If you don't find anything, is my medicard going to cover this? I mean, is it going to cost me anything?"

"Cradle to the grave, Mr. Goodale," the doctor said, twitching open the medical record. "Say, you know you write backwards too?"

"I do?"

"Yes indeedy. Say, this isn't a put-on, is it? You weren't hired by one of my associates, were you?"

"It's very interesting, in a way," Mr. Goodale said, gently tapping himself on the chest with the flat of his hand. "*Yaw eno,* for example. I never realized the beauty of road signs until I saw them reversed coming in to the hospital. *Nrut tfel on.* I live on *eunevA nosidaM.*"

"Here," the doctor said, handing Mr. Goodale a ballpoint. "Write something. Use the paper on the desk."

Mr. Goodale took the pen and made a few flourishes in the air. "What shall I write?"

"Anything. Sign your name; that'll do for a start." He watched as Mr. Goodale carefully scrawled his name in mirror-writing, from right to left. "Have you always been left-handed? Can you write at all with your right hand?"

"Left-handed?" Mr. Goodale sounded puzzled. He lifted the hand which held the pen. "*Right*-handed, you mean!"

"Curious," the doctor commented, mostly to himself. "Medula? Frontal lobe, perhaps. Well! Let us start at the beginning, and keep going until we reach the end, and *then* diagnose." He took a disposable stethescope from its plastic bag, pincered one end onto his ears and waved the other end toward his patient's chest. "Unbutton your shirt," he said. "Breathe," he said. "Hmmm!" he said. "Well!" he said. He clutched convulsively for the record folder and started flipping pages. "One thing about the computerization of hospital records; you sure get to know more about a patient than you want, or can use. But somewhere in this mountain of socialized facts there should be a statement—some simple notice—nothing! You'd think someone would have noted ... After all, a man's heart ..."

"My heart, Doctor? What's the matter? There's something wrong with my heart?"

"Not that way, no. It's just on the wrong ... Aha!"

"Aha?"

"You've had your appendix removed!"

"That's right. At this hospital. It was two, no three, years ago."

"Let's see it!"

"The appendix? I'm sorry, I didn't keep it. I didn't know you were supposed to."

"No, Mr. Goodale; not the appendix: the *scar*."

"Oh. Here it is, Doctor." Goodale pulled his shirt up and indicated an almost invisible hairline scar.

"Right!" the doctor said, a satisfied smirk on his face. "Now if *that* was abnormal they'd have to have mentioned it. Mr. Goodale, I know what's wrong with you."

"You do? What?" he asked, clutching his hands together over his belly. "Is it malign?"

"Sit down."

"That bad?" He sat. "I'm ready."

"Mr. Goodale, you've been turned inside out!"

"What?" He stood. "I've been what? What does that mean?"

"I have no idea," the doctor told him. "Inside out is perhaps inexact: you've been flipped right for left. Your heart has changed sides, your appendix scar has changed sides, your brain, apparently, is comprehending in reverse. Luckily you can understand speech, since it's a linear function; but anything with bilateral symmetry you've reversed."

"I don't exactly, understand." Mr. Goodale looked frightened.

"Mr. Goodale, raise your right hand."

Mr. Goodale complied.

"Very good. Now, to you that's your right hand. Always has been, always will be. But to me, and to the rest of the outside world, Mr. Goodale, that's your *left* hand. Sometime in the recent past you've flipped over, like a fourth dimensional flapjack!"

"Is this, ah, common, Doctor? Is it covered by my medicard? Is it curable?"

"I don't think there's anything I can treat," the doctor said. "It seems to be harmless, if annoying. You'll have to learn how to read again; and you'll have to get a medicalert bracelet or something similar. Just a simple statement: *'Heart and other internal organs on wrong side.'* Just in case you get in a car accident or something."

"What causes this?"

"I don't know. Not common, I assure you. Have you done anything unusual recently? Unusual for you, I mean. Doesn't have to be unique."

"Well, I've been on this diet my wife found: the Eat, Drink, Throw Up, and Stay Slim Diet. This doctor found it in some research he was doing on the ancient Romans. Been on it for two weeks now. Funny, I haven't been hungry until we broke the diet last night for that Chinese dinner. Since then I've been getting hungrier and hungrier. Every time my wife goes on a diet, I go on a diet."

"I don't see how the diet could have anything to do with this," the doctor told Mr. Goodale, "but I must say that I think this particular diet is medically unsound. What about the Chinese dinner?"

"Tell that to my wife, Doctor, not me. The idea of barfing after dinner doesn't grow on you even after you've done it for two weeks. The only thing unusual about the

Chinese dinner was that we had it in Shanghai. That's getting pretty common these days, I guess, with the Transgate; but it's still new to us." "Aha!" the doctor said. "The Transgate!"

"Could that have done it?"

"I think it's safe to assume that anything which can flip you from place to place electronically can turn you inside out—or wrongside around—or whatever. We'll look into it. Any other symptoms you've noticed since last night—anything at all?"

"Nothing but being hungry. I guess it's either the Chinese food or the diet, but it is something new."

"We'll check you out. How do you feel now?"

"Hungry."

[continued]

PLAIN: Vibrations, you say, Professor? The transporter turns a person into a bunch of vibrations? Something like a symphony, or a cantata?

WITNESS: (Professor Harold Vanspeepe) That is an incorrect statement of what I told you, sir. We are—all matter is—merely a complex pattern of vibrations at all times. What the Vanspeepe Matter Transporter does is to transmit these vibrations through space—a high-order space, you understand—in the form of an energy analog of the matter. Surely . . .

PLAIN: It turns matter into energy. We understand that, Professor. Would you say it turns us into, like, radio waves, then beams these waves to a new location?

WITNESS: No, sir; I most assuredly would not say that! That is a gross oversimplification, and contains several errors in fact.

PLAIN: But Professor, bear in mind that I and the other people present in this courtroom are non-technical people, and not distinguished scientists like yourself. For our untechnical brains, in a grossly oversimplified statement that we mere laymen can understand, wouldn't a description of beamed waves be fair?

WITNESS: Well . . .

PLAIN: Thank you, Professor. Now, where in this beam, in which matter is destroyed, converted into energy and then reconstructed at the other end, is the soul?

WITNESS: But . . .

PLAIN: If we were to think of a radio or television program, Professor, we would realize that the real person is not there in front of us; merely the reproduced sight and sound of that person. By the same analog, Professor, is it not fair to state that in the Vanspeepe Transporter it isn't the real person who comes out to us on the other end, but merely his reproduced body?

WITNESS: I have no idea what that means. It isn't scientific.

PLAIN: Thank you, Professor. You may step down now.

[more]

"The fucking Vanspeepe Transporter," Edith X said, savagely throwing a tray of papers into the wastecatcher, where they disappeared with a popping sound and a slight smell of ozone, "has caused more troubles than any other five inventions in history lumped together!"

"Don't bitch, Edith," said her executive assistant, a dumpy little man named Clovis; "it has also created the power base that's made this office the most important political position in the world. 'City Manager of Earth,' they call you. Stop throwing the trays away with the papers, they're getting expensive to replace."

"But it's such a goddamn uphill fight," Edith said. "Every time something new happens somebody else wants to close down the system or set up barriers or something. We'll be back to passports and border guards pretty soon; only they'll be at the gates instead of at the borders. Who the hell crosses borders any more?"

"A little imagination, that's all it takes," Clovis said. "You've got to keep one step ahead of them, that's all. Like those kid gangs; the metal detectors at the gates stopped them cold. It's no fun to rumble in some strange city if you've got to do it bare-knuckled and the local hoods have all the firepower."

"You are imaginative and effective, I grant you, Clovis; the best damn executive assistant I've ever had. I've always said that men make the best secretaries. But every time we solve one problem, there are two more wagging their stubby little tails around the corner."

"That's known as life, Edith. You want no problems— drop dead. Don't take that personally; I meant it illustratively only."

## HOMETOWN JAIL BILL PASSES GENERAL ASSEMBLY

NEW YORK, Monday (cns)

In an example of that international spirit that is rapidly making the United Nations a true World government, the General Assembly today passed the so-called Hometown Jail Bill by an overwhelming voice vote.

The bill provides that any person convicted of a crime anywhere on Earth in a country not his own can be sent back to his place of citizenship to serve the sentence, the cost being defrayed by the sentencing authority. This "bill," in reality a draft treaty, is designed to halt the wave of misdemeanors committed by people from the poverty pockets who gate to rich-nation cities for the sole purpose of spending a few weeks in jail.

The bill is expected to be ratified and passed into the ever-expanding body of International Law within a matter of weeks.

[continued]

JUDGE: The jury having found for the plaintiff, I have no choice but to so declare. I award real damages in the amount of one million dollars, and exemplary damages in the amount of one dollar. Will counsel for the plaintiff please step forward.

I find no choice, Mr. Dollivan, but to conclude, on the basis of the jury's findings, that you are not a true person, but a sort of *doppelgänger*, without a soul, or essence of whatever it is that makes one human. Personally I think that this is a ridiculous finding, and one that should not be used as a precedent. I intend, Mr. Dollivan, to see that it isn't by discouraging such cases in the future.

PLAIN: I don't understand, your honor.

JUDGE: Mr. Dollivan, a jury of your peers, at your insistance, has found you to be not human. Therefore I find that you are, and must be, a chattel of the Vanspeepe Transporter Gate Web Corporation, in whose apparatus you were first discovered.

PLAIN: But, your honor, you can't . . .

JUDGE: You no longer have any standing in this court. This case is closed.

"I'm sorry, Mr. Goodale, it isn't going to be as simple as I first thought."

"What do you mean, Doctor? What's the problem?"

"I neglected polarity. I mean, it's not something that comes up every day. As a matter of fact, it's never happened before. Never. Mr. Goodale, you are now left handed *all over*. All those nice little right-handed sugar and protein molecules can no longer be utilized by your body for food. Mr. Goodale, no matter how much you eat, you're starving to death!"

"You mean it's not this crummy diet? How the hell do you like that! So what do I do?"

"I admire your faith, Mr. Goodale. As a matter of fact, there *is* something you can do, and I'd suggest you do it right away."

"Great. What's that?"

"Sue the Transporter Gate Web Corporation for a lot of money. And don't lose!"

"How's that?"

"Mr. Goodale, we're going to have to synthesize everything you eat. You're going to live on a thick broth of the worst-tasting left-handed amino acids ever made out of coal tar. In a couple of days you're going to look back nostalgically on the worst diet your wife ever dreamed up. And I think we can keep the price down to four or five thousand dollars a day."

"If you think the Goodale case is bad," Clovis said cheerfully, "I got a worse one for you now!"

"That poor guy," Edith X said; "what a hell of a thing."

"Yeah, but at least there's a chance of a cure. If they can figure out what happened to him, exactly, they can do it again and he'll re-flip. But this new one—guy called Langart—*he's* got a problem."

"Another transporter case?"

"Right on!"

"And they can't stick him back in the machine to cure it?"

"Don't see how. Which one would they stick back?"

"Which . . . ?"

"Yup. There's two of him. He left Beunos Aires and arrived in New York. At the same instant, he arrived in Shenyang. Then he went home. Both of him. His wife is about to have a nervous breakdown, and neither of him is looking too calm either."

"I resign," Edith said.

"You can't," Clovis told her. "You have a lunch date with the Secretary General. Right now Professor Vanspeepe is here to see you."

Edith took a deep breath. "Show him in," she said.

Professor Vanspeepe advanced like the Hun taking Belgium. "I have it all solved!" he yelled.

"Everything?" Edith asked.

"It is all clear! Why didn't I see it before? Another two years and everyone will have one!"

"One what?"

"Vanspeepe Personal Transporter. Just wear it around your waist like a girdle. Self-power. *Poof!* You are where you want. No receiver necessary. It will change the world!"

Edith leaned back. "No doubt," she said.

# SYDNEY J. VAN SCYOC

## and

## R. BRETNOR

# WHEN PETALS FALL

## Sydney J. Van Scyoc

The appearance of a story by **Sydney J. Van Scyoc** is always a special event, whether it is short, as this is, or a novel, such as her **Saltflower** and **Assignment: Nor'dyren,** both from Avon. Both in miles and in thought, she is a long way from the Indiana town she was born in.

Her husband and the Air Force took her to the Pacific, where she studied briefly at the University of Hawaii, and it was there that she really set herself to writing. Her first story appeared in **Galaxy** in 1962, and in 1967 she buckled down to a rigorous writing schedule in spite of the demands of her two young children.

Today she lives in Hayward, California, and her output is increasing each year. She is also active in a local group concerned with birth defects, and her general concern for the human condition and individual rights to health are reflected in this story.

•

It was 2 A.M. when Kelta pushed the night buzzer at the personnel entrance. A minute later a narrow night face, male variety, appeared at the opening door. Kelta palmed her credentials at him. "Federal Inspector." Quickly she stepped past into the corridor, a tall, lean girl with straight brows and purpose in her voice. "Take me to the central desk please."

The orderly stared at her incredulously. "You can't come in here."

"I have. Now examine my credentials again and take me to the desk."

"You—" He frowned at the credential case in her hand, shook his head, reluctantly surrendering to her authority.

The corridor turned, branched, and they approached a broad counter behind which appeared another night face, female variety, sandwiched unpalatably between stiff white collar and bun of rusty hair.

"Miss Hastings, this—"

"This Federal Inspector is bumping the aide on Ward Seven for the remainder of the shift," Kelta finished for him, presenting her credentials, sliding out of her coat. Beneath she wore white.

Hastings gaped at the emergent uniform, at the tall girl inside it. She turned the credentials, digested them biliously. Her face pulled itself together. "You can't enter this facility at this hour. Inspections are scheduled through Director Behrens herself. For daylight hours."

"Well, my approach is a little different. I'm Inspector West, transferred out of Federal District Four six months ago."

Intelligence invaded the stony eyes. "So."

"So," Kelta agreed, confident her reputation had preceded her. "I'm sure you know that if a Federal Inspector is denied entry, the facility may find its license suspended upon twenty-four hours' notice. That would involve relocating a number of patients very rapidly."

Hastings' face underwent a second unpleasant rearrangement. She moved to the end of the counter, punched at the commset there. She molded the privacy receiver against her ear. "Director, I'm sorry to disturb you at home, but there is a Federal Inspector here. West. She is trying to enter Seven." Her glance returned to Kelta. "Director wants the name of your superior."

"I'm sure she knows Pallan Holmes has been Supervising Inspector in this district for several years. But she may not know that if I'm not conducted to Seven within five minutes, my report to Holmes will reflect your lack of cooperation. Combined with what happened here three nights ago, that could have a deleterious effect upon the licensure of this institution."

Quickly Hastings relayed the ultimatum. A moment later she proferred the receiver. "Director Behrens will speak with you herself."

Kelta shook her head. "Tomorrow, after I've completed my inspection." She retrieved her credentials, dropped them into her bag. Deftly she flipped her dark hair off her collar, rolled it, and pinned it to her head.

Waited.

Five minutes later the door of Ward Seven slid and Kelta stepped in. Her eyes swung up the steep walls. Tiers of care cradles, serviced by narrow, railed catwalks, reached to the ceiling. A deserted monitor desk commanded a view of both cradle walls of Ward Seven.

Hastings' voice rattled up the walls. "Ames?"

A face appeared upon an upper catwalk, eyes large.

"Inspection. You're dismissed for the night."

The aide's eyes slid to Kelta. She pattered down the stairs, stepped quickly behind the desk to retrieve her coat. Vanished through the sliding door.

Kelta stepped to the desk. Her eyes moved across the display of monitor panels. Over half those panels were dark tonight. The ones that were illuminated, indicating occupied cradles, were scattered randomly. "I see you haven't consolidated the survivors on the lower tiers."

Hastings glanced at the display without comment.

"Didn't it strike you at the time of the raid that there

was an unusually high survival rate? Normally when a Messenger strikes, 95 percent of the patients are lost. In this case, better than 40 percent were salvaged."

Hastings' eyes were impenetrable. "Evidently the girl failed to pull the tubes early enough in her shift."

Kelta nodded. "Possible." She dropped her coat over the back of the seat. "But I'm very interested in that survival rate." Her mouth moved in a quick, impersonal smile. "Please don't let anyone interrupt me tonight."

Hastings moved to fortify her position. "Director Behrens instructed me—"

"To see that I don't turn in an unfavorable report. And I'm telling you I don't want to be annoyed by anyone while I'm at work. I will sign out when day shift arrives at 6 A.M."

There was a recoiling in the stony eyes. "Night shift terminates at 4 A.M. on these wards."

Kelta's eyebrows rose. "Oh? Who takes the load between 4 and 6?"

"Monitor readout is switched to the central desk. I take it myself."

Kelta's eyes narrowed. "I see. Well, I'll relieve you of this one ward tonight."

The rocky eyes turned briefly to lava. Then Hastings withdrew.

Alone, Kelta dropped her bag beside the desk. She sat, touched the surface of the desk. Here, only three nights before, a Messenger of Mercy had sat watching these readout panels while her patients died in their cradles. Then, shortly before her shift ended, she had disappeared into the night. She hadn't been seen since.

Not by anyone who hunted her.

Kelta stood and mounted the catwalks, walked the tiers. The old lay in their cradles swaddled in senility, entubed at every orifice, gaping eyes deserted, lax mouths wordless. Forty-two of them doggedly fighting out the last moments of personal existence, blood circulated by machinery, minds erased by age, they waited for the miracle that could restore them to function, however minimal. Waited for someone, somewhere, to make the immortality-breakthrough before their bodies deteriorated to the point where even the machinery of Ward Seven would be useless to them.

But these particular patients seemed to have an edge on the elderly in other nursing homes across the country. Because when the Messenger had disentubed this ward three nights ago, forty-two of these patients had resisted death. Forty-two of a hundred had remained warm and breathing.

Now Kelta examined those forty-two. In most she found several unusual conditions. The skin that stretched across the wasted muscles and prominent bones was leathery, lacking the typical fragility of age. Turning the patients she found no sign of bedsores. In these same patients, Kelta found the surfaces of the eyeballs subtly mottled. In most there were perceptible deformities of the limbs, bones of the forearms and forelegs oddly bent.

When Kelta had examined all the present occupants of the ward, she selected her three test cases. Grimly she disconnected them from the equipment that maintained them, leaving their tubes arcing loose like so many strands of half-cooked spaghetti. Then she returned to the monitor desk and sat.

Waiting.

Watching.

In all three cases, blood pressure fell—and stabilized. Heart action appeared—and stabilized. Temperature fell, four degrees—and stabilized. No distress lights flashed. Within their cradles the three patients drew breath without artificial aid.

Just as they had three nights before.

Kelta frowned, bobbed up to make visual check. She found respiration barely perceptible, pulse light but steady, skin surfaces slightly cool, but not with the chill of death. This was the chill of life.

Unnatural life. The lines of Kelta's face lengthened. Her lips set.

At 5:50 A.M. she reconnected her three subjects and settled behind the desk again. At 6 the door slid. A thirtyish woman in white stepped through, eyes anxious. Kelta stood. "Day duty?"

"I'm—yes, I'm Fisher." Fisher's eyes moved nervously up the tiers.

"How long have you been on Seven, Fisher?"

Fisher probed dry lips with pale tongue. "Three years."

"Notice anything unusual about the patients who survived the Messenger call?"

Again Fisher's eyes made the anxious trip up the tiers. "They're—well, they're different. They're—" Her voice died uncertainly.

Kelta nodded. "Any idea whether they're on special medication?"

Fisher shook her head. "A registered nurse administers medications. I'm not qualified."

Kelta nodded again, stood, flipped her coat off the back of the chair. "Well, I think you'll find everything in order. There were no emergencies."

Upstairs Hastings waited stiffly behind the desk while her relief moved busily behind her. "What time does Director Behrens normally sign in?" Kelta asked.

"Director arrives at 9:30."

"Good. Leave word that I'll be in to speak with her then."

Outside the world was dim, the walks almost empty. Kelta plunged through the dawn-fogged loneliness toward the transit stop, preoccupied. At the hotel she shelled out a dozen water tokens and showered. It refreshed her little.

Immortality. Someone was on the verge of the breakthrough, perhaps had already penetrated the barrier. There could be no other explanation. But she was not helpless in the face of this development. Not if the patients on Ward Seven, and probably on other wards as well, had been used in the way she suspected they had been used.

At 8:30 she hit the commset and reached the district headquarters. "Supervisor Holmes, please."

Pallan Holmes appeared upon the faceplate, a big man with curly locks that tumbled over his forehead and a vague expression. It became less vague when he met Kelta's eyes. "West," he acknowledged painfully.

"I've run across something a little unusual in my present assignment. I'm scheduling the day to deal with it. I may have to requisition someone to back me up later in the day."

Alarmed, Holmes pawed at his desklog. "You're at Leisure Gardens in Cincinnati?"

"No. Taylor-Welsh Home in Cleveland. I rearranged my schedule. I wanted to observe the aftermath of the Messenger strike three nights ago."

Holmes' voice rose in alarm. "West, Taylor-Welsh is one of the higher caliber homes in our district. We've never had cause for complaint there. Management has always been fully cooperative with the department, and the department in turn—"

"The department has always been fully cooperative with management. You've even allowed Director Behrens to schedule 'impromptu' inspections at her own convenience."

Holmes swept at his curls, his eyes lost in agony. "West, it's our policy to cooperate with reputable facilities whenever we can. Particularly when they're as ably administered as Taylor-Welsh. I've known Director Behrens personally—"

"A convenient arrangement for everyone, though sometimes I think that philosophy has something to do with the way I'm bounced from district to district. I'll call later if I need help. I'd appreciate it if you would hold Napp available."

Holmes' face twisted. "West, you're not—"

"You'll probably have a call from Director Behrens later this morning. I haven't interviewed her yet." Quickly Kelta broke connection, retreated from the commset.

It summoned a moment later. Kelta did not answer. Somehow she recognized the wounded tone of its cry.

At 9:35 she was admitted to Director Behrens' private office.

Director Behrens was a middle-aged woman with glossy green hair. Matching nails lay upon her desk. "The type of off-hours inspection you subjected this facility to last night would be far more appropriate to some undercapitalized vegetable farm," she snapped, green nails tapping the desktop once in sharp emphasis.

"Well, I guess you've already heard that I don't tailor my visits to suit management," Kelta said, sitting. "And I thought the Messenger raid unusual enough a circumstance to warrant an unusual type of visit."

Director Behrens' face creased bitterly. "Inspector, no home in the nation is invulnerable to those fanatics. I learned that three nights ago. Despite every precaution, they slipped through to work their devastation upon our business."

"And not upon your patients?"

Behrens' face colored slightly. "Our patients *are* our business. They've entrusted their futures to us. In the past years, our district association has watched this scourge concentrate first upon one district, then upon another. Now apparently it is our turn. Seven homes ravaged in a bare four months. I completely fail to understand why the authorities have not prosecuted these people."

"The fact that none of them have ever been apprehended may have something to do with it."

"And *why* have none been apprehended? Over a period of five years? After thousands of deaths?"

Kelta shrugged. "The operation appears to be very well managed. The Messenger appears with an apparently valid certificate from a local aide training school. She works for a day, maybe for two or three days, even four. Then, before anyone on the staff has had time to become acquainted with her, she pulls the plug and disappears, never striking again. It later develops that the girl who actually graduated from the training course has disappeared too. The local girl whose name and background both Messengers borrowed is always found to be in complete ignorance. Presumably both Messengers change their appearance and resume their former lives.

"The leaders of the movement issue periodic statements of philosophy and intent—but never in such a way as to point to the identity of any member of the organization. You know, I've even heard it suggested that any member who has delivered her Message is immediately and permanently disaffiliated."

Behrens nodded impatiently. "Oh yes, I've heard all the theories. And I feel it should be made adequately clear to the public that when an incident of this nature occurs, the home is in no way at fault. Despite all my media releases, this home is losing patients at the rate of two dozen a day."

"Unfortunate." Kelta's tone became remote from the topic. "Now. My first question concerns the two hour gap between night shift and day shift on the wards."

Behrens' green nails disappeared beneath whitening knuckles. "During those two hours all monitor systems are read at the central desk, Inspector. The nurse on duty can attend to any emergency within moments. Our patients are in no way endangered by this simple economy measure."

Kelta nodded. "I see. But I wonder why you economize in that particular way when no other reputable home leaves wards unattended during the early morning hours."

"Inspector, there is nothing within regulations to prohibit this particular arrangement."

"No. As a matter of fact, there isn't. Now, I'm interested in the patients who survived the Messenger raid. Have you examined them yourself?"

"I never enter the wards."

"But I'm sure you know these patients show some interesting physical manifestations. A difference in skin texture and thickness, a mottling of the ocular surfaces, limb deformities. Are these attributable to some medication these patients receive?"

"You may speak with our staff physician tomorrow. He is out today."

Kelta shook her head. "I think I will learn just as much by examining your patient files."

Behrens stared at her. Her face whitened. "The condition of the patients on our wards is testimony enough to the care we render here."

"Well, I'm going to see the files anyway, Director. Immediately."

Director Behrens sat, stark and still. Then, abruptly, she stood, her eyes fierce. She stalked out.

Kelta sat back in the chair to wait. There would be a delay, she knew, while Director Behrens called Pallan Holmes. In a few cases, Kelta's Supervising Inspector had actually summoned her back to district headquarters before she had completed inspection. But she doubted that Pallan Holmes would respond that vigorously or directly.

Ten minutes later the door opened. A secretary tapped across the floor, pressed the control that brought the microviewer up from Director Behrens' desktop, inserted a plate of microrecords. "You'll be able to view better from this chair."

"Thank you." Kelta installed herself in the Director's chair. "Do these include files on the patients who died in the raid?"

"Why, no. These only include patients who are on Seven now."

"I want the others too."

The secretary wheeled, addressed a silent question to

Director Behrens, who stood at the door. Tight-lipped, Behrens nodded.

Kelta flashed through the files in half an hour. Then she stacked the two plates. "Wrapping paper and tape, Director?"

Behrens stared at her, grappling for voice. "For what purpose?"

"I'm going to take these records with me. They're quite interesting."

"They're—you can't."

Kelta stood, tapping the plates. "I don't find any mention here of the medication being administered to the patients who survived the raid and not to the others on Seven. Something else I don't find is signed consent forms."

"Consent? For what?"

"For the drug that obviously *is* being dispensed to those patients sometime between 4 and 6 A.M. It's a criminal offense, you know, to use experimental drugs on patients who haven't been apprised of all details and who haven't signed consent forms while in clear mind."

"This home—Inspector, Taylor-Welsh would never risk the welfare of its patients in the fashion you intimate."

Kelta shook her head. "I'm not intimating. I'm stating. Studying these records, I see that the patients who survived the Messenger strike are actually on the average older than the patients who died. I disconnected several of the survivors myself this morning—for three hours. From their medical records, and from my personal observation, I can say they should have expired almost immediately. They didn't, anymore than they expired when the Messenger disentubed them. They're receiving a drug that enables them to survive. But there's no such drug on the market. Therefore it's experimental. And there are no signed consent forms in these files."

Director Behrens' eyes flashed. "Young woman, it would be much more to the point for you to attempt to find the person who killed over fifty of our patients than to persecute the administration of a reputable home."

"I'm a facility inspector, Director. My job is to police the management of nursing homes. The local and state police forces will have to track the Messenger for you."

"And they'll never catch her! They never do! These children—they come into our facilities, devastate our business, and then they drop from sight! Idealists they call themselves!"

Kelta's brows rose. "Well, there *are* a lot of ways the time and money you expend here could be put to better use."

"These children might think differently if they were old themselves."

Kelta shrugged. "Wrapping paper and tape?"

There was another delay. Then the requested items appeared. Kelta secured the two plates into a small package. "I'm filing departmental action immediately to insure that those patients aren't removed from the facility. If you need me, I'll be at the Southside Hotel for the rest of the day."

Before proceeding there, however, she locked the microplates into a box in a security vault. The key to the box she mailed to herself at district headquarters.

Reaching her room, she called Pallan Holmes again. He flashed on screen in a state of agitation, curls bobbing distraught. "West, I've had two calls from Director Behrens at Taylor-Welsh in the past hour."

"I'll fill you in later," Kelta said quickly. "I have some very interesting evidence in safekeeping, but I need a backup man immediately. Is Napp available?"

"West, Taylor-Welsh is one of the most respected homes for the aged in our district. I've known Director Behrens—"

"Yes—personally for a number of years. Is Napp available? I want sound equipment with him, and I want him now."

Discussion ensued. Kelta prevailed. Napp was scheduled on the next flash west.

He arrived an hour later, appeared at Kelta's door, a burly young man with reddish-blond hair creeping up from his chest and back from his forehead. "You jarred me off write-up on a week's work. You're offering thrills?"

Kelta grinned. "I'm offering. You have the sound equipment?"

Napp nodded, stepping into the room, glancing around. "Here?"

Kelta chewed her lower lip. "No, elsewhere, I think. I want a remote button."

Napp nodded, setting down his case, rummaging in it. Kelta studied the top of his head, hoping her evaluation of him had been accurate. "How much stock do you hold, Napp?"

Napp's brows furnished brief warmth to his balding upper forehead. "Pardon?"

"Stock. United Textile East. Singer Diversified. General Paper and Plastics."

Napp's grin cleared a dozen and a half solid white teeth. "You know, West, I've observed that ownership of stock tends to interfere with pursuit of duty. So I don't own any stock. But I hear others in the department own a little. I guess you've run into that, as much as you've bounced districts."

"Repeatedly. Now I think I'm about to be offered some myself." She accepted the small blue sound button along with his appraising glance. She clipped the button into the hair at the base of her neck. "Has this equipment been checked out recently?"

"I checked everything while I was waiting for flash time."

The call came minutes later. A smooth masculine voice, a matter of mutual interest to be discussed, a rendezvous arranged.

A rendezvous kept. Kelta arrived at the hotel bar,

where a reserved booth awaited her, five minutes early. She wore a brief dress with buttercup skirt strips that flapped across her long thighs. She had touched her lips with color, but her brows remained straight and uncompromising.

That fact she obscured temporarily with a bright false smile when two sleek men in business blue were conducted to the booth, suits glossy, smiles glassy. "Miss West?"

"Yes," she agreed, sitting again.

Prosperity on their jowls, shrewdness in their eyes, they were Patrick and Nussman. "Our colleague, Dr. Vincinzi, will meet us in a few moments," Nussman reassured Kelta smoothly. "I think we may order without him."

They ordered. Drinks arrived.

Nussman leaned earnestly across the table. "Now, Miss West, it has been suggested that you are an excellent prospect for investment counseling. You hold a civil service position with good salary and security prospects. You're young, dedicated, very much involved with your profession. Too involved, I'm sure, to make careful analysis of the market yourself or to spend much time watching your stocks as they must be watched to derive maximum benefit from your investment program."

Kelta tilted her drink, examined the bottom of the glass through it, nodding. "My time is so completely filled I've never gotten around to investing at all. Which counseling service do you represent?"

"Ah." Nussman flourished an embossed card. "Actually we represent Robard Wheels East, a diversified industrial and service firm. Casters, utility wheels, rubber products—"

"Nursing homes."

Nussman's glib attempt to gloss over Kelta's interruption was interrupted in turn by the arrival of an elderly man, slight and visibly withdrawn. Patrick and Nussman bobbed up. "Dr. Vincinzi, Inspector Kelta West. We were just discussing Miss West's investment program."

"Which is currently non-existent," Kelta added, her eyes on the older man. He joined them with obvious reluctance. "Do you represent Robard East too, Dr. Vincinzi?"

Vincinzi's forehead creased faintly. "Not in the way Patrick and Nussman do." His eyes met Kelta's briefly, then moved away, avoiding his associates.

Nussman reasserted himself. "Miss West, we're here because a mutual acquaintance suggested you might appreciate being introduced to a new investment plan. Our plan, you see—it's still in the pilot stage—is designed to help responsible younger citizens find their way into the market by granting them substantial blocks of Robard at very nominal prices. In addition, you will be introduced to one of the investment firms we have found reliable in our own trading. They will handle your account without fee. In fact, it might be possible to arrange an extended program, a certain number of shares of Robard East being entered upon your account semi-annually over a decade. Of course, you would be in no way obliged to retain the stock. You could trade or sell, although your counselors would advise you that Robard is a diversified concern with many excellent prospects."

Kelta nodded gravely. "Are you in the pharmaceutical line, Dr. Vincinzi?"

The older man's eyes came up, faded, wary.

Nussman hastened into the gap. "Now, Miss West, we can't discuss certain aspects of our enterprise at all. Pharmaceuticals are a very touchy field. If the nature or direction of certain researches are leaked too soon, the opportunity to sweep the market—at enormous profit—could be lost forever. That would considerably diminish what you might otherwise expect to realize from your own block of Robard."

"I see. How many nursing homes does Robard hold?"

Nussman's smooth forehead was briefly marred by irritation. "Robard holds half a dozen of the better homes in this state."

"And in how many of those are experiments in extended longevity being conducted?"

The three men were silent. Perspiration appeared upon Nussman's forehead.

"Only in the Taylor-Welsh home and Walden Gardens," Dr. Vincinzi said quietly, finally meeting and holding Kelta's eye.

"And how far has the research progressed, Doctor?"

Vincinzi's pale eyes were troubled. "I have developed a serum—with the help of my assistants and research staff, of course—that produces, as nearly as we can determine, virtual immortality. Unfortunately it does nothing to deter the progress of senility. It does not delay the onset or ameliorate the more distressing manifestations of senility even slightly. Virtually all it does is enable the body to survive as a body, not as a viable personality."

"Are your subjects vulnerable to accidental death?"

Vincinzi nodded slowly. "They are. Severe blood loss— loss amounting to 80 percent or more—will produce death. Incineration of body tissues likewise will produce death." He shrugged. "Little else will. I have in my possession mice who are up to twenty years old. They are helpless. Hopeless. But alive."

"Like the patients I examined this morning, on Ward Seven."

Nussman moved uneasily. "Inspector, this is no place to discuss these matters. We made this appointment in order—"

Kelta's eyes were grave. "This is where we are going to discuss them. Doctor, have you considered the social aspects of your serum?"

"Present? Or future? I've considered both. I'm still considering them." Vincinzi shook his head. "When I went into this branch of research, I was a young man on the trail of conquest. Immortality—the unexplored frontier. If a breakthrough came in my time, it was my ticket to the future, to the centuries that lie ahead. My personality could survive, participate, contribute.

"Now I'm old. I see my development purely as a holding measure. There are hundreds of thousands of my generation in homes across this country, waiting. Most of them, if there were no startling development within the next few years, would die despite everything. But if my serum is marketed soon, they can continue to live. They can continue to wait—for the miracle that may someday restore them to consciousness and function." His eyes were sudddenly intense. "Perhaps they will never contribute much to the future—perhaps *I* never will. But the sun shines. Water flows. Children play and roses bloom. The simple pleasures continue. Can we deny ourselves them? Could you deny yourself, after your productive years are past?"

Kelta was aware of Nussman and Patrick's alert silence. She frowned. The personal case, always the personal case. The two entrepreneurs hoped Dr. Vincinzi's personal case would persuade her.

She could only give the personal answer. She reached for her bag, flipped out a handful of tokens, spread them before her. "Water flows, Doctor Vincinzi? This represents my water allowance for the next week. It will get me through two showers, some personal laundry, and hopefully I'll be able to wash my face each morning. Of course I don't drink from the tap. I don't like to use sick leave unnecessarily.

"Personal Exhibit #2, a photograph. My brother. He's twenty-two years old. He doesn't leave the apartment. That's because he's allergic to air—or to what passes for air. My parents have invested thousands of dollars in air filtration devices so he can survive inside the apartment.

"Exhibit #3, my radiation badge." She slipped it from around her neck. "It registers normal now. That's because I was reissued fourteen years ago, after the Dallas pile disaster. You'd be surprised how many young women are devoting themselves to careers or social causes because they'll never bear normal children."

She shook her head. "Your generation invested its time in a number of worthwhile purposes and in a number of frivolous ones. It created a number of problems we've all had to live with. Now, instead of passing on and leaving the one heritage any generation can leave—a clear field for the next generation to deal with those problems—it wants to linger. It wants present and future generations to maintain it indefinitely in thousands of storage homes all over the country. It wants precious resources expended upon it—water, power, pharmaceuticals, rubber, plastic, and metal products."

Kelta smiled grimly. "You're not just asking for moral support. You're asking for our drinking water, our oxygen, our children playing. I say no. You've had your roses, Doctor. I hope you enjoyed them. You've had your time on Earth too. Now it's our turn."

Nussman's features contracted ominously. "That sounds like the Messenger line."

"Is there anyone in the country who hasn't heard the Messenger line by now?"

Vincinzi touched Kelta's hand, his face grave. "You've answered my question, the one I've been asking myself—and sometimes these gentlemen—with increasing frequency these past few years. No man wants to go. But several mornings ago I stood on Ward Seven and saw fifty-eight dead. Fifty-eight, stiff and cold in their cradles. And a strange thought, an alien thought almost, entered my mind: death *is* a part of life."

"The rose petal drops." Kelta swung her head to meet two other pair of eyes. They glittered, stark and cold. "As I see it, Robard has a choice. It can face charges of illegal experimentation upon human subjects and attempting to bribe a federal officer—I have a sound man upstairs recording this conversation—or it can close down its immortality project. Immediately."

Nussman and Patrick sat very still. Finally Nussman creaked back to life. "You can't prove anything. Even with sound tracks."

"I can prove a lot. I *will* prove a lot if I have to. You can make your stock offer to every member of the district staff—and it won't keep *me* quiet." Kelta stood. "The reason the department keeps me bouncing from district to district is that I don't silence."

"But we have a massive investment in this project!" Patrick exploded. "We've dropped billions into this!"

Kelta smiled tautly. "Now you're going to lose billions. Either way. If the government prosecutes, your chance to grab the market dissolves. Along with your corporate image. If you turn off the project, you might salvage at least the image."

Nussman shook his head stubbornly. "No. You misread public climate. Federal funds support our nursing homes. The old have public sympathy. Our serum will have public sympathy too, even if there has been some infraction of the law."

"Oh? Which public? For how long? Nursing homes originally drew public funds because their clients were human beings. Now the nursing homes have created a clientele of objects, and I see public sympathy changing. I see the public resenting the flow of money and resources into the maintenance of corpses. I see the public beginning to realize, with each Messenger strike, that the only parties who benefit from the present arrangement are the owners of these homes." She shook her head. "You have a choice. Dr. Vincinzi, I think maybe you've made yours."

The older man spoke through dry lips. "I believe I have now."

Upstairs Napp repacked his equipment. Kelta twitched the remote sound button out of her hair, dropped it into his palm, sagged into a chair. "I want the sound tracks dropped directly into a security vault."

"Done." Napp's eyes were bright. "What do you think? Which light will they blink?"

Kelta shook her head. "I don't know. But I think we have them either way."

"You do?" Napp's brows went north, surprised. "Well, I can see Nussman and Patrick wading right through your charges and going ahead with their project, even from prison. There's still profit in corpses, even if it has to be shared."

Kelta shrugged. "In that case, I can see Messengers doing more than pulling tubes. I can see Messengers reversing blood flow back into the circulating equipment. Or creating a series of funeral pyres. And releasing more public statements, especially on the subject of the increased costs of maintaining the tubers.

"And I can see Vincinzi publicly denouncing the project if necessary. Maybe even delivering a Message to his experimental subjects himself. As a public demonstration of his feelings."

Napp's eyes widened. "Ah." His legs folded and he sat, on the floor. "That *was* the Messenger line you were unwinding downstairs."

Kelta's eyes rested upon him. The normally decisive line of her mouth drooped with weariness.

"The Messenger line—you've been in this district what? Five months?"

"Six."

"And four months ago we began getting heavy Messages. As many in a few months as we'd gotten in two years before."

Kelta's expression remained opaque.

Napp frowned intently. "You know, a facility inspector would be an ideal coordinator for Messenger operations. A facility inspector has access to everything, schedules, floor plans, personnel records, the facilities themselves. A facility inspector—"

Kelta unfolded from her chair, rummaged in her bag.

Came out with a handful of water tokens. "Napp, would you mind if I took a shower?"

Slowly Napp shook his head. "No. No, I'll go find a security vault." He grinned. "On the way back maybe I'll pick up a rose."

Kelta smiled. "All right. Buy a yard of sunshine, too. We'll spread it on the floor."

"And a puddle of rainwater? Enjoy it while we can."

"And one child playing." She touched her radiation badge, trying to keep the smile on her lips.

# PAPA SCHIMMELHORN AND
# THE S.O.D.O.M. SERUM

### R. Bretnor

**Reginald Bretnor** is a formidable British-looking person
of imposing stature and bearing. This remarkable exterior
conceals the soul of one of nature's few remaining gentlemen. He is deeply interested in military science, and in
1969 Stackpole Books published his theoretical study,
**Decisive Warfare.** He wrote the Encyclopedia Britannica
article on science fiction and is currently editing a sym-
posium on modern science fiction for a major hardcover
publisher.

A scholar of compleatist convictions and an avid Sher-
lockian, he has the singular distinction of having attended
a long list of private and public schools and colleges
without ever having acquired a formal degree of any
kind. This all began in Vladivostok, Siberia, where he
was born, and moved with him to Japan, where he spent
several years.

Reg is widely known for his science fiction humor. His
two most notable contributions to this subgenre have been
the adventures of Ferdinand Feghoot and the creation of
the redoubtable octogenarian genius lecher, Papa Schim-

melhorn, who first appeared in the pages of the second issue of **The Magazine of Fantasy and Science Fiction** in "The Gnurrs Come From The Voodvork Out." Imagine the editors' feeling of wild triumph when Reg volunteered to bring Papa from the retirement of so many years into a dizzying adventure involving longevity serums, an "X"-rated cuckoo clock, and a female mafiosa named (what else?) the Godmother.

●

It was Mama Schimmelhorn's own fault that, at the ripe old age of eighty-plus, in the very prime of his manhood and virility, Papa Schimmelhorn invented his longevity serum, designed to extend the human life span—or at least the Papa Schimmelhorn life span—by five hundred years. Had she not surprised him *in flagrante* with the lush, forty-year-old Widow Siracusa, and had she—when her suspicions were confirmed—refrained from inviting Pastor Hundhammer to witness the intensely painful confrontation, the Pastor would never have delivered his vitriolic diatribe on the imprudence of old men who wasted their declining years in lust and lechery, Papa Schimmelhorn would not have taken it so much to heart, and Bambi Siracusa would have had no reason to call in the Mafia Family to which her late husband, Jimmy "Fickle Finger" Siracusa, had belonged—though that, of course, was only after she and Mama Schimmelhorn had formed their infamous alliance.

As soon as possible, after listening to his wife recite the endless catalogue of his infidelities, Papa Schimmelhorn took refuge in his basement workshop. It was there, in his leisure hours, when he was neither working at his job as foreman at Heinrich Luedesing's cuckoo-clock factory nor pursuing his more serious hobby, that his soul found solace and his genius its full fruition. On this occasion, he remained uncomforted. Tenderly touching his bruised left ear, by which Mama Schimmelhorn had led him home, and ruefully feeling his injured ribs, which had felt the impact of her black umbrella's pointed ferrule, he sat down on his workbench. There, before him, was his 1922 Stanley Steamer touring car, painted British Racing Green, in which he planned to install an anti-gravity device of his own invention. There was his treasury of old bicycle frames, eviscerated typewriters, snaggle-toothed gears, and tangled springs. Beside him were his drills and chisels, vises, wood-shavings, and unlikely power tools seemingly derived from dead vacuum cleaners. And next to them was his old friend Gustav-Adolf, lashing his long, striped tail, purring loudly, and obviously enjoying the plump mouse he was devouring.

"Ach, Gustav-Adolf, you do not undershtand!" Flexing his mighty biceps, Papa Schimmelhorn groaned dismally. "Look at me! I am as good as new—chust ask my lidtle Bambi if you don't beliefe! But old Hundhammer iss right. Maybe only ten years, maybe fifteen—then no more chasing pretty lidtle pussycats. It iss all ofer—such a vaste!"

At the thought of all the ladies, young and middle-aged and even well-preserved elderly, now destined to be irremediably deprived, a tear appeared at the corner of his bright blue eye; and Gustav-Adolf, who understood him perfectly, growled in sympathy, pushed the remains of the mouse toward him with a paw, and said, "Go on an' eat it, chum—you'll feel lots better!" in Cat. He waited for a moment and, when his offer was ignored, philosophically polished off the mouse himself.

"But it iss not chust pussycats," sighed Papa Schimmelhorn. "It iss der vorld. Remember, Gustav-Adolf, I am a chenius. Vhen I vas chanitor at der Geneva Institute Für Higher Physics, efen Herr Doktor Jung came to shtudy me. Und for a vhile he paid for me to sit und listen, and read der old books and a lot of foolish new vuns, and vhen I asked him vhy he vould chust chuckle und say, 'Don't vorry, Papa. Someday from der subconscience it pops out.' Und he vas right. How my chenius vorks I do not know, but I haf invented der *gnurr-pfeife* to blow so die gnurrs come from der voodvork out.[1] Und also a time-machine. Und der anti-grafity so someday maybe ve fly der Stanley Shteamer. Und also—" He pointed at a newly contrived and splendid cuckoo-clock hanging on the wall. "—also I am an artist. Look! I make it for my lidtle Bambi—der vorld's only X-rated cuckoo-clock, adjusted mit tvelve positions, und vith a qvartet of cuckoos instead of only vun."

Sadly he turned the hands to twelve o'clock. The quartet of cuckoos—two tenors, a baritone, a bass—obligingly came out and sang the hour.

Gustav-Adolf tensed; then, remembering previous experiences with the Schimmelhorn variety of avifauna, relaxed disgustedly.

The cuckoos went back in. A larger door beneath them opened wide; a tiny Louis XVI bedstead emerged luxuriously; on it, in miniature, lay Mrs. Siracusa and an anonymous young man. Papa Schimmelhorn watched them sentimentally for quite a while. "I do not put myself," he explained to Gustav-Adolf. "It iss modesty, because I am a chenius." He sighed. "Und now Mama has made my lidtle-Bambi angry, und Pastor Hundhammer has lowered der boom." He shook his head self-pityingly. "A trachedy—imachine! Eferything cut off chust vhen I feel good for maybe fife hundred more years—"

He stopped. That subconscious which had so fascinated Jung—and which probably would have proved even more intriguing to Herr Doktor Freud—had slipped swiftly and silently into top gear. His eyes narrowed calculatingly. *"Und vhy not?"* he asked Gustav-Adolf. "Fife hundred

---

[1] "The Gnurrs Come From The Voodvork Out," in *Fantasy and Science Fiction*, Winter-Spring 1950. Reprinted *Special Wonder*, Random House 1970 and Beagle Books 1971.

years perhaps iss no more difficult than anti-grafity or
gnurrs!" He paused to contemplate the possibilities. The
number of pretty pussycats who could be chased successfully in half a thousand years seemed pretty much unlimited. He beamed. "Maybe it vorks!" he exclaimed delight-
edly. "Anyhow ve try. Und if I fix it, Gustav-Adolf, also I
giff you some. Maybe it lasts you vun hundred years only,
because you are a cat, but dot's better than chust two or
three, *nicht wahr?*"

*"Mrrrow!"* declared Gustav-Adolf emphatically.

Papa Schimmelhorn winked at him. He pointed warn-
ingly at the floor above. "Only remember!" he whispered.
"To Mama, not a vord!"

For several weeks, he was a model husband. When he
was not toiling at the cuckoo-clock factory, most of his
spare time was spent either in his workshop or at the public
library poring laboriously over treatises on genetics, cytol-
ogy, cytogenetics, biochemistry, and any number of other
subjects he did not understand—but which his subconscious
absorbed very effectively indeed. He dipped into learned
works on the mating habits of the bower bird, the decoc-
tion of ethers and esters and imitation Irish whiskey, the
electronic marvels of the Space Age, proctology made
easy, hypnotism, herpetology, and the magical and thera-
peutic properties of the ancient Chinese pharmacopoeia.
Occasionally, he made mysterious small purchases, and after a while Mama Schimmelhorn began to notice strange
vapors coming from the basement, some pleasant and actually enticing, others noxious and repellent, but his behavior lulled her suspicions temporarily. Every Sunday, for
the first time in their sixty-three years of married life, he
now accompanied her to church, and much to the astonishment of all it was his mighty voice that took the lead in
every hymn. Indeed, on his first visit, when Pastor Hundhammer abandoned his prepared sermon to deliver an ex-
temporaneous one on "Sodom"—which in Biblical times
had been a wicked city, but now could be taken to mean

"Shame On Dirty Old Men"—the AMEN! to which he gave utterance was positively heart-rending.

Mama Schimmelhorn's female friends rejoiced, with Pastor Hundhammer, in his reformation. The male members of the congregation, including his employer, old Heinrich Luedesing, began to whisper gloatingly that Papa was finally losing the powers they envied him. And in the meantime the R & D program in the basement proceeded toward its triumphant dénouement.

Naturally, Papa Schimmelhorn was excited—but he was not a man to leave anything to chance. "Ve giff it first to mices," he told Gustav-Adolf, eyeing a murky, evil-odored fluid in a pickle-jar. "Maybe you vork hard und catch? At first ten or tvelve vould be enough." He glanced into his friend's green, unwinking eyes, sighed, and went out to buy white mice from a pet shop. We need not detail either the ingredients that went into his final product or the seemingly disconnected and decidedly unsanitary processes by which it was arrived at, but there had been contributions from his own anatomy, one or two minor ones (reluctantly) from Gustav-Adolf's, and a variety of others from unlikely areas of the animal, vegetable, and mineral kingdoms. Finally, the pickle-jars had been subjected to subtle treatments under an antique X-ray machine, the veteran of several dentists' offices, before which a strangely twisted crystal did a clockwork dance over what looked like a drunken diffraction grating. Three fluids had resulted: the one already mentioned, another like a liquid Gorgonzola with things wiggling in it, and a bright red preparation which threw off fumes, sizzled slightly, and smelled of shrimp.

The first white mice arrived, were left with no protection but a shoebox, and perished promptly when Papa Schimmelhorn left the room for a few minutes. The second batch, given the yellow fluid while Gustav-Adolf was digesting their predecessors, rolled up their beady eyes and died immediately. The third absorbed the liquid Gorgonzola, flickered eerily for about thirty seconds, and disappeared.

"Ach!" murmured Papa Schimmelhorn. "I haff made der mistake vith der wrong dimension. Okay, ve try again!"

The fourth batch, approximately of platoon strength, drank up the shrimpy preparation greedily. Then, one by one, they weakened rapidly. They shrivelled. Their fur thinned and dulled. Their eyes grew dim. They too gave up and died.

There was just one exception—a rather bristly mouse a bit larger than the rest. He too had seemed to shrivel. His fur had changed its texture and its hue. But his eyes had kept their brilliance, and now he actually seemed stronger than before.

Papa Schimmelhorn picked him up with a glad shout. He flung the door open to admit a much irritated Gustav-Adolf, exiled since the debacle of the first mice.

"Look, Gustav-Adolf!" he cried out. "Maybe it vorks! Herr Maus iss alife and vell!" He put the mouse down under his cat's nose—and the mouse squeaked once, stood up, and bit it savagely.

Never, not even in his rough-and-tumble kittenhood aboard a Scandinavian merchant vessel or his waterfront adventures in such places as Port Said and Marseilles, had Gustav-Adolf been bitten by a mouse. Shocked to the core, he yowled, leaped backward, and crouched, growling suspiciously. The mouse jumped from the workbench and escaped through the door.

"*It vorks!*" shouted Papa Schimmelhorn. "For mices, it giffs maybe ten years, for cats vun hundred, for me fife hundred—imachine! Fife hundred years of chasing pretty pussycats!" He danced a jig. "Blondes, Gustav-Adolf! Brunettes and redheads und shlender vuns und plump vuns and maybe lidtle girls from China und Chapan!"

He looked down. Gustav-Adolf, forgetful of the mouse, was just lapping up the remaining liquid in the saucer.

"Mein Gott!" Papa Schimmelhorn reached out to stop

him. "Not yet, Gustav-Adolf! First ve make experiments!
It iss too dancherous—"

He was too late. Gustav-Adolf gave the plate a final
swipe, and sat up to lick his chops. Papa Schimmelhorn
regarded him with trepidation—and nothing happened. He
did not shrivel. His fur and eyes retained their accustomed
brilliance. Perhaps his chops seemed suddenly a little
grayer, but even that was not quite certain.

The truth dawned suddenly on Papa Schimmelhorn.
*"Okay!"* he roared, lifting the pickle-jar like a Viking drinking horn. "It vorked on Herr Maus because he vas a
Dirty Old Man maus! It vorks for Gustav-Adolf because
he iss a Dirty Old Man tomcat! Ach, because of Hundhammer, ve must call it der S.O.D.O.M. Serum!" The
bright red liquid fumed and bubbled. "So down der hatch!
Look—chust like Herr Doktor Chekyll und Mr. Hyde!"
He took a mighty gulp.

It went down very smoothly, hit bottom, vibrated,
bounced, and diffused instantly throughout his system. He
felt it in every nerve and muscle, in every organ, in each
blood vessel. Abruptly, he felt revitalized. He had not
changed; it was just that suddenly his warranty had been
renewed—and unconditionally.

He stretched as he had not stretched since he was sev-
enteen. Gustav-Adolf followed suit. They stared at each
other conspiratorially.

"Tonight ve go to see my lidtle Bambi," said Papa
Schimmelhorn. "Vhen I giff her X-rated cuckoo-clock, und
tell how I am full of vinegar for fife hundred more years,
maybe she forgiffs me for not saying I am married und
about Mama. But now—" He hoisted Gustav-Adolf to his
shoulder. "—ve haff all afternoon, so ve take a valk to
visit Cherry Blumenheimer, who iss nice und pink und
who has a pretty lidtle Siameser pussycat. Ve both haff
fun."

And in the dining room directly overhead, Mama
Schimmelhorn removed the microphone of an otherwise

unnecessary hearing aid which she had pressed against the floor, straightened in her stiff black dress, brandished her stiff black umbrella, and hissed, "*So!* Shtill you vant to feel naked vomen vithout die clothes, und for fife hundred years! You chust vait—ve fix!"

For a moment, she simply stood there, breathing fire and looking like a cross between Whistler's Mother and the Day of Judgment. Her doubts had reawakened a few days previously, on the Sabbath, when Papa Schimmelhorn had absentmindedly pinched the invitingly round bottom of Miss Jasmine Jorgensen, Heinrich's secretary. She had begun to wonder, not only about the sincerity of his conversation, but just what he was up to. Now she knew. "*Traitor!*" she muttered. "So you do not tell dot you are married!" And suddenly she found herself regarding Bambi Siracusa—her *bête noire* of the weeks just passed —not as a home-wrecker, not as the quintessence of female depravity, but as a frail sister equally betrayed.

She waited until she saw Papa Schimmelhorn and Gustav-Adolf turn the corner. Then she phoned Mrs. Siracusa. She was not warmly greeted, and it took some minutes for her to convince Bambi of her good intentions. She declared that she did not know that Papa Schimmelhorn had been posing as a bachelor. She apologized for invading Bambi's boudoir, for doing so in the company of Pastor Hundhammer, and for assaulting her with an umbrella. She expressed her sympathy for an innocent young woman who had so cruelly been deceived.

"You really got yourself a handful, Mrs. S.," said Bambi, stretching her warm hundred and sixty pounds reminiscently inside her pink peignoir. "I'm sure glad you called. It's real tough when an old goat like him, with all sorts of experience, takes advantage you might say of a little girl like me, who was a for-real virgin almost till I got hitched to Siracusa, God rest his nasty soul!"

"*Experience?*" cried Mama Schimmelhorn. "For sixty-three years, and vunce in der old country vith a female shtring qvartet! Und now he fixes it so he lasts fife hundrd years more. It iss an oudraitch!"

Bambi choked over the beer she was sipping, sputtered, and finally said, "*H-how's that?* Come again?"

"He iss a chenius," Mama Schimmelhorn informed her—and then she told her all about how the Schimmelhorn subconscious operated, and about his inventions which even great scientists couldn't understand, but which always worked, and she detailed the successful experiments she had overheard.

"You wouldn't shi—I mean, kid me? Would you, Mrs. S.?"

Mama Schimmelhorn assured her that she would not.

There was a sudden silence. Bambi Siracusa was a high-survival type in an extremely tough society. Where Papa Schimmelhorn saw only five hundred years of good clean fun, and Mama Schimmelhorn the threat of five centuries of sordid sin, she at once smelled money—and a lot of it.

Her mind began to function as swiftly and efficiently as any Schimmelhorn invention. *"Why, that dirty, lowdown, horny male chauvinist pig!"* she exclaimed. "Mama, you got any notion what the old bastard's up to?"

"He vants to live fife hundred years to play with naked vomen," replied Mama Schimmelhorn accurately enough.

"You're goddam well right! And that's not all. He and the rest of the old goats are going to keep it all themselves! You tell me, like why can't he give some of it to us girls? Why can't *we* go screwing around for five hundred years? I'll tell you why! Because that's how they've always treated us, that's why!"

"Vomen's Lib!" proclaimed Mama Schimmelhorn. "Dot's vhat ve need!"

"You can say that again, Mama! And I know just the girl can help us out. Her name's Val Canicatti. She heads up the Fa—that is, she's the Woman's Lib boss in these parts. I'll get it set up right away. We'll get together and have a snort. She'll tell us what to do."

"I vill not shnort," said Mama Schimmelhorn, "but I vill maybe drink a cup of tea."

"Okay, we'll have ourselves a tea party. You just stay put, honey. She'll send a car for you. You think the old man's going to be around?"

Mama Schimmelhorn replied that the old man had gone out chasing pretty pussycats, and Bambi, indignantly, promised that Women's Lib would snake her safely out of there before he could show up again.

They broke off the conversation with mutual expressions of affection and esteem. Mama Schimmelhorn, taking a drop of Mogen David to quiet her nerves, phoned Pastor Hundhammer and poured out her sorrows to him also, shocking him profoundly and causing him to cry out against Papa Schimmelhorn's profanation of the Biblical three score years and ten. However, he did remark that it would indeed be miraculous if a man could live five hundred years to serve the Lord—and Mama Schimmelhorn, reminded just in time of his masculinity, said nothing to him about the part the Women's Liberation Movement was going to play in the chastizing of her husband.

In the meantime, Bambi very excitedly had phoned Vala Canicatti, of whom—like everybody else—she stood in terror. Born somewhere between Macao and Harbin, of ancestry unknown, Mrs. Canicatti had grown up speaking any number of exotic languages—each with a vaguely foreign accent—and practicing any number of little known and illegal arts. Her finishing school, where World War II had found her, had been one of Shanghai's fanciest and most expensive bordellos. There, after the Liberation, she had been discovered by a quartermaster colonel, who had purchased her, taken her back to Kansas City as a trophy of war, and married her. He had survived for several weeks before perishing in a household accident, and had been followed, in rather swift succession, by a Little Rock dentist, a Phoenix real estate broker, and a Beverly Hills investment consultant, all of whom had obligingly left her everything of which they died possessed. Finally, in New Haven, she had married Luigi "Lucky Looey" Canicatti, of whom she had been genuinely fond, and whose willing helpmate she had been until he too passed on, surprisingly of natural causes. At that point, she had simply taken over, and one or two male chauvinists who had disputed the succession had ended up in concrete coffins under several fathoms of polluted water. She was known as "the Godmother", and her word was law.

Perhaps because she had done very nicely in what was ostensibly a man's world, the idea of posing as the local head of Women's Lib delighted her. As those who knew her knew better than to trick her, she never doubted that there was at least an element of truth in Bambi's tale. But where Bambi had smelled only money, she instantly smelled power. Graciously, she promised to send a limousine after Mama Schimmelhorn, and to join them for tea.

First though, she phoned the representative of a discreet but prosperous South American import-export firm, headed by a former executive of the S.S., which traded in illicit pharmaceuticals. Then she called up an unlisted number and made arrangements for an old acquaintance, now working for a major Iron Curtain country, to get in touch with her. Finally, after issuing the necessary orders to her mafiosi, she rummaged through her wardrobe for clothing which would make her more plausible in her new role, and settled on a pair of striped bellbottomed pants, a turtleneck red-white-and-blue sweater with a peace symbol on it, and a loudly checked sports coat of the late Mr. Canicatti's.

In the meantime, Pastor Hundhammer had not remained idle. As soon as Mama Schimmelhorn hung up, he had called his favorite parishioner and financial mainstay, Heinrich Luedesing, to tell him the exciting news, and Heinrich had immediately pounced on the trans-Atlantic phone to inform his wife's Cousin Albrecht, Managing Director of S.I.V.A., a gigantic chemical combine in Zürich. Miss Jasmine Jorgensen, listening in on her extension, had at once taken a coffee break so that she could tip off a groovy boy friend named Howie, who worked for a dubious detective and industrial security agency, and whom she had managed somehow to confuse with James Bond. And a young man in Cousin Albrecht's office surreptitiously sent a coded cablegram to the Vice-president of a Dutch cartel which was S.I.V.A.'s most formidable rival. By the time Vala Canicatti's limousine arrived to pick up Mama Schimmelhorn, forces of an astonishing rapacity and ruthlessness were zeroing in on Papa Schimmelhorn and his S.O.D.O.M. Serum.

Bambi Siracusa's tea party was a great success. Mama Schimmelhorn had more or less expected the head of Women's Lib to be a truculent, masculine creature with a deep bass voice. Instead, she found a woman who in her youth had certainly been very beautiful, and who even now—except for her wide Finnish cheekbones, her strange garments, and her cigar—looked like the expensively well-preserved widow of a successful broker or neurosurgeon. The Godmother was decidedly feminine. Even her black eyes did not betray her—as quite a number of interested males had discovered to their sorrow. Very demurely, she drank her tea—which she laced heavily with Lemon Hart rum—and listened to Mama Schimmelhorn's tale of woe, commenting sympathetically in a softly musical voice. Her agate-eyed male attendants, who had served as chauffeur and footman aboard the limousine, showed by their deference exactly who was boss; and when she spoke of the cruel oppression so long endured by her sex, she gave no hint that her own interest in the male animal was, aside from its financial aspects, a bedtime one, or that she found Papa Schimmelhorn's reputed potency quite as intriguing as his serum's.

It took her only a minute to arrive at her decision. "That serum's not all *his*, dear," she told her guest. "Don't ever think it is! There's a community property law in this state, and you own half of it. Women's Lib has lawyers who'll handle all that for you. All you need to do is give me what they call a power of attorney so we can act for you."

Mama Schimmelhorn, very much impressed, replied gratefully that that would be very nice indeed.

Mrs. Canicatti beckoned one of her mafiosi. "Get Woozy over here right away," she ordered. "Tell him it's for a power of attorney." Then she poured Mama Schimmelhorn another cup of tea. "And I guess we'd better get your Dirty Old Man out of circulation for awhile," she continued, with a twinkle in her eye. "I've got a sort of— well, a *rest home*, out in the country. The boys'll take him there and keep him safe, just so he won't have a chance to sell the serum out from under you. We'll tell him how we're acting in your behalf. Then, if he won't give us the formula, we'll get some of our women scientists to analyze it."

"It serfes him right!" Mama Schimmelhorn said grimly. "But maybe you find it easier if die boys shtay home und you send a pretty girl inshtead."

Both the Godmother and Bambi at once saw the wisdom of this argument, and Bambi—perhaps a bit too eagerly—volunteered to serve as decoy.

"Mama said a pretty *girl*, dear," murmured Mrs. Canicatti. "We'll send Diane from the—er—nightclub. She's blonde, with a delicious figure—prime old-goat bait. . . . Pete!" she called over her shoulder. "You go get her. She can use my car to make the pickup. How soon can you have her here?"

"Maybe twenty minutes, Mrs. C.," Pete grunted, "if she's got her clothes on and no customers."

The Godmother snapped her fingers, and he took his leave.

"But how's she going to find him?" Bambi asked.

"He vas on his vay to visit Cherry Blumenheimer," spat Mama Schimmelhorn. "She iss a bad girl who lives on—"

"I know the name," interrupted the Godmother, her eyes narrowing. "She used to peddle—well, never mind." She turned to the remaining mafioso. "Get on the horn, Romeo, and tell her what the score is. Tell her if he shows up to keep him till we call, then boot him out... Don't worry, honey," she said to Mama Schimmelhorn. "He's in the bag."

The doorbell rang, and Bambi admitted Woozy the attorney, a long, cold, hairless being with the personality of a baited rat-trap and a briefcase of imitation lizard-skin. He listened to Mrs. Canicatti's explanation, and quickly prepared a power of attorney in triplicate. Mama Schimmelhorn affixed her signature triumphantly, and Romeo and Bambi also signed as witnesses. Then Woozy slithered out, and the tea party resumed.

Very genteelly, the Godmother poured the tea, and Mama Schimmelhorn graciously accepted so generous a dollop of Lemon Hart in hers that, when Diane was ushered in a few minutes later, she was able to regard her not just dispassionately but with approbation.

"Chust right for der Dirty Old Man," she declared. "You vill haff no trouble."

Diane's briefing was short and to the point. She and her driver were to lurk near Cherry Blumenheimer's residence until they spied their quarry. Then Diane was to flirt with him, tell him how muscular and masculine he was (a move suggested by Mama Schimmelhorn), and invite him to a week-end house party. She was to phone them as soon as the mission was accomplished.

When she was gone, Mrs. Canicatti poured again, and began asking questions about how the Schimmelhorn genius functioned. These, of course, Mama Schimmelhorn could not answer. She repeated what she already had told

Bambi—that, great as his inventions were, neither he nor anybody else had ever duplicated one of them.

"In that case," said the Godmother, "we'd better not take any chances, had we? When we drive you home, I'll just pick up the serum he's already made, so our scientists can start in analyzing it. You do know where he keeps it, don't you?"

Mama Schimmelhorn replied that she did indeed—that she had hurried to his workshop as soon as he left the house.

They toasted the cause of Women's Liberation in tea and rum, and in less than half an hour Diane called in. She had had no trouble persuading Papa Schimmelhorn, she informed Mrs. Canicatti breathlessly, and—My God! who was this super-Santa anyway? They'd been in the car together only five minutes maybe, and here she was already black and blue *all over*—and he'd—he'd brought along his *tomcat!*—and anyhow they were on their way back to the Mansion, and here he was *trying* to p-p-pull her back *out of the phone booth!*

The Godmother hung up, commending her, and told Mama and Bambi what she'd said; and Mama Schimmelhorn, now slightly tiddly, commented that Gustav Adolf vas a good cat, who caught rats und mices. All the way home, in Bambi's car, she chuckled wickedly at the thought of how she and her allies were going to fix Papa, and without hesitation she delivered the pickle-jar with its remaining contents to the Godmother.

"Bye-bye!" she called after them. "Pretty soon I call you ofer und ve haff tea again."


The Mansion of the Canicatti Family was precisely that—a great, pillared house built in the mid-nineteenth century by an ex-Governor of Connecticut and inhabited for many years by a Chief Justice of the State Supreme Court, whose whiskered portrait—to the amusement of its present residents—still glared disapprovingly from the far wall of its great dining room. Now its spacious grounds were fenced forbiddingly and closely guarded.

As the car, driven by Romeo, turned into its shaded drive, Bambi looked a little apprehensively at Mrs. Canicatti. "Are—are you going to—?" she began uncertainly. "I mean, Mrs. C., is there any chance of the old guy getting, well, like *hurt!*"

The Godmother smiled dreamily. "Bambi honey, I'm going up to change into something a lot more comfortable. Let's see—there's that mutation mink housecoat out of Neiman-Marcus, the one that's split up to my waist each side and right up from my bellybutton in the front. And *then* we'll find out if what everybody's saying about your antique friend is true, and if it *is*—well, Women's Lib won't do him any harm, I promise you!"

Bambi suppressed a sentimental sigh. The assurance of Papa Schimmelhorn's continued physical well-being did not quite console her for the fate she saw immediately ahead of him.

The door was opened by Georgie "Goofball" Capotino, big and broken-nosed and very carefully tailored, who came as close to being a second-in-command as the Godmother would permit. "Hey, Jeez, Mrs. C.," he grunted, "you sure latched onto a weirdo this time. Diane's got the old cluck upstairs. You won't believe it—they're playin' *games*. What is the deal, anyhow?"

"Big money," snapped Mrs. Canicatti. "What else's new?"

"Howie phoned," he told her. "Just a quarter hour ago. I don't get it, but he said the old lady called her preacher and talked about some medicine like it makes you live a thousand years, and the preacher he rang up the old guy's boss, and *he* got right through to some great big outfit back in Switzerland. Howie said to tell you the word's out."

"*Merde!*" said the Godmother under her breath, adding a Cantonese expletive so imaginatively pornographic that, translated, it would have shocked even her present audience. "I didn't think of that! Well, we'll do the best we can. Bambi, you phone Mama right away and tell her a crew of male chauvinist bastards are after Papa's secret, and she's to make sure they get in touch with *me*. Give her my personal number. Now get with it!"

Bambi got with it.

"We're really going to have to hurry," continued Mrs. Canicatti. "I'm giving a big house-party, Goofball, and it's going to be bigger than I thought—though it won't last as long. I want you to round up my top boys—" She enumerated five of her most wanted men. "and they can bring their chicks. You can keep enough of the rest around to guard the grounds, but tell 'em *nothing* and send everybody else away on jobs until it's over. Oh, and tell Chong tomorrow night we'll have an all-out banquet."

Goofball grunted obediently.

"Okay, then. I'm going up to undress. And then I want to meet our senior citizen."

Humming a pretty tune, she took the stairs two at a time, quickly secreted the pickle-jar in her personal wall-safe, bathed, powdered, scented, touched her beautifully groomed hair approvingly, and slipped into the housecoat. It showed a great deal of her, and she went downstairs again elated. Her plans for a quick financial killing and for adventure of a different sort were practially complete, and they were progressing famously. She waved happily to Bambi—

And abruptly, from behind her, came a piercing feminine squeal, a booming *ho! ho! ho!* of male laughter, a rush of running feet—and in a flash of flesh-tones and blonde hair, Diane had passed her, closely pursued by Papa Schimmelhorn, beard streaming in the wind, and wearing spectacularly a pair of pink and green striped shorts. He caught up with Diane, who was wearing exactly one pair of shorts less than he, lifted her squealing in his mighty arms, and shouted, "See? I vin!"

Bambi Siracusa saw the Godmother's eyes widen as she beheld his masculine proportions—and at once narrow calculatingly and hungrily. At that instant, "Bambi!" he cried out, spying her. "You haff come also to der party? Look, Diane and me, ve play der hide und seek, und I haff von der prize!" He bounced the prize up and down affectionately. "Now ve haff lots of fun!"

Then, simultaneously, he and the Godmother for the first time really saw each other. He dropped Diane, who squeaked and darted off. His countenance radiated pleased astonishment. He opened his arms wide.

*"Lidtle Vala!"* he roared joyously. "My lidtle Vala! After so many years!"

And, *"You!"* hissed Mrs. Canicatti.

For a fraction of a second, her face was a Medusa's mask of such malevolence that Bambi shuddered, but the expression vanished just as suddenly, replaced by a smile whose artificiality Papa Schimmelhorn obviously failed to recognize. He embraced his lidtle Vala. He held her at arm's length. "Ach!" he exclaimed. "Chust imachine! Diane, und Bambi, und now you! It is chust like Old Home Veek!" Then he remembered that his prize had fled away, hugged the Godmother once again, promised that he would return to her as soon as he had time, and rushed off in pursuit.

"My Gawd, Mrs. C.," cried Bambi, "you *know* each other?"

Immediately, the Medusa mask was back, and this time it stayed put. "Know him?" she hissed again. "*Know* him? That is the only man who ever got it for nothing from Vala Canicatti—for *nothing*. Not one thin dime! And for a solid week. And then he left me—*me!*—for a crumby little beer hall waitress. We were in Switzerland, me and my third husband, the one who left me all the money when he fell off the cliff. And that old son of a bitch yodelled at me." Mrs. Canicatti was now breathing hard under the stress of her emotion; she had abandoned instantly all thought of such legalities as powers of attorney, and Medusa was even more frightening than before. "Bambi, I'll tell you this—*his* five hundred years are going to be the shortest ones on record! I've got to keep him on exhibit until I pull off this caper. Then back he goes to the ecology!"

Pale and trembling, Bambi muttered something about how she didn't blame her.

The mask dissolved, and at once the Godmother was her cold self again. "He mustn't guess what's going on," she said. "As long as possible, he's got to keep on thinking it's just a house-party where he can chase his pretty pussy-cats. But I don't think Diane can do the job, not if she lets him chase her naked through the halls. Our party's got to be respectable. Bambi, it's up to you. We'll send Diane back, and you take over. You'd like that, wouldn't you?"

"If you s-say so, Mrs. C.," answered Bambi, torn between terror and anticipation and trying hard to keep her cool.

"It's lucky the old ape has his mind on just one thing, and you've got lots of it. But you're not just to play around together. I want you to find about that formula."

"You—you mean so you won't have to have the serum analyzed?"

The Godmother regarded her contemptuously. "So I can make damn sure Mama told the truth. Remember? She said he hadn't any notion how he made it, and nobody could ever figure out how his inventions worked. Wake up, for Christ's sake! You don't think I'd ever let that formula get out, do you? I'm going to live five hundred years, and so are a few guys like Goofball, whom I can handle, and maybe so are you, because you let me know about it. I'm going to peddle whatever we don't need to these guests we've got coming here, for cold, hard cash—but they're going to swallow every drop of it before they leave. There's no percentage in letting *everybody* have it, stupid—not just for quick bucks. This way, after a while the few of us can rule the world! The competition'll get old and die, *but we won't.*"

The first guests arrived just before the cocktail hour, having had to travel only from Washington, D.C. One of them was Mrs. Canicatti's Iron Curtain contact; and she immediately sized up the other as someone far above him in the secret apparatus. His eyes were even stonier than those of her own mafiosi, and he seemed more ominous because he spoke no English and kept growling comments in his own Slavic tongue. They showed up carefully camouflaged, riding inside a poodle beauty parlor panel truck which vanished into the estate's one-time stable before decanting them.

"He is a Colonel-General of the Special Secret Police," whispered his subordinate as the Godmother greeted them, "but he remains incognito. You will call him by his code name, *Quicklime.* He is much interested in what you have for sale."

"What an interesting name," said Mrs. Canicatti. "He sounds like a man after my own heart." She offered vodka, which they turned down in favor of her most costly Scotch, and then she made it plain that no business would be transacted until the rest of her intended customers arrived. After that, though their glasses were frequently refilled, the conversation languished until dinnertime, when Papa Schimmelhorn showed up attended by a nervous and much-rumpled Bambi, who had rearrayed him in his shorts and sports coat.

Only a man with five hundred good years ahead of him could have displayed so uproarious a *joie de vivre* in so grim a company. He had told Bambi about his S.O.D.O.M. Serum, giving the tensions of its manufacture as his reason for having forgotten to confess that he was married. He had described the X-rated cuckoo-clock in detail, explaining that he had made it in her honor and as a gift to her; and, deeply touched, she had forgiven him affectionately. Now, in splendid spirits, he described graphically how Gustav-Adolf, confined to quarters and provided with a flea-collar by orders of the Godmother, had disgustedly rejected the cat-box installed for his convenience. He ate with gusto. He drank deeply and enthusiastically. Several times, he walloped Mr. Quicklime on the back, informed him that it vas too bad he vas a cold fish vith no vinegar, and assured him that if he vished to restore his youthful vigor all he had to do vas vatch Papa Schimmelhorn. On each of these occasions, Mr. Quicklime's subordinate turned pale; and finally, when told to translate, could hardly gasp out the reply that Mr. Quicklime had, in his country, heard much of the achievements of the great Academician Schimmelhorn, that he admired the products of the Academician's genius, which were incomprehensible to lesser men, but that now, to his infinite regret, he would have to bid the great Academician a warm goodnight.

As they left the room under the hostile stare of the dead Chief Justice, Papa Schimmelhorn thumped the table and roared with laughter. "Now I am der Academician I vill tell you how I haff become vun! Vunce in Geneva there vas an academy for die young vomen, und—"

Sometime later, after intercepting several poisonous glances from the Godmother, Bambi managed to entice him upstairs again. She watched him dismally as he undressed, and for the first time in her adult life experienced a true crisis of conscience. Never before had she met a lover of such prowess, but that was not the most important point. Never, *never* had anyone, anywhere, made her so much as a special mousetrap, let alone an X-rated cuckoo-clock. She slipped out of her things, sat down quietly on the bed beside him, and started sniffling.

Papa Schimmelhorn sat up. "But you are crying!" he exclaimed in astonishment. And even Gustav-Adolf, underneath the bed, temporarily stopped his indignant growling.

Bambi sobbed a little louder.

He reached for her. She shrank away—and suddenly the whole story poured out of her. She whispered brokenly how Mama Schimmelhorn had phoned, how she herself had called the Godmother, and about the t-t-tea party, and who Mrs. Canicatti really was, and her plans for the S.O.D.O.M. Serum and its ill-starred inventor.

Except for a burst of laughter at the idea of Vala Canicatti as a Women's Lib leader, Papa Schimmelhorn listened silently. He made no protest at his wife's course of action, saying only, "Poor Mama! She does not undershtand me or my serum, or how I like vunce in a vhile a goot time." He was convinced; he was even impressed; but he was in no way dismayed. After she had pointed out the peril into which loyalty to him had plunged her, describing gruesomely the fate of Mrs. Canicatti's enemies, he reached for her again, dried her tear-moistened cheeks against his beard, and said, "Vhat a shame! Und it could haff been a party chust for fun! Vell, don't vorry, shveetheart, tomorrow I pretend I do not know, und ve vill get avay."

"H-h-how?"

"Ve send Gustav-Adolf to tell Mama, so she can call der F.B.I."

"You mean your—your *cat?*"

"He iss a shmart cat," replied Papa Schimmelhorn, getting out of bed. "He brings der F.B.I., und ve are safed, und also they shtop Vala from playing vith der serum. It iss dancherous." He found a pencil and a scrap of paper. "Bambi, now you must talk to me like ve are making luff—maybe somevun listens. I write a note." *Dear Mama,* he wrote laboriously, while Bambi made appropriate noises,

*I am a prisoner of der Mafia und die Mafia lady tomorrow shteals my serum und sells it, und her hoodlums kill me. So you must phone der F.B.I. und HURRY! To safe my life!!!!*

He signed it *XXX Papa*, then passed it on to Bambi, who added a PS:

> *dear Mrs Shimelhorn its all true, DONT phone Vala just call in the Feds. Its all TRUE Mrs Shimelhorn I'll try to keep her off of him till they get down Love Bambi*

Under the bed, Gustav-Adolf responded churlishly to all entreaties. "What th' hell is this, chump?" he growled in Cat. "Lugging me to this lousy joint with a goddam pantywaist sandbox, for Pete's sake! Y' think I'm queer? You play your own games. I'm gonna stay right here!"

He reacted the same way to Bambi's honeyed, "Nice kitty-kitty-kitty!"

Finally, lying on his stomach, and at the cost of a scratched wrist, Papa Schimmelhorn fetched him forth, still swearing. He removed the flea-collar, wrapped the note tightly round it, and tied it firmly with a thread from Bambi's pantyhose. Then, ignoring Gustav-Adolf's imprecations, he replaced the collar, and carried his friend over to the window.

"Suppose it just won't open?" whispered Bambi, pulling up on it.

"A lidtle harder," whispered Papa Schimmelhorn.

She heaved. The window opened a bare six inches.

"So we can't get away," she explained fearfully.

"It iss enough!" He put Gustav-Adolf on the sill; and Gustav-Adolf, uttering one more reproachful epithet, went out into the night. For an instant, he simply crouched there, reconnoitering. Five feet down and perhaps eight feet off, there was a branch. He tensed. He leaped. And he was gone.

"Now ve don't need to vorry," said Papa Schimmelhorn. "Ve can go back to bed."

Bambi allowed herself to be escorted there, but she did not share his resiliency. Again she sat down. "You said your serum's *dangerous,*" she whispered. "Why's that?

You—you told me it'd make people live five hundred years!"

"It iss not goot for *all* people," he replied patiently. "Only if you are old und full of vinegar like me it vorks. If you are not, first it makes you very qvickly old—but if you get old vithout der vinegar it iss too bad!" He told her about his experiments *in vivo* with the mice, and about Gustav-Adolf, and how he himself had downed the fateful draught.

Beside him, Bambi shivered. "I—I wouldn't like that!" she declared. "Jesus, I never thought I'd sit here prayin' for the F.B.I., but I sure am now. What'll we do if they don't make it?"

"Ve shteal back der serum."

"I don't see how. She told me she'd locked it in her safe, behind that WANTED picture of old Looey in her bedroom."

"I am a chenius, but not at opening safes." For the first time, Papa Schimmelhorn sounded a bit concerned. "Vell, ve maybe vork it out tomorrow."

There was a silence, and presently he felt Bambi creep under the covers next to him. "I—I never told anybody this before," she said into his ear, "because Augie made me promise never to. He was my boy friend before I married Siracusa, and I guess you'd say he was a safecracker, sort of. Anyhow that's what they called him at the trial. But it was him that taught me how. He said it was like, well, giving me real social security for my old age. I—I could open up that tin can of Mrs. C.'s in no time if I could get at it, but her suite is always locked except when she's there."

Papa Schimmelhorn patted her bottom reassuringly. "Goot! Now I know ve do not need to vorry—only vun more lidtle problem, und tomorrow I vill solfe it!"

He slept soundly and dreamed many a pleasant dream of chasing pretty little pussycats. Bambi, however, not being a genius and having a more intimate acquaintance with the Godmother and her ways, passed a restless night and rose with deep, dark circles under her brown eyes.

When she and Papa Schimmelhorn came down to breakfast, they found Mrs. Canicatti in high spirits, greeting them as though her intentions were thoroughly benign. "Well, I can *see* you really had yourself a ball," she twitted Bambi. "And I've been sort of busy too. Almost all my guests are here already, and they're eager to meet your Papa Schimmelhorn. Later on, I'll introduce them."

She did not mention that four uninvited guests had come in the small hours of the night, that they had been representatives of a rival Family (tipped off by Howie for a fat fee), and that they had been silently and efficiently disposed of, partly for the edification of Mr. Quicklime, who for professional reasons had been invited to attend.

Mrs. Luedesing's Cousin Albrecht had flown in from Zürich, bringing his company's chief of security, whose personality was reminiscent of Mr. Quicklime's. His Dutch rival, named van der Hoop, had come over from the Hague, accompanied by his own hulking security chief. And Mama Schimmelhorn, of course, had duly given them the phone number. The one-time S.S. man from South America had not yet arrived, but he was on his way, bringing with him a most important personage. All of them, having access to unusual sources of accurate information, had briefed themselves thoroughly on Papa Schimmelhorn's inventions, and they were eager to do business.

The S.S. man showed up just before luncheon, and his companion turned out to be no less a figure than the Dictator-Generalissimo of the small country where he had found refuge. With them came the nation's Minister of Internal Tranquility, who looked disquietingly like Robespierre.

They all took each other's measure instantly, and those not already acquainted with the Godmother assessed the situation accurately as soon as they were introduced. She, in turn, wasted no time in levelling with them. Having sent Papa Schimmelhorn and Bambi out to play in the swimming pool, she called a conference in the Chief Justice's library.

"Some of you," she said, over the polished mahogany of his table, "came here thinking you were going to buy the formula for a five-hundred-year serum. You aren't. Nobody is. Even old Schimmelhorn doesn't know what's in it, and—believe me!—no one is going to get a chance to analyze it. The situation's simple. I won't try to snow you with a lot of garbage about overpopulation. You are practical men. The entire supply is in this house. There is enough for maybe twenty people. And even twenty people with a five-hundred-year life span could be too many. I will be one of them. A few of my assistants, on whom I can rely, will join me. So will you, unless you turn down the opportunity—something both you and I would infinitely regret." She paused to let all this sink in. "We'll be the most powerful and exclusive club the world has ever seen. Our competition will be temporary, but *we* will not."

She sat back and let them buzz. There were questions and hypocritical objections, but from the outset it was obvious that she had made her point. Finally, looking down at his broad, well-manicured fingers, Cousin Albrecht quietly said, *"How much?"*

She smiled. "A price each of you can afford. From you, M'sieu, one million dollars worth of S.I.V.A. stock. From you, Mynheer van der Hoop, the same amount of stock in your cartel. From His Excellency the President and Generalissimo, from my old friend who was so kind as to bring him, and from my esteemed colleague Mr.—er—Quicklime, one million dollars each, in cash, deposited at my Swiss bank. My fees are modest, especially as they'll include free doses for your trusted colleagues here." She beamed at the Minister of Internal Tranquility and the security men, and felt the balance of good will shift in her direction. "You will arrange the transfer of stocks and funds this afternoon. Make each transaction irrevocable, to take effect automatically on your return. Tonight we'll have a banquet to celebrate. Then we shall drink a toast to one another in Schimmelhorn's liqueur. '*Long* life!' I think would be appropriate."

"And how do we know, Madame," demanded van der Hoop, "that we will get what we are paying for?"

"Mynheer," she said, "I am the big frog in this little puddle. Here, what I say goes—but only here. Once you leave, any one of you can squash me easily—except that when you find I've kept my word you'll see that we can all be very useful to each other."

"How can we be sure," asked Mr. Quicklime's translator, "that this serum made by Academician Schimmelhorn will not poison us?"

"It didn't poison him. It didn't even hurt his tomcat, who drank a lot of it. And you can sit and watch—I'll drink it first. Okay?" She surveyed their faces, and read what each was thinking: *five hundred years*—a future by human standards virtually unlimited, in which to gain experience, amass personal fortunes, maneuver enemies to their destruction, build empires.

"A million dollars, that is nothing!" said the Generalissimo. "My people are hard-working. But I do not want to buy this serum and then find that more of it is made for any *cholo* with the money."

Abruptly, Medusa showed her face again. "I promise you—" The Godmother spoke softly. "—that *no* more will be made. Schimmelhorn is too dull-witted to grasp the potentialities of his invention; all he can think of is his pussy-chasing. He's also much too stupid to realize that I have plans for him. You understand?"

"Mr. Quicklime says *he* understands!" the translator cried. "He says is good, yes, yes! He stays to watch. Also he says okay, one million dollars!"

It took only a few more minutes for all of them to reach agreement, to make their inter-continental calls, to send their coded radiograms. Then Mrs. Canicatti, again the gracious hostess, summoned them to lunch, where they were joined by Bambi and Papa Schimmelhorn, the latter still attired in one of Mr. Canicatti's striped beach-robes, which was much too short for him. Throughout the meal he discussed his favorite topics, compared the physical endowment and state of preservation of the others—especially Mr. Quicklime's—unfavorably with his own, and flirted outrageously with the Godmother, occasionally introducing pointed little innuendos about the jolly time they had had in Switzerland.

Mrs. Canicatti sat through it frozen-faced, and only Bambi, watching, realized that Papa Schimmelhorn's popularity was dropping to an all-time low—and speculated tremblingly on the dreadful destiny which this might bring not only to him, but her.

The afternoon dragged endlessly. There was no sign of the F.B.I., and poor Bambi took turns praying to half-remembered saints, worrying about the misadventures which could overtake even an experienced tomcat with several miles to travel, and wishing that Papa Schimmelhorn would at least make some effort to behave decorously and not push quite so hard. He was in fine fettle. He offered to race anyone the length of the pool and back again, and enraged the Generalissimo by beating him and then shoving his head under water. He challenged all the younger men to Indian wrestle, proved to them that none could last longer than thirty seconds against his hairy forearm, and then advised them that they had been enfeebled by not chasing enough pretty pussycats. Finally, at the cocktail hour, Mrs. Canicatti took Bambi to one side and told her, in a flat and absolutely deadly voice, *"You*—you get that miserable old bastard out of here! You were supposed to keep him simmered down. Take him up to your room, *and lock him in.* Then get yourself down to the kitchen and help Chong. I'm going up to take a bath and try to get relaxed."

Bambi obeyed her mutely, tactfully separating Papa Schimmelhorn from Mr. Quicklime, whom he was pounding on the back, and almost dragging him upstairs. She told him what had happened and what her orders were.

Papa Schimmelhorn embraced her warmly. "It vorks," he whispered in her ear. "I tell you I am chenius!"

"Wh-what do you mean?" asked Bambi.

"I haff worried maybe a lidtle about Gustav-Adolf," he confessed, "dot maybe he has shtopped to haff a fight or chase a lidtle pussycat. So ve must shteal der serum. Und dot iss vhy I make my Vala angry—you vait und see. How can ve tell vhen she iss in der tub?"

"Her—her suite is right next door, and I remember sort of how we could hear the water in the pipes. It'll run quite a while for that big marble tub of hers, and she'll get in as soon as it gets full."

"Okay, ve vait," said Papa Schimmelhorn.

"B-b-but I'm supposed to—to lock you *in*," she bleated.

"You lock me in und go downshtairs mit der Chineser cook. Maybe in fife minutes you come up again, und unlock. Vhen I go out und get into her rooms, you follow me. I keep her busy till der safe iss open. It takes how long?"

"M-m-maybe a minute, m-m-maybe two. It's a lead-pipe cinch, and once I saw her opening it and caught the first two numbers. B-but I'm *scared!*"

"Don't vorry!" He clasped her to his bosom. "Alvays you can trust Papa Schimmelhorn!"

She did as she was told. She locked him in and, hurrying to the kitchen, greeted Chong, a tall, elderly Chinese whom the Godmother had known in her Shanghai days. When asked how she could help, he pointed at a simmering kettle on the stove and informed her courteously that, in a few minutes, she could stir the soup. Its fragrance told her that it was a famous lobster bisque of his own invention, but she was in no mood to appreciate his artistry.

Hastily, she told him she'd just remembered something. and she'd be back directly, and rushed upstairs.

Papa Schimmelhorn was waiting for her. "Listen!" he whispered.

Bambi listened, and heard the murmuring of the pipes. They waited. Presently it ceased. He beckoned her over to the door, and peered out cautiously. No mafioso was in evidence. Then he tiptoed massively down the hall to the door she indicated, and opened it without a sound. She pointed tremulously at another door leading off the sitting room. It was partly open, and from behind it came the sounds of soft music and a muted splashing.

"H-her *bathroom*." Mutely, Bambi formed the words, and she pointed nervously at the framed WANTED poster on the wall.

Papa Schimmelhorn urged her on towards it. He himself gained the bathroom door, pushed it just a little.

"Who's there?" called the Godmother.

Coyly, he peered around the edge, and spied Mrs. Canicatti seated luxuriously in the sea of bright pink bubbles in her marble bath. "Peek-a-boo! Und I see you!" he cried out cheerily.

"Get *out* of here!" Caught off balance, the Godmother was not yet at her fearsome best. "What's wrong with you? Can't you see I'm in the tub?"

He chortled. "Natürlich! Dot's vhy I came! Ach, Vala, remember how in Schvitzerland sometimes ve took a bath together aftervards?" Sighing sentimentally, he dropped the beach-robe from his enormous shoulders. "How you vould rub der soap on me und I—"

At that point, Medusa did not flicker. She came on full force. The Godmother rose to her full height, dripping, and it was obvious that she was indeed well preserved.

"How beautiful!" exclaimed Papa Schimmelhorn. "Chust like Venus on der Half-Shell, only not so shkinny. Und vot a lofely tub, mit marble, und enough room inside for both of us. It vill be chust like old times!"

The last thing Mrs. Canicatti wanted at that moment was an uproar. What started as a scream of hideous rage she managed to compress into a banshee cry distinguished, not for its volume, but for its chill lethality.

In the bedroom, Bambi heard it just as the wall safe opened for her. She panicked. Almost dropping the precious pickle-jar, she pushed the safe quickly shut, shoved the picture of Lucky Looey back over it, and then, clutching the serum to her capacious breast, took off. All she could think of was that the Godmother must not find her there—that she must somehow gain the safety of the kitchen, where she had been ordered to remain. Down the back stairs she ran, luckily unseen. Chong had his back to her, busily chopping something with his Chinese cleaver. She glanced round desperately—and suddenly heard masculine voices in the hall. Without a second thought, she unscrewed the top, emptied the contents of the pickle-jar into Chong's lobster-bisque, and dropped the jar itself behind the stove. By the time Goofball and Romeo entered, she was stirring desperately away, flushed and perspiring as though she had been at it for some time.

They in—and a shrill bell pealed, twice and twice again. "Jeez!" grunted Romeo. "Mrs. C. sure wants somebody up there. Listen at her!"

"We better get right on it, like!" Goofball agreed, and they took off, leaving Bambi even more frightened than before.

Meanwhile, in Mrs. Canicatti's bathroom, Papa Schimmelhorn had continued to appeal to his one-time inamorata in terms of a passion she obviously did not reciprocate.

Standing there wet and naked, she cursed him in Russian, Chinese, and Sicilian, pointed her finger at the door, and said, "Get . . . out . . . of . . . *here!*"

"But ve could haff such fun." He shook his head regretfully. "Und you haff such a pretty bottom shtill! Vell, maybe you haff lost der vinegar, und it iss now too late."

"GET . . . OUT! *GET OUT, I said!*" Mrs. Canicatti was stabbing fiercely at a bell-push. *"You are going . . . to be locked up . . . in Bambi's room!* And by God, this time my guys'll see you stay there!"

"Okay," said Papa Schimmelhorn, putting the robe on again. "I know vhen I'm not vanted. But it iss shtill a shame!"

"*And that stupid damn Siracusa bitch is going with you!* I ordered her to lock you in your cage—and she *forgot!* Or did you talk her out of it so you could get in here? Anyhow, the two of you can wait in there together—*then* you'll find out what I'm going to do to both of you!"

"Anyhow it vill be fun to shtay vith Bambi," he remarked philosophically. "Bye-bye, lidtle Vala."

He encountered Goofball and Romeo in the sitting room, and within five minutes he and a sobbing Bambi, who had been dragged up from the kitchen to face Mrs. Canicatti's wrath, were locked in together, with Romeo standing armed guard at the door.

"You haff der serum?" he asked her.

She nodded silently.

"It iss here?"

"N-n-no," she whispered. "I—I got real scared. Goofball and Romeo were coming in, so I—I just got rid of it where they can't ever find it."

"Goot!" He patted her. "Now eferything vill be okay. Vala cannot hurt anybody vith der serum, und pretty soon comes der F.B.I. You think maybe she looks inside der safe before?"

Bambi stifled her sobs. "N-no. I—I don't think so. She won't take any chances with it in the open till she's about to serve it. Then she'll go get it, with Goofball and a couple others to help keep it safe. I—I h-h-hope!"

"Don't vorry," said Papa Schimmelhorn. "Gustav-Adolf brings der F.B.I. For a cat, he also iss a chenius!"

Gustav-Adolf was, as a matter of fact, much superior to

most cats. Having reached the ground, he first availed himself of the great cat-box Nature had provided, then took off on a beeline for his home where, he knew, he would be welcome to sit on Mama Schimmelhorn's stiff black silk lap and purr, and listen to her comparing him more than favorably to her wayward husband. Unfortunately, however, he was soon distracted by the lilting love song of a little tortoiseshell, whom he found complaisant and for whom, as a memento of his favors, he caught a mouse. In the process, he found it necessary to teach good manners to two lesser tomcats and an intrusive springer spaniel. Then he caught another mouse for breakfast, watched for two hours at a rathole, napped for an hour or two, and went his way after the sun had risen. The day too was full of its distractions, and it was late afternoon when finally he meowed at Mama Schimmelhorn's back door. Indeed, his entrance coincided precisely with Papa Schimmelhorn's and Bambi's attack upon the wall safe.

"Vhere haff you been, you vicked cat?" demanded Mama Schimmelhorn.

"With yer old man, that's where," Gustav-Adolf said in Cat, and went on to complain about how Papa Schimmelhorn had tried to make him use a goddam cat-box.

"Poor Gustav-Adolf," crooned Mama Schimmelhorn. "Und now he comes home hungry? Poor lidtle kitty-cat."

"Damn right!" He rubbed against her, purring raucously. "A hunk o' liver would go down real good."

Suddenly, reaching down to pet him, she spied the collar. "Vot iss?" she exclaimed. "Nefer haff ve put a collar on my Gustav-Adolf! Maybe die Vomen's Libbers? Und vith a dirty piece of paper—" She pulled the collar off over his head, and untied the thread. "—probably mit cherms!" Then, on the point of tossing the paper in the wastebasket, she glanced at it and frowned. "Ach! *A note from Papa?* Maybe he makes a joke." She read it slowly, frowned, read it aloud to Gustav-Adolf. "Vhat does it mean, der Mafia? Und der F.B. und I.? Der Mafia iss against der law. I think about it, but first I giff mein Gustav-Adolf some nice beef heart."

She sliced up the beef heart, placed it on a platter, and watched with pleasure as it was devoured.

"Vhat vill I do?" she asked. "If it iss chust Papa, I know it iss a joke. But also there iss Mrs. Siracusa, who is a good girl." She thought about it until Gustav-Adolf, having cleaned his plate, began to wash himself. Then she made up her mind. "Okay, because of Bambi better I take no chances. I phone der F.B. und I."

She looked the number up, dialed it, asked if she could speak with Mr. Hoover, was told that he was no longer available, and condescended to discuss her problem with someone less impressive. The agent listened to her not-too-clear account of something that sounded like a kidnapping by Women's Lib or perhaps the Mafia, though she didn't really think so. Then he asked her to explain the motive. To get her famous husband's serum, she informed him, which would make people live five hundred years.

"And what did you say your husband's name is?" the agent asked.

"Papa Schimmelhorn," she told him. "He iss a chenius."

Something rang a bell, and the agent transferred the call to his superior. The Agent in Charge also listened politely. Then, having recognized the name, he patiently explained to Mama Schimmelhorn that his office could not take the alleged motive seriously. "Madam," he said kindly, "I'm sure your husband is a very clever man, but you must remember that after the episode of the so-called *gnurrs,* a joint Congressional committee investigated the affair and determined that his *gnurr-pfeife* had nothing whatsoever to do with it, and that actually it was nothing more than a plague of lemmings. We can scarcely base any action on the presumed value of another such invention."

"Nonsense!" snapped Mama Schimmelhorn. "Lemmings do not eat people's pants! Und der head of Vomen's Lib

herself beliefes in it—a shmart voman named Val Canicatti, who vears trousers und shmokes cigars. She has
taken my Papa to a house party, und now he writes he is
der prisoner of der Mafia."

There was dead silence at the other end. Then somebody
said *Whee-ew!* and the Agent in Charge was on the line
again.

"Why didn't you *say* Vala Canicatti?" he barked.

"I chust did!" answered Mama Schimmelhorn.

"Well, never mind. Mrs. Schimmelhorn, you sit tight
right there. Don't phone anyone. Don't open your door no
matter what until we get there. And *save* that note saying
he is a prisoner. I'll pick you up directly."

"But I do not know vhere Papa iss!"

"Never mind," he told her grimly. "*We* do. Let's hope
we get out there in time!"

Within ten minutes, a car full of F.B.I. agents picked
her up, tightly furled black umbrella and all, and sped into
the newly fallen night to rendezvous with others of its
kind, with sheriff's deputies, and state investigators, and
other less well known enforcement officers.

She was escorted from her house just as the Godmother's banquet got under way. The table in the great
dining room was laid with damask and with Haviland,
with precious crystal and fine sterling silver. Rare wines
were ready for the pouring. Mrs. Canicatti's five lieu-
tenants flanked her, uncomfortable in evening dress not
worn since Lucky Looey's splendid funeral, their molls
strangely bedecked in spangled evening gowns, extraordinary wigs, ill-gotten diamonds and orchidaceous corsages.
Her several guests faced her across the table, Cousin Albrecht and Mynheer van der Hoop striving to suppress superior smiles, the Generalissimo sniffing the air hungrily,
and Mr. Quicklime and the rest staring with varying degrees of amazement at the panoply before them. The
Godmother herself, attired expensively and in excellent, if

somewhat splashy, taste, greeted them and gave the signal for the feast to start.

Two or three minor mafiosi and their girls had been pressed into service as waiters and waitresses. Now they wheeled in a cart bearing a magnificent tureen, and—Romeo presiding—ceremoniously began the service of the soup. "Jeesus, Romeo," one of them muttered as he held a plate, "old Chong sure must've been workin' hard. Boy, all of a sudden like does he look old!" And Romeo answered that was the way it was with Chinamen. "Christ, you can't tell how old the buggers are by thirty years! Anyhow, this soup smells real good."

The soup was served out quickly and efficiently, while the Godmother told them how she had rescued her great chef from his career as a river-pirate, and how he had named this special dish *Lobster Bisque à la Vala Canicatti.* And she added that she was serving it to them because it was so celebrated, even though she herself was now allergic to the lobster. She would, she said, take her pleasure in watching their enjoyment.

There was a quick round of polite applause, and they set to—

And upstairs, Bambi clung to Papa Schimmelhorn, and asked him again when the F.B.I. would come.

"Gustav-Adolf alvays comes home for supper," he assured her. "Soon they are on der vay. If they arrife before she comes upshtairs to get der serum, ve are okay. You are sure she cannot find it before then?"

Bambi nodded tearfully. "I—I dumped it in the soup," she sobbed.

"Gott in Himmel!" he cried out. "Bambi, do you realize vhat you haff done? Dot soup they are now maybe serfing! In a few minutes der Mafia all vill know! Und then vhat happens?"

Bambi moaned dolefully—

And in the dining room, the Godmother stared at Goofball's hand, holding its silver spoon a foot away. She glanced aside at his lady's too-deep decolletage—surely her skin had not hung in such crêpe creases when she first came in? Surely the flesh on her full arms had not hung so revealingly from her large bones? She looked from left to right. She saw gray hair where there had been black. She heard the shrill, senile crack of Cousin Albrecht's laughter—

And suddenly she knew just what had happened. She knew instinctively just how the serum worked—and how it worked on whom. She knew that for the second time in her life a man had tricked her—the same man. Rage and pure horror animated her. She stood. She called to Romeo. He had noticed nothing. He came to her. "Take your two boys," she ordered, in a voice no follower of hers could disobey. "Get up to Bambi's room *right now*. Don't wait for anything. Wipe out that *Schimmelhorn*—I don't care how. *And finish Bambi too*. Then bring their heads or something down to me!"

Gesturing to his men, Romeo left the room hurriedly. Now certain other lesser folk started to realize that something strange was going on. There was commotion: shouts and frightened exclamations and runnings back and forth. Only the company around the table noticed no change, detected nothing wrong.

The noises carried to the prisoners on the second floor. They heard the heavy running footsteps of Romeo and his boys, the scraping of a key inserted in the lock. Bambi whimpered pitifully. Papa Schimmelhorn braced himself against the door—

And suddenly there were a dozen shots outside, some cracking sharply from pistols and revolvers, more booming from buckshot-loaded riot guns.

"Vot did I tell you?" cried Papa Schimmelhorn exultantly. "Comes der cafalry!"

The Mansion was invested, assaulted, occupied in minutes, the morale of its defendents shattered by what had happened to their leaders. In no time, law officers were everywhere. Romeo and his surviving fellows had been taken into custody. Papa Schimmelhorn and Bambi had been rescued and brought downstairs. Finally, with everything secure, Mama Schimmelhorn was escorted in to greet her husband and to view the victory.

The dining room was a distressing sight, for the S.O.D.O.M. Serum worked as swiftly and relentlessly with people as with mice. Around the table sat, and stood, and capered a croup of aged men and women strangely and pathetically overdressed, their finery hanging from their wasted frames. A third of them had fallen to the floor or collapsed over their place-settings, having obviously just perished of old age. A few others were quite as obviously about to. Mr. Quicklime, toothlessly drooling now, was fumbling foolishly with a Tokarev automatic, which an agent gently took away from him. The Godmother, all Medusa, stood handcuffed to an enormous deputy, cursing in a variety of unknown languages.

Mama Schimmelhorn strode in between two agents. "Vell!" she exclaimed at the sight. "So dot's vhat Vomen's Lib iss all about!" She caught sight of her husband. "You should be ashamed," she said. "Iss not enough you play vith naked vomen. Now you make silly shenanigans vith old people!"

Beaming, the Agent in Charge came up to her. "Thank God you called us, Mrs. Schimmelhorn!" he told her fervently. "You have performed a great service to the community and in the cause of law and order and clean government. This Canicatti woman's committed every crime in the book—murder, dope, blackmail, you name it. Now, thanks to you, we have her dead to rights!"

"That's God's truth!" echoed a state investigator.

"Vhat for?" asked Mama Schimmelhorn.

"Running an old folks' home without a license!" He slapped his notebook. "Failure to provide adequate medical assistance. No licensed dietitian on the premises. No certified gerontologist. Hell, we'll get her on about twenty counts. This is the sort of job you *really* get convictions on!"

Again they thanked her. They informed her that nurses and doctors were on the way to care for the victims of the Godmother's neglect. They assured her that letters of appreciation would be sent to her at least from the Governor and Attorney General.

Generously, she told them that Bambi Siracusa also deserved credit. "Und now," she stated, "I take Papa home."

"We'll drive you," the Agent in Charge told her respectfully.

Papa Schimmelhorn was whispering in the ear of an ancient but robust Chinese who had come out of the kitchen, and who was listening to him with every appearance of delight. "On Herr Chong it vorked," he announced to all and sundry, "because he iss full of vinegar like me!"

The room was emptying. The mafiosi had all been removed. The Godmother, squalling hideously, had been led away.

Mama Schimmelhorn's eyes flashed fire. She lifted her unbrella threateningly. "Ve go!" she announced.

"Goodnight, Bambi," Papa Schimmelhorn said sadly.

"You are a nice girl, Bambi," declared Mama Schimmelhorn. "Soon you come ofer und ve drink some tea." She shooed her husband to the door. "So now der serum iss all gone?" she asked him when, for a moment, they were out of earshot.

Papa Schimmelhorn, conscience-stricken, stuttered apologetically that it was a shame, that he did not mean to use it all, that had he even dreamed the way things would turn out, he would never have hurt Mama's feelings by chasing so many lidtle pussycats.

"So," she said, "now you are sorry because you liff fife hundred years und Mama liffs maybe only ten, *nicht wahr?*"

He blew his nose unhappily into a red bandana handkerchief.

"Vell, shmart guy, I find out something in der basement you do not know." She reached up and grasped him firmly by the ear. "Your serum, *dunderkopf*, is not chust a S.O.D.O.M. Serum. It iss a C.O.W. Serum also."

"Vot iss, a C.O.W.?"

"It iss a serum for Clean Old Women vith lots of vinegar," said Mama Schimmelhorn. She smiled grimly. "Papa, ve shtay together now a long, *long* time!"

# GEORGE ZEBROWSKI
## and
# TAMSIN ASHE

# ROPE OF GLASS

## George Zebrowski

Austrian-born Pole **George Zebrowski** grew up in Britain and New York City and makes his home now in upstate New York. This polyglot beginning may account for his great success in a second language—rare in any writer, and all the more surprising in a man as young as George Zebrowski. He has amassed an astonishing number of credits: his 1972 Ace novel **The Omega Point** has won him wide acclaim and his upcoming novel **Macrolife** will, we predict, establish him firmly in the front ranks of major science fiction writers.

When not busy with storytelling, he lectures, has done translations, and is the editor of the **Bulletin** of the Science Fiction Writers of America. Energetic, he oozes presence that should make even Charlton Heston look to his laurels.

•

Sam Brickner was halfway down the block, walking slowly to his apartment building on the corner, when the diagnostic van rolled past him and slowed down.

Sam stopped. The light on the corner turned red, a

small porthole into hell. The van was standing behind a food ration truck, directly in front of the entrance to his house. He had the sudden fear that they were waiting for him to come near enough so they could force him inside where the medics could take his blood count. He tensed and waited, knowing that it was a long light. He looked at the scratched paint on the rear doors, fearing that his luck was over and they would find out. A muscle near his knee twitched nervously, and he felt his face tighten into a rigid grimace; sweat began to form on his brow.

The light turned green and the medical van moved away. He walked the rest of the way home shaken, feeling as if he had just crossed a glass tightrope and miraculously it had not shattered.

He paused outside the front door to his building. The air of the city was oppressive, a mass composed of exhalations from a billion human throats and the wastes from inhuman machine processes. Sam went inside and up the creaky wooden stairs to the second floor. He opened the old latchlock to his apartment with a key and stepped inside. He closed the door, pushed in all the bolts, and lay down on the large bed in the center of the room. He was still shaking a little.

He tried to calm himself. It had been nothing, he told himself. No one was after him. The man who had jostled him in the crowdjam on 34th Street was a nobody—despite the fact that he had run into him again at the hospital last night. He was probably a subnormal janitor tunnel worker for the New York Hospital complex. The man had shown no sign of recognition when Sam had come out of Katherine's makeshift treatment room in the branch of the hospital's underground transfer tunnel. Kathy would have known if he were a euthanasia cop, but she had told him that the man was an orderly in the hospital, probably on an errand.

Kathy loved him. She loved him despite his age, Sam knew that, because he made her feel like a human being and not a trapped animal. They had their own world together, at least once a month, the uncrowded, unregulated world of each other's presence. She loved him enough to risk saving his life, believing with him that the bootleg Poly-IC drug would in time induce a permanent remission of his body's mimic-leukemia. Twice the drug had almost succeeded, boosting the percent of healthy cells in his bone marrow, running the hemoglobin count in his blood to supernormal levels, making him feel twenty years younger than his fifty-three years. But the bad cells had come back and Katherine had put him through a new series of treatments. "Sam, you've got to hang on," she had said; "it may be a matter of just waiting long enough. The remissions are lasting longer." She had pleaded with him, trying to coax him out of his depression, using words and looks, her body, and all the bootleg drugs and knowledge she could steal for him as a nurse and paramedic.

They would have their years of happiness. She had promised him that, for as long as he lived. He was safe with her; she was the one person who would never turn him in to the death cops. She could not do it without revealing herself as an accomplice in concealing a chronic disease. They would take her life and his for that. She was silent because she loved him.

Calmer now, he fell asleep.

*The man with the flamethrower aimed it at him. The fire leaped out, burning his face, melting his eyes and flesh, scorching the bones of his skull, purging him of all infection.*

Sam woke up with the sun in his face, shining at him through the hole in the dirty window shade, warm and blinding. He got up and staggered into the bathroom. His face was pale in the mirror. He looked at it carefully, searching for signs of last night's fear. I have to see real dangers, he told himself as he took off the clothes he had slept in, and not torture myself with imagined ones. I found out soon enough to save my life and justify my existence. I do my job with no trouble. I'm useful. No one complains about me. I am not unfit. No one can tell the difference from day to day, not even the law. And I'm going to get better, maybe even next week. They'll never know what I had, not even after I'm dead.

He took a quick sponge bath in the shower stall with his saved water ration. After shaving he had enough water left for two cups of coffee. Before going out, he took a look at himself in the long mirror on the back of his front door. His hair was thick and black and streaked with gray. His green city worker's uniform was neatly pressed, and the buckle on his black belt was still shiny. He felt reassured by the sight of himself, and he felt definitely stronger after the previous day's Poly-IC treatment.

He opened the door and went down the stairs. On the sidewalk he looked around and saw no crowdjams yet at any of the corners, although traffic in the street was increasing.

He started walking toward the food ration center where he worked, four blocks down-city. As he walked the noise grew louder around him and people began to fill up the sidewalk from the doorways of the apartment buildings. By the time he reached the center ten minutes later, he was walking slowly behind a mass of humanity at least a mile long, each person moving forward at the same time to avoid a jam. He cut out of the crowd and went inside the ration center and up to the second floor where his office was a desk between two partitions on a balcony overlooking the huge warehouse floor below.

He sat down at his desk and stared down into the huge floor area where endless lines of humanity had stood for more than thirty years of his life while he kept records and checked shipping orders, occasionally catching a counterfeit ration ticket and sending it up to the third floor to the men he had never seen. The only contact he had with them was through the intercom and the air tube which carried papers between floors.

Two years ago Katherine O'Faolian's name had appeared on a counterfeit ration ticket. He had looked up from his desk and had seen her staring up at him, her eyes pleading. The look on her face had been one of unexpected horror. He had picked her out from all the thousands of people on the floor, and it had seemed obvious to him that she had signed the ticket unknowingly. He had torn it up in her sight and had sent down a blank form to replace it.

After work he had found her waiting for him by the front entrance. She had gone home with him, holding him up with her arm when he stumbled along the way. He had been right, he had told himself later; he could not have lived with the thought of her becoming a subnormal laborer for passing the ration ticket. The world lived by rigid rules of productivity, and it was anxious to use up human beings completely.

He remembered the night she had come to his apartment in the middle of winter to find him sick and weak. He remembered a small woman with brown hair and blue eyes wearing a nurse's uniform. As she had leaned over him, he had noticed how pale her face had seemed, making her freckles more prominent than he had ever seen them. Later that night she had brought a doctor to him, and had covered his face while he was being examined and diagnosed, and he had wondered if that was to protect him or the doctor. He had never found out whether the doctor had been a legal practitioner or not.

He remembered how gently she had told him what he had a few days later. It had become fairly common recently: a mimic-leukemia, something which could start like a cancer of the blood, disappear suddenly and return just as unexpectedly to kill the marrow's capacity to make fresh blood cells. The Poly-IC drug could prod the bone marrow into new production, and might eventually stimulate the organism into a complete remission, but he had to have intravenous doses of the stuff whenever his healthy cell count went down. The drug's side effects were flu symptoms, high temperature, and severe shivering during the treatment, but they went away in reasonable time.

He had avoided the end, but complete remission had not taken place. The world wanted him to die. There were too many human cells to make a healthy humanity; failing cells had to be flushed out of the organism. In one or two generations the patient might begin to live again.

Sam sat up straight in his chair and picked up a pen from his desk. He picked up the first sheet of paper from the pile in front of him and tried to read it, but his eyes wandered to look out through the glass instead. A line was forming by the first trough below; workers dressed in green coveralls were coming in to dispense the day's first rations. Suddenly Sam was looking at the same man who had jostled him in the crowdjam and whom he had seen at the hospital. The man was staring up at him blatantly, deliberately torturing him with his presence. Sam tried to look as if he were doing his job, but his eyes refused to limit their attention to the paper on his desk. The man continued to stare at him. Sam knew the man was sensing his fear, and when he smiled at him Sam almost cried out inside, sure that the other's gaze had penetrated into him and had seen everything.

He knows, Sam said to himself; but I won't lead them to you, Kathy. He hid his sweat-covered face with his hand, hoping that somehow he might die right there, that his circulatory system would shatter like glass, spilling his diseased fluids into his body cavities and leaving nothing for his heart to pump. He remembered how strong he had been after the first few treatments. Kathy had been delighted with him, vowing that she would never want anyone else. He remembered the first time he had made love to her and how she had cried out. The sleep he had shared with her then seemed so very precious now, and he wished that he had died in it . . .

He took his hand away from his face and looked for the stranger below; but the man was no longer looking at him. Suddenly he seemed just an ordinary man waiting passively for his rations to be doled out.

At four o'clock they put the news on over the building's loudspeakers. Sam tried to ignore it as he checked through some files in the cabinets in the rear of the balcony, but he listened to the last few minutes of the commentator's daily inspirational when he got back to his desk.

". . . and finally I say to all good Americans who want to see a better America—the world is out of control, but *we* have closed our shores, stopped all pollution, cut our population growth to hold steady under two billion this year; our death rate is the highest in the world this year *and* last. And we will have our Horn of Plenty! Our best scientific minds are working day and night to perfect the universal matter synthesizer which will give us anything we want from basic raw materials—anything from a ham sandwich to a chunk of steel. Unlimited fusion power— power to rip matter apart at its basic level and put it back together into anything . . . fusion power and laser scanning of matter to form the image and the reality of a better world, a planet free of the need for agriculture and the tasteless synthetics we eat now. Money and time and mind will free mankind, as long as the research continues, as long as the unfit pass from our midst. Those who cannot serve the future with healthy bodies must contribute by quitting the game. They too are patriots and heroes, here by a mistake of nature or the curse of the past. We must set things right, purging humanity of sickness so it may survive into better times. The Horn of Plenty is just around the corner. We cannot hesitate now and waste all those who have died. Courage . . ."

It was the same speech every day. Only the voices

changed. Sam knew it by heart, like he knew the prayers of his childhood. He had grown up at the end of the good times near the turn of the century. He had seen all the good ideas die in their application to life. He had lived through the drug resistant plagues, through the brief reprieves of the 1990s, through the tyranny of the innovations control boards and their stifling of new technologies, through the global depression following the world crop failures. He had seen UN-enforced migrations, culminating in the complete isolationism of the big powers after the pogroms and expulsions. He had been a plumber and electrician, a union official. At fifty-three he held his job in the food ration chain because national employees were never fired. They worked until they died or contracted a disease. He had lived to see his union pension and social security turn into ration tickets. At work he tried to look fit enough to avoid suspicion that might lead to a spot medical check. In many cases old age was defined as a terminal and chronic disease. The death cops could arrest you directly for that, diagnose you at the euthanasia terminal and send you on your way, saving everyone time and money.

But Kathy lived in this world with him, making it bearable. She was there at night when he felt most alone and afraid, and she would never hurt him. She was exactly what he needed her to be. She was for him; for now.

*"This way please. Don't worry. It's all arranged. Lie down. Give me your arm."*

*The straps tightened around his body. The nurse's face fell away and he saw that it wasn't Kathy O'Faolian. It was the face of a death cop, a skull with glass eyes leaning over him, attaching the gas mask to his face and leaving it there, leaving it forever, and nodding back and forth as it turned on the flow of oblivion with white fingers, making him taste the gas in his mouth. He screamed into the mask, gasping the mixture into his lungs . . .*

He woke up and Kathy was mopping his face with a

cloth. He shivered under the blankets. The empty intravenous bottle hung on its post near the bed.

"How do you feel?" she asked, and smiled.

"Like before," he managed to say. "Maybe—maybe this time will be the last."

She nodded, smiling. Her eyes were so clearly blue in the lights of the small room, so completely without guile or despair, so young.

"I love you," he said and shivered again, so violently this time that he shook the metal bed.

He heard someone take hold of the doorknob and turn it back and forth loudly, followed by a knock on the door.

"In the hall, Kathy, someone's there," Sam said.

She stood up and turned her back to him. He looked up at her, but the low overhead light blinded him partially. "They've found us, Kathy—who could it be?" She paid no attention to him.

"Open up, Kathy," a voice said from beyond the door; "open up or I'll bring help." Sam knew that he couldn't even get up to defend her; and she didn't seem to care.

She went to the door and opened the lock. Someone pushed the door open, and Sam saw a figure shove Kathy back.

"Harry, how did you find this place?" she asked, and her voice sounded strange to Sam, as if what she was saying was for his benefit and not for the intruder.

The man did not answer. He came over and looked down at him, and Sam recognized the face which had terrified him.

"Old man," Harry said, "I'm going to kill you the easy way. I'm going to turn you in. A thirty second call is all it will take. They'll never know who did it. Maybe tomorrow morning—"

"Harry, for God's sake please leave!" Kathy said.

The man turned suddenly to face her. Sam heard the silence and then Harry saying, "You dump him and I'll let him live . . . Kathy, I love you, I've known you a long—"

And he heard Kathy, his Kathy, whisper back, and he knew she was hoping that he wouldn't hear. "Okay, Harry, but go now, I beg you. I'll come to you later for sure, but go now."

In a moment the other man was gone and Sam heard Kathy close the door to the dark hallway. He shivered again, less violently now. He felt like stretching all the muscles of his body in one long motion. "Sam, I'm sorry I'm not what you want me to be," Kathy said somewhere far away. "It was all real between us, everything, believe me." It was all a bad dream. Nothing to worry about. Abruptly there was nothing underneath him. He fell and was slowed to perfect stillness by a liquid sleep.

In the long moment before he woke up he dreamed of soaring birds and swift gazelles leaping against a background of graceful trees. He opened his eyes, losing the clearest sky he had ever seen; but he was left with a sensation of physical well being that he had not known since his youth. He knew it was the drug, but he could almost believe that this time the remission would be complete.

He sat up and saw that he was alone in the room. He threw off the covers, got up, and had started to put on his pants when the door opened with a key from the outside and Kathy came in wearing her nurse's raincoat.

"Oh, you're up," she said almost coldly.

He finished dressing and sat down on the bed, remembering and waiting for her to speak. He wanted to believe anything that she would say but something inside him was transfixed and screaming.

"I had to go to him," she said, "to save your life. I went while you slept."

He looked up at her. It was someone else speaking to him, not Kathy. "While I slept . . .?"

She nodded. "Sam, forgive me," she said in a low voice, "but you see I had to do it. It's been going on for a long time, from before I met you, from when he and I first started at the hospital. He says he can't stop . . ."

He looked at her, saw the half-formed tears in her eyes, but no shame. He felt old despite his borrowed health, a survivor from a different world, draining the life from . . . this child with the last kicks of his diseased body. He was lying to her, revealing to her what he wanted her to see of him—the way he was inside under all the old flesh, the way he could never be again. And hiding behind even the youth inside him was an old man, buried deeper than he would admit to himself. That was the person who wanted her, who needed her with the attachment of a jealous child and would do anything to keep her.

He stood up and looked at her, wondering what the two of them said to each other about him. "Who is he, Kathy; where does he live?"

She looked at him and the possibility of tears was gone from her eyes. He came up to her and shook her. "Where does he live, Kathy, what's his name? Choose now, love, do you hear me?"

"What are you going to do?"

"Nothing," he said.

"He's an orderly—Harry Andrews, across the street . . ."

He went past her and out the door. "Sam!" she shouted after him. "Come back. Don't you see it's over with him . . . Sam!" He ignored her cries and walked down the branch corridor to the main passage which ran up to street level a quarter mile away. There he went through an old door which let him out into an alley in back of the hospital. It was a seldom used exit, and even if anyone noticed him his green uniform would get him by.

He came out into the street from the alley and noticed the old brick apartment building across the street from the hospital, where many of the hospital staff lived for as long as they could hold their jobs. Harry Andrews probably shared rooms with a dozen other men.

Sam crossed the street, feeling a remarkable new lightness in his step. He stopped in front of the entrance to the building and checked the names on the mailbox panel. *Harry Andrews—4L* was the third name he looked at. He pushed the buzzer and held it until the reply buzzer sounded and he was able to push through the front door. He started quickly up the stairs instead of using the elevator.

He turned around on the third landing and Harry Andrews was standing there staring at him from the next floor. The younger man's surprise quickly turned to a look of contempt. Sam felt the muscles in his own face tighten and tremble slightly.

"Now what's this, old man? Coming to beat me with your fists?" And he laughed, echoing in the space of the stairwell. "Look, old man—I could kill you right here, or turn you in. But if you go nice-like and leave Kathy and me be, I'll let you live out your days in peace. And no more peekaboo at the ration center either, deal?" And he smiled a winning smile.

Sam screamed and rushed up the stairs, his body a knotted mass of hate and pain. He clutched at Andrews' throat. The younger man kicked him in the stomach. Sam doubled over and fell on his back.

As Sam tried to get up, Andrews turned and went through the door back into the building. Sam stood up and staggered after him through the swinging door. He stepped into the hall just in time to see Andrews pause in front of the door to his apartment.

"Andrews, listen good!" Sam shouted. "You'll never get rid of me—it's me she wants. There's nothing you can do."

Andrews ignored him. The younger man opened the door to the apartment and went inside. Sam leaned against the wall in the hallway and tried to catch his breath. In a moment Harry Andrews came out again. There was a gun in his hand.

"I'm taking you down to the nearest police station on a

citizen's arrest," Andrews said as he came down the hall toward Sam. "They can check you over at the euthanasia station after I tell them I caught you trying to break into the hospital. You tried to bribe me for some drugs . . ."

Sam turned and pushed through the door to the stairs and started down quickly. As he turned on the second landing, Andrews shouted after him. "If I shoot you trying to escape, like, it'll be easier—especially after the autopsy shows your sickness!" Sam reached the ground floor and burst out into the dark street. He started running uptown. He looked over his shoulder. Andrews was not there.

Sam knew then that Harry Andrews was playing with him, that he intended to kill him and maybe say nothing to the police or anyone; not even Kathy.

As he ran Sam thought of Kathy. How far away she seemed now, like someone he had known in another life on a different world. If Andrews killed him, Sam Brickner would disappear from Kathy's life and no one would look for him. In an overcrowded city he was not important enough to qualify as a legitimate missing person. A check of his age would be enough for the police to close his file. Even if Andrews let them find his body, and he would not, it would be unprofitable to search for the murderer of a fifty-three-year-old man.

Sam stopped and listened for footsteps behind him. He looked around at the run-down buildings of the old east side. He was near the river; many of these buildings had been condemned a hundred times, and a few blocks ahead had recently been sealed off. The air smelled of brick dust and sewage-polluted river water.

He heard slow footsteps somewhere behind him. A thought pushed into his mind like a cold icepick. There had to be more to Kathy and Andrews, more than Andrews using him to put a leash on Kathy.

Sam turned a corner and ran toward the river, a suspicion forming in his mind. The footsteps turned into staccato running sounds behind him, echoing out of step with his own.

Suddenly to his right the block ended, turning into a rubble-filled lot and a view of the dark river flowing dead toward an unseen ocean. Sam stepped into the moonlight shadow of the last building and waited. He reached down and picked up a rock. The steps grew louder. In the east the coming dawn was a sickly gray stain of light, and the last quarter moon was a bloated grainy yellow balloon sitting on a rooftop.

The figure came by Sam and stopped with its back to him. Sam hurled the rock at its head and the mannequin crumpled. He did not feel as angry as he thought he would be.

He dragged the still-breathing body into the empty lot near the wall of the building. He sat down next to it, removed the man's gun, and waited.

Harry Andrews coughed and the cough turned into a laugh.

"That's good, old man—but you don't have it to kill me."

Sam pointed the gun at the man's head, saying, "Now tell me what you and Kathy are really up to."

In the faint morning light Sam saw the look of uncertainty in the man's face as he looked at the barrel of his own automatic. Andrews shrugged. "I really do love her too, you know."

"What else?"

"It won't do you any good to know."

"Out with it!"

"Katherine feeds me the regular medication-type drugs, like insulin, for instance. I sell them on the street to those who are hiding things, like you for instance. I set up your doctor's appointment when you needed it, old man." Andrews shrugged again. "Who would have thought Kathy would fall for you? She was mine before, you know, and will be again after I sing about you. I have too much on her. There's a chain of illegal medical practice and medication that runs clear into Canada, and she's plugged into it. You should kill me now. but you won't, you can't." Andrews coughed again, and Sam saw him touching the back of his head. "You bastard," Andrews said, "you've opened my scalp!"

Suddenly Andrews swung at the gun, knocking it from Sam's hand. It clattered in the rubble. Andrews crawled, half leaped onto Sam, reaching for his face. Sam tried to kick and fell backward, the sharp debris pushing into his back. Andrews grasped him tightly around the middle and pulled himself into a sitting position on top of Sam's chest. Then he reached forward and put his hands around Sam's neck. Sam saw him—a dark figure towering against a pale sky. Slowly the hands tightened their grip, until Sam started gasping for breath. A voice said, "I gotta do it, old man—it's the only way. You're two headaches for me. You know too much and I couldn't stand living without her. You too, so it'll be easier on you this way." Sam was climbing a rope of glass winding into a black sky. The rope was suspended over an abyss. The glass crumbled in his hands like sugar bloodying his palms, and he fell . . .

Sam thrashed around desperately, trying to get some air into his lungs. His hand closed on a rock and he brought it up and hit Andrews in the temple, caving it in with a crunch. The younger man's grip loosened and he fell on top of Sam.

Sam lay still for a moment, taking in greedy mouthfuls of air. He crawled out from under the corpse embracing him and rested next to it. He thought about Kathy. He had known only a carefully selected portion of her, what she wanted him to see,what he wanted her to be.

The sky grew lighter. Everything seemed so calm now, so peaceful. Maybe he could take Harry's place, if he recovered. Harry had tried to kill him, but he had also helped him live. How many others had benefited? Someone would have to take his place.

Maybe Sam Brickner deserved to die, after all? Maybe he should never see her again, take no more treatments, and let only the strongest survive in a roomier world? That world might have a chance to look outward again to the stars, dream again, and maybe love better than he had. It could all be arranged.

He got up and covered the body with stones. As he worked he realized that he had not known Harry Andrews very well; they had both known only each other's hate and violence. When he was done it was almost fully light. He looked down into a small pool of rainwater in the rubble, wondering how he could ever explain to Kathy how he felt. The face which looked up at him betrayed nothing, a face wrapped in shadow, a silhouette against a white sky.

# THE QUALITY OF MERCY

## Tamsin Ashe

Although **Tamsin Ashe** is new to science fiction, her presence is a welcome addition to the growing number of women in the field. In her mid-twenties, she lives with her husband and daughter out in the rural and lovely town of Bolinas, California, a stone's throw from the Point Reyes National Seashore and the site of a disastrous oil spill two years ago. She, along with several hundred others, worked around the clock for almost a week in an effort to save not only the lagoon but the birds that had been trapped by the oil.

Deeply concerned with environmental issues, Tamsin runs her own small organic farm, where she produces sufficient food from her garden to provide over half of the family's vegetables the year round, as well as raising chickens and, naturally, eggs.

She is also an avid music fan, with truly catholic taste. If you're lucky, you might some day get to hear her sing blues, which she does to perfection.

All this may seem strange when you consider the story that follows, but no one lacking her concern for the people of the San Francisco Bay Area could have come up with the vision she has created.

•

The door closed behind him with a sharp crack.

"Ah, Joseph, m'lad . . ." Bevis Mayhew-Streich extended a flat, long-fingered hand across a desk formidable enough to befit the Director of the Bureau of Human Natural Resources Preservation for the Pacific Quadrant of the Northern Hemisphere. "I'm so glad you found time to accept my invitation."

"More in the way of a summons, wasn't it, Bevis?" Joe met the professional smile warily.

"Now really, Joe," he laughed deprecatingly, "the Genetics Conservation Board keeps you bright young scientists pretty busy. Who knows when you might have found the time for a casual visit."

Joe Freyer managed to keep from clenching his teeth, and instead, offered a small twitch of his lips and an off-hand shrug. Socializing with this unctuous slug, Joe felt, was a pain in the ass. And how he hated Bevis' condescending references to "Joe Freyer, Boy Scientist."

"Let me offer you a cup of syn-caf, Joe, my boy." The jovial grin spread froglike over his face.

"No thanks, I simply don't have the time. There's quite a bit of work waiting for me back at the lab." What does he want? he wondered.

"Oh, come now, you'd think all you gencons boys were conscripts."

"All right then, Bevis." What the hell is he after?

"Have you heard the news about old Kyle?"

"No." Joe found it difficult to sound interested. He felt he would really rather be back in the lab, and away from this dangerous, smiling man.

"Well, he's announced his retirement this spring. I fully intend *and* expect to move up and take his place."

Jonathan Kyle, Coordinator for the North American Sector, was indeed, planning his retirement. Joe was sure that Bevis was the most likely man to take his place, though not necessarily the best.

"I really don't think I'll have much trouble with the competition," Bevis chuckled, almost coy.

Bevis' opinion of Harcourt Sinclair, Director of the Atlantic Quadrant, and the only other man in line for the position of Coordinator, was no secret to anyone. Sinclair was a quiet, methodical little man. He was little interested in keeping in the public eye, and he seemed to move through his job, day by day, with the slow and steady pace of the proverbial tortoise. Bevis maintained that the man had reached his present post by the purest of accidents.

"I suppose, if Kyle is really considering retirement, you're the obvious one for the job." Why the friendly chatter? thought Joe. We've never been on what you'd call "good terms," so what does this little scene mean?

"Of course he's retiring, man! It isn't that odd you know, a man in his position, with the credits he makes. And he's not so young anymore. He'll be fifty-four this March."

"Getting on, isn't he," Joe admitted.

Bevis sighed. "Not like the old days when a man could look forward to sixty, seventy, even eighty productive years. Regrettable turn of events, don't you think?"

"Bevis, did you call me over here just to discuss your plans for the future?"

"Well, no. You see, I've found myself at a loss as to how to tell you this."

"Why don't you just say it, Bevis? I have to be getting back to the lab." And he waited.

"Joe, it's about Holda. . . . You see, I've discovered she has psycho-motor epilepsy."

Oh God, Joe thought, suddenly alert.

"You realize this means she'll have to be brained, don't you, Joe?" He peered at Joe, almost slyly.

"But . . . are you sure?" The man's talking about Holda, his own wife. How can he be so matter of fact?

"Very sure. I confronted her and she admitted it. It seems she's been keeping it hidden for quite a little while now. Funny we didn't notice it sooner. She must have had help somewhere. Look, Joe, I wanted to tell you this personally because I know you were a very special friend to her."

"But, couldn't she be wrong? She hasn't the training to diagnose herself." He thought of that first morning a year and a half ago, when he had awakened to find her propped up on her elbows, chin in her hands, gazing down at him. "You're real," she'd said, with a kind of wonder. He'd drawn her down to him and kissed her. He'd felt the same kind of wonder.

Bevis sighed and gazed at Joe with a look of infinite patience. "You understand, she was quite upset when she realized I knew. She had a seizure, Joe. I saw it. It was unmistakable."

"There must be something you can do, Bevis." As he said it, Joe knew how foolish it was. Bevis would be the last to try and save Holda.

"The law's the law. My hands are tied."

"The Hoffmahn Precedent. What about that? Have you applied for her testing?"

"I didn't think it applied in her case. Holda was really nothing special."

"Genetic testing is her right."

"She should have applied when she first found out about her condition. My duty's clear."

"Your *duty* should be to discover first if she carries any valuable genes and to preserve them." Joe discovered that he was beginning to shout. He couldn't allow Bevis to see what kind of effect this was having on him. Bevis is getting satisfaction enough out of this, he thought, and I can't afford to lose control.

"Believe me. Holda had nothing worth saving. Besides, I sent out the order for her pick up ... oh, nearly two hours ago," Bevis said, glancing at his disk chronometer.

I can't let them take her, thought Joe. My God, two

hours. He's been stalling me here. I've got to get out, got to stop it if I can.

"I realize this is quite a shock, Joe, but it's done and the van is on its way by now."

Joe nodded woodenly.

"I know this seems rather sudden to you, but it wasn't an easy decision." Bevis stood. "Now I've got to get back to work, so if you'll excuse me. . . ."

I'll stop it, so help me God, I'll stop it, thought Joe as he walked from Bevis' office with studied calmness.

Joe entered the auto-taxi and spoke his destination into the cabbie. "Fast," he added. The cabbie informed him that it couldn't exceed the legal speed limit and asked him to please fasten his seat belt. Seething with frustration, he complied.

The Mayhew-Streichs lived in a nicely appointed high-rise apartment in the still fashionable Carmel, an enclave of money, position, and power.

The small crowd of people milling around the entrance to the apartment building when he arrived told Joe that the van had probably been and gone. Crowds always gathered when the pink day-glo van arrived in a neighborhood. Its presence usually meant a free show to liven up an otherwise boring day. These vans carried no anesthesia and the crews took sadistic pleasure in carting away the panicked victims.

Joe stuck his head out of the window, "Has the van left yet?" he shouted to a man on the edge of the crowd.

"You a friend of Mrs. Mayhew-Streich?" the man asked.

"Yes, have they taken her yet?"

"Who would have thought Mrs. Mayhew-Streich . . . ?" The man shook his head, disbelieving.

"Look Mister, just tell me. Has the van gone?" Joe could not help showing his impatience.

"Well, pardon me. Sure, it left about a half hour ago."

Cursing, Joe turned to the cabbie and asked it to take

him to the Embarcadero Exchange. The van had left a half hour ago, and still these people milling around. It reminded him of the way flies will sometimes hover over a scent on a dock where a dead fish has lain.

A half hour, thought Joe; I can still make it. It will be a good hour and a half or so to take her through processing. He tried to keep thoughts of what lay beyond processing away. But they came. Holda had psycho-motor epilepsy. "A chronic or debilitating disease," the law said. Under that law, she was subject to euthanasia.

Euthanasia, he mused, such a harmless sounding word. A merciful killing. Oh, the body's terminated painlessly enough. But the brain, Holda's brain would be removed and kept "in vitro," hooked to a computer. And she would still be Holda, he knew, never resting, considered more productive "dead" than alive. But her beliefs, her unrealized hopes and dreams, her memories, would all still be there. Buried under the clicking efficiency that runs the slide walks, shuffles the Bart cars, and keeps the factories turning out nice consumer goods, but *there,* and alive as the brain itself. Damn Bevis, damn him!

"My God! What am I thinking? I've got to call the Bureau," he said, sitting up with a start.

"Repeat please, sir," stated the cabbie.

"I want to be connected with the Admitting Office of the Bureau of Human Natural Resources Preservation."

"I have your party, sir."

"Hello." He made it sound like a command.

"Bureau of Human Natural Resources Preservation, Admitting. May I help you?"

Funny, thought Joe, that the receptionist should sound so cheerful, working in a place like that. "You have a van coming in soon. It will be carrying a Mrs. Holda Mayhew-Streich. I want her held until I can get there," he said.

"What is your authorization, sir?"

"This is Doctor Joseph Freyer. I want Mrs. Mayhew-Streich held for genetic testing."

"I'm sorry, sir. You will have to come in and present your ID card and fill out the necessary forms."

"Can't you just hold her for a half hour, until I get there?"

"Not without the proper procedures."

"Can't you people do anything?"

"Sir, you're shouting."

"I know it, dammit! Goodbye."

He slumped down into the seat. Yes, he said to himself, business as usual. Holda's just another case to them, one of hundreds they will see today. Poor Holda. How terrified she must be! And I promised her I wouldn't let it happen.

He remembered that day in the redwoods. He had taken her up the coast to the Redwood Preserve run by the Genetics Conservation Board. How awed she had been by their beauty! Holda had never seen a living tree, as few had. Exhilarated by the clean, fresh air, there among the trees, she had wanted to climb the steep rise that led up to the head of the ravine. For a better view of the beach, she had said. He remembered how lovely she had been, laughing and running in the undergrowth of ferns, her short dark hair catching the shafts of sunlight filtered through the branches and flashing copper. She had never been more beautiful.

It was there in the trees that she had had the attack. Afterwards, she had tearfully admitted to him that, yes, it was epilepsy. She had only known herself for a few weeks. She had begged him not to let them take her brain. He had held her close in his arms and had promised himself to take care of her, to get the needed drugs through the underground. Promised to keep her secret safe.

The taxi stopped with a sudden jolt. "What is it?" asked Joe.

"Couldn't say, sir," replied the cabbie. "Some kind of holdup ahead."

Joe opened the door, and with one foot on the taxi floor, he raised himself as high as possible to see over the other vehicles. All he managed to see was a large crowd of people blocking the entire road.

"Can't see a thing," he told the cabbie. "Wait here."

He made his way to a yellow-suited traffic controller, who was trying valiantly to disburse the crowd.

"What's the delay, officer?"

"Suicide. Man and a woman managed to get to the roof of that building and jump. It's a mess," the man answered, pointing.

"How long do you think it will take to clear things up?"

"I've got help on the way, a whole squad. Twenty minutes I'd guess."

"Can you help me get through?"

"Are you kidding? I can't get you through this mob. I'll be lucky if I'm not trampled to death myself."

"I've got to get through. You've got to help me."

"Mister, I told you, it's impossible. There's nothing I can do. Look, why don't you try going around? Take another route."

Joe turned, mumbling to himself. "I'm losing my mind. I should have tried that in the first place." He tried to run back to the taxi, but found he had to push and squirm his way through the crush of curious bodies. The crowd had grown by at least a third while he had been soliciting the aid of the controller.

Reaching the taxi, he found it confined on all sides by late-arriving vehicles. Oh Lord, he sobbed inwardly, I can't wait ... can't just sit here and wait ... got to help her. Breathing deeply, he fought for control.

"Get me the office of the Chief of Traffic Control, Kurt Horne." Horne was a friend of Joe's and would surely help him.

"Traffic Control, Mr. Horne's office. May I help you?"

"Let me speak to Mr. Horne, please."

"What is this in reference to, please?"

"I'm at the corner of El Camino and Peninsula. There's been an accident."

"Personnel have been dispatched to clear that area, sir."

"Yes, I know. I'm stuck here. I *must* get through."

"Sir, Control *is* doing its very best."

"Look, Kurt Horne is a friend of mine; I know he can help me."

"Mr. Horne has just gone to lunch."

"Why didn't you tell me before?"

"He's *just* left, sir."

"Damn you! You knew he was going to lunch. Why didn't you connect me?"

"Sir," the secretary said with a deep sigh, "Mr. Horne is a very busy man. He doesn't have time to take every call. Is there something I can help you with?"

"I want to requisition a chopper to get me out of here," Joe answered, thinking quickly.

"I'm afraid that's impossible. You would have to present your ID and fill out forms 37925-A and -B."

"Can't you do anything without forms?"

"I'm sorry, sir."

"Where is Horne lunching?"

"He didn't say."

"All right, thank you anyway." Joe put his face in his hands. "Oh, shit," he moaned; "what am I going to do?" Looking up, he saw the arrival of the Traffic Control chopper in the roof-port of a building near him. Clearly distracted, the controller he had talked to was making his way in that direction. Joe, weaving in and out between the immobile vehicles, intercepted the fellow.

"How much longer?" he asked.

"You that same guy? Boy, you don't give up, do you?"

"How much longer?" Joe repeated through clenched teeth.

"About forty-five minutes."

"Ten minutes ago you told me it'd be about twenty."

"Ten minutes ago, we didn't expect the crowd and the traffic to more than double."

"But, you said . . ."

"Okay, Buster, take it easy. Go back to your vehicle and keep out of the way," snapped the controller as he entered the roof lift.

Stunned by this news, Joe stumbled back to the taxi. Leaning into the window, he asked, "Where's the nearest Bart Station?"

"Behind us. El Camino and Third," answered the cabbie.

Joe fed his ID into the cabbie. It read his number and the appropriate credits were deducted from his account.

"We have not yet reached your destination, sir," protested the cabbie. "Surely you're not going to leave now?"

"Yes," answered Joe, retrieving his ID. He took a slide walk down the El Camino to the Bart Station. The Bart was always crowded, no matter what the hour. Joe couldn't remember the last time he'd been lucky enough to sit. So, this trip, he strap-hung, staring at blurry faces and grumbling impatiently with every jostle and station stop. Leaving the train at the Embarcadero Exchange, he hurried to the hover-cab stand. Hover-cabs were one of the few forms of transportation not automated. They were an expensive item. The B.H.N.R.P. complex was situated on Yerba Buena. A hover-cab would be faster and much less trouble than the shuttle from the main Bart tube on the bay's floor.

"I'd like to engage a cab, please," Joe asked the gaunt, bespectacled man attending the stand.

"There will be a ten minute wait, sir. All cabs are out at the moment."

Joe presented his ID. "I want the first cab returning," he said.

"Your destination?"

"Yerba Buena."

"Do you wish the cab to wait?"

"Yes."

"And will you be returning to the Exchange?"

"No. The roof-port of the Genetics Conservation Board."

"Very good, sir. Thank you," he said, returning Joe's ID.

Across from the cab stand was a bank of visi-phones.

Maybe I can get in touch with Willis, thought Joe. Maybe he can help somehow. It's a long shot, I know. He can't do anything officially, but he might be able to stall them.

"I'd like to speak to Dr. Jake Willis, B.H.N.R.P., Virology." He waited.

"Bureau of Human Natural Resources Preservation, Virology. May I help you?"

"Let me speak to Dr. Willis."

"May I say who is calling?"

"Dr. Joseph Freyer."

"Thank you, I'll see if Dr. Willis is free."

Joe waited only a moment before Dr. Willis' face appeared on the screen. He and Jake Willis had been friends since the university. Joe hadn't seen much of him in the past year.

"Joe," he grinned, "you old reprobate."

"Listen, Jake, I need your help."

"Sure buddy, what can I do?" Willis' brows came together.

"Your people are processing a Mrs. Holda Mayhew-Streich. She's probably there now. I want you to get down there and stall them until I can get there."

"I can get down there in about fifteen minutes. I'll see what I can do," Jake said.

"I'll be there by then; I want you to stop them now!"

"Calm down, Joe. I don't know what's going on, but I can't leave the lab now. I'm waiting out a reaction."

"Jake, this is important. You've *got* to help me."

"My job is important too. I can't walk out on this test."

"But you can walk out on a friend, eh?" Joe said bitterly as he broke the connection.

"Sir, there's a cab available now," called the man behind the cab stand.

Soaring in a low arc toward the island, Joe looked down at the bay. Yerba Buena seemed strangely isolated. He could remember when it was linked to either side of the bay. Since the completion of the Bay Area Rapid Transit, the various bridges spanning the bay had fallen into disuse and disrepair. Most had been demolished, although both the Golden Gate and Bay Bridges had been designated landmarks. But the quake of '94 had left them both so damaged that they too were finally demolished.

Joe glanced at the white-on-white decor of the Admitting Office. It seemed to reinforce the detached attitude of the personnel.

"Ahem," he said, standing at the main desk. The woman behind the desk paid no attention. "Ahem," he said again, a little louder. She still did not look up. "Hey!" Sharply this time, slamming the flat of his hand on the desk. Now, she raised her head, facing Joe with a look of indignation and reproach.

"May I help you?" she said stiffly.

"I want the release of Mrs. Holda Mayhew-Streich."

"Fill out these forms and present them with your ID to the gentleman in room 12-C," she said with a bored sigh, ignoring his demanding tone.

He sat down in a very functional chair and began to fill out the forms.

What? he said to himself. What do they need my height and weight for? How long have I been at my present job? This is utterly ridiculous. Eight pages of unnecessary information, he thought in disgust as he went down the corridor marked *11-C to 14-C*.

The man in room 12-C was small and owlish. He

quickly scanned the forms. "I see you are employing the Hoffmahn Precedent," he commented.

"It's not unusual," Joe said.

"Yes," the man agreed, "Not that unusual. Well, your release seems to be in order, Doctor, but I'm afraid Mrs. Mayhew-Streich entered Processing some while ago. She must be well on her way by now."

"She can't be," snapped Joe.

"Well, suit yourself."

Joe raced through the hallway, sliding on the slick floor, and fairly broke down the door of Processing. Here the white walls were trimmed in icy blue.

"Mrs. Mayhew-Streich, I have her release," he panted to a woman in O.R. greens.

"Oh, I *am* sorry, sir . . ." She spread her hands.

Joe managed to get halfway down the hall when his knees buckled under him and he collapsed, sobbing, to the floor.

Seated at his desk, Joe tried to think of the ride from the B.H.N.R.P. complex. He could recall little. It's probably due to the sedative, he thought. He could remember the hard faces of the nurse and two attendants as they administered the sedative, and helped him into his hover-cab, at his insistence. He didn't like the idea of sedation. He knew it would be entered into his psycho-medical profile. The law required this of everyone. Every instance of psychological or physiological importance that could be officially observed was recorded.

Joe tried to fight down thoughts of Holda, but they would not be quelled. Oh, Holda, I promised you. I tried, Holda, I tried. He thought of Bevis, sitting in his downtown office. I'll kill him, he thought. I'll take that self-satisfied grin off his face. No, he thought again, I can't do that. They'll catch me. It's sure. Then I'll be brained too. Even if I fail. No, I can't do a thing. Oh, Holda, forgive me. Sobbing inwardly, he laid his head in his arms.

He stayed like that for a while, consciously thinking of nothing. He sat suddenly upright. "Christy, come in here, please," he called to his secretary over the intercom.

"Yes, sir?" she said, standing in the doorway.

"I want you to arrange for the release of the body of Mrs. Holda Mayhew-Streich. I want it brought to the lab for testing, immediately." He reached into his desk. "Here," he said, signing in the required places; "these are the post-mortem testing forms. Fill them out for me please."

"Yes, sir, I'll take care of it right away."

"Christy," he said, "this takes priority over everything else."

She nodded and left.

Joe spent the rest of the afternoon pacing his office. It was nearly quitting time when the lab report came. He read it greedily. Finishing, he fell into his chair, stunned. It's true, he thought with surprise; I only hoped, and it's true. Now I have what I want. Holda carried not one, but two of the genes on Gencons's "save" list.

Joe began to giggle. This was all that he had hoped for and more. Gencons carefully guarded the gene pool. To deliberately cause the loss of valuable genes was a felony. All convicted felons were brained. "Brained," Joe tittered to himself; "Bevis is going to be brained." He held his sides and rocked in his chair. Abruptly, he was himself again.

"Christy," he said into the intercom, "I need you again. Go over to the Hall of Records and get a copy of the braining order for Mrs. Mayhew-Streich. Quickly, before they close," he told her.

After she had gone, Joe wrote out a formal statement. He gathered up the test results and the statement and took the lift downstairs.

He met his secretary at the entrance when she returned. "Thank you, Christy. You can go home now. It's past time," he said, taking the papers from her.

"Thank you, Doctor," she said as she left the building.

Giving the papers a cursory glance, Joe's eye was caught by the line marked "Assignment." "Bart: Sausalito-Cloverdale," read the precise print of some unknown clerk.

That's my line, he thought as an almost overwhelming feeling of nausea swept over him.

"All in a day's work, eh Bevis?" said Joe, the nausea quickly replaced by rage. He stood, shaking, for a moment. Then, his composure regained, hurried to the computer room.

It was well past quitting time now, and the only person in the room was the night attendant. Joe handed the man the papers he carried. "I want you to send these off right away," he told the attendant. "Send them to Mr. Harcourt Sinclair."

Joe watched, satisfied, as the man fed the information into the computer. Sinclair will know what to do, he thought. He won't waste any time either. He wants the position of Coordinator as much as Bevis does. He'll know just how to use this information.

You played your clever joke, Bevis, Joe thought, pity you won't be free to enjoy it. It was swift for Holda. One moment, her secret was known, and the next, she was riding in that pink van on her way to braining. It won't be quite that fast for you, Bevis. You'll have to wait it out, hoping every minute for an acquittal. But it won't come, no, not with your big, bold signature on the testing waiver. Joe walked outside to meet the evening.

Joe began to chuckle softly as he realized he was actually seated. He stopped when he saw the startled expression of the man seated next to him. "I'm sorry," he said to the man, "But it's only fair you know. It *is* her train." The man watched Joe carefully from the corner of his eye until his station was called. As he rose from his seat, Joe put a restraining hand on his arm. "Do you know where this train is going?" Joe asked, "really going?" But the man jerked his arm free and squirmed his way into the crowd and towards the door.

A tired-faced woman dropped down into the vacant seat. "Do you like this train?" Joe asked her. "She'd like you. She always liked people," he told her. He cocked his head, listening. "You can hear her, can't you? She used to sing to me all the time." But the woman didn't answer. She made every effort to get as far away from Joe as possible and still remain seated. Humming softly to himself, Joe began to caress the cold walls of the train. "I'm right here, Holda. I'm going to take care of you."

# CHELSEA QUINN YARBRO
## and
# HARLAN ELLISON

# UN BEL DI

## Chelsea Quinn Yarbro

Erstwhile statistical demographic cartographer, actress, and counsellor for mentally disturbed children, **Chelsea Quinn Yarbro,** presently voice teacher and author, is rapidly becoming one of the most sought-after younger writers in science fiction. Not content with that list of talents, she is currently directing a satirical fairy tale which she wrote and composed for a local San Francisco dinner theatre.

She excels as a gourmet cook and as an intimate friend of Gildenstern (survivor of the famous team of Rosencranz and Gildenstern), a tomcat of singular mien and accomplishments.

Quinn is married to bearded Don Simpson, artist and inventor, whose list of talents is equally formidable, and whose work regularly wins top prizes at science fiction art shows.

Short and with a bubbling enthusiasm, she is at her best when wedding science fiction with her other love, opera.

As his terrifying smile widened the Janif Undersecretary watched the procession of Papi wind its way up the far side of the valley. "They're like fine children, perfect children, every one of them." The Undersecretary licked his outer lips; it was a furtive darting movement. "So sad they aren't truly intelligent. If they were . . ." He broke off. If they were . . .

His companion almost put a hasty hand on the Undersecretary's auxiliary arm. "We are still in doubt about that here. We have not run many tests yet. They might have greater potential than we know." The Ambassador made a weak gesture of apology.

Undersecretary Navbe waved him away in an offended manner. "Certainly, certainly. Keep your ambassadorial pride. I myself look for signs of genius in my pets. You are free to do the same."

Instead of the accepted answer the Ambassador raised a primary arm slowly and remained rigidly silent. He then bowed with maddening propriety to the lengthening shadows.

The Undersecretary closed the screen, stepping back with a gesture of regret. It was a great pity that he had to be so very isolated. And the Ambassador was just as bad as the others of his status. He would be tolerant to absurdity of the locals, then become unyielding and moralistic with the others of his kind. Navbe had seen it often in his post, and bitterly rued having to deal with such perversity.

But the Ambassador was speaking. ". . . for the Papi, in this instance. You will want to observe them while you are here, Undersecretary."

Privately the Janif Undersecretary thought this a lamentable state of affairs. "Of course. I look forward to it," he said.

"This is quite a unique place," continued the Ambassador, warming to his subject.

*They all are,* thought Navbe.

"We've found not only that the Papi have a highly de-

veloped social order, but that they surgically alter their
young to fulfill specific cultural functions." Here the Ambassador hesitated.

"Oh?" Navbe managed the illusion of polite interest.

"Yes. They can make truly amazing changes. Each of
the modifications has a definite place in the culture, although a couple are odd, dependant creatures."

"They can actually do this?" Navbe asked lazily.

"It appears so," answered the Ambassador cautiously.

"Before or after birth. How?" Under his meticulous exterior Navbe felt a deep elation. Perhaps his temporary
exile would not be as terrible as he had feared it might be.
There could be great solace here after a few special arrangements.

"I am sorry to say that we have not yet discovered their
reproductive mechanism. They are probably ovovivipa-
rous." He moved uncomfortably, knowing how far he had
stepped beyond the bounds of allowable ceremony. It was
also a blot to his record that he knew so little about the
people he lived with.

At this Klin Navbe all but laughed. So there was a mystery, was there? That made for a challenge. And this
sniveling diplomat had not found it out. "Probably?" He
was scornful, but not so much as to discourage the Ambassador from talking. As all others of his status, Navbe
despised the Representative status. Yet there was a chance
that his host knew the reason for his temporary exile, and
he dared not put himself in a compromising position with
such a person.

"As I have told you, we cannot do the tests. We lack
the full authorization to do so. I do not know how we
shall function if we are not properly authorized."

"Precisely." What was this fool's familial name? Lesh?
Yes, Ambassador Lesh. He wanted the authority to proceed with tests and Navbe could give him that authorization. Plans blossomed in his mind.

It was perhaps fortunate that the Meditation Bell rang

the summons to the Third Cycle just then; it provided cover for the awkwardness between the two officials. Their Janif formality asserted itself, and they strode silently down the hall together.

When they had completed their ritual exercises, Navbe put Ambassador Lesh at his ease with that age-old question beloved of off-planet Janif officialdom: "How did you come to serve on Papill, Ambassador?" And he masked his boredom at the too-familiar tale of a diplomat's career.

In the long twilight the two Janif sat together on the terrace listening to the distant Night Song of the Papi. In the valley below Ambassador Lesh's estates the waning light shifted, slid, and was gone, and the soft white fogs followed the shadows to wrap the valley in sleep. On the ridges the tassled, angular trees sighed in the wind, their hard thin leaves clicking endlessly above the fog.

"A beautiful place, Lesh, even with just the two stars. It is like a children's story." Navbe watched the valley's soft change, dreaming absently of violated children and the strange Papi, intense pleasure hidden in the formal set of his face. He had picked a flower and was stroking it with the extending sensors of his thumbs. "You are to be envied, Ambassador—to be surrounded by all this loveliness."

"I have thought so myself," said the Ambassador in an unbecoming burst of familiarity.

Navbe ignored the solecism. "And the Papi are such pretty people. So delicate. Not like those creatures on Tlala or Isnine. You have beauty here, and tractable natives."

The Ambassador, lulled by the Undersecretary's flow of remarkable condescensions and innocuous questions, was betrayed into elaborating on the Papi. "They are a gentle people. It is of great importance to them that they bring delight to their neighbors. It is unfortunate that they do not recognize the laxness of their social order, but their errors are charming. They have made almost a religion of their kindness. Over the years I have observed their spirit of self-sacrifice." He became aware of his blunder. "But it is nearly impossible to take advantage of them. They know their own order." His confusion led him to a further mistake and he showed his primary hands as he shifted position.

Irritated, Navbe wondered how many more insults he would have to endure at the hands of Ambassador Lesh. He savagely desired to humiliate his host, but he wanted information more so he forced himself to respond with calculated ease: "Certainly, to see the Papi is to want to protect them from abuse. They must be greatly in your debt."

"Not at all," Lesh said hastily, looking wretched.

Navbe flung back both pair of arms in his best offensive manner. "You must not fear me, Ambassador Lesh. Surely you know the Judiciate would not have allowed me to come here if they had found any real basis to the scandal. But such talk, especially about High officials, is dangerous. I have willingly elected to leave Jan to come here in order to allow the tale to be forgotten."

The Ambassador twitched uncertainly. He had heard tales of the Undersecretary's strange perversions, but was loath to ask about them. Even to admit he had heard the rumors would be more shame than he would deliberately bring on himself.

"Come, come, you must not be afraid. You have heard something of me caught alone with the children of Sub-council Hariv. No, you needn't deny it. The grosser strata, disobeying every Janif law, have repeated the story, elaborating and embellishing it, if the versions I have heard are indicative. That I have been allowed to see the children is true, and I am fully aware of the honor done me in this, but how, in a High House, would I have obtained that access to the completely sequestered offspring of such an official? Only think of the obstacles and be reasonable." It had been difficult to get to them, but Navbe was well-aware that the task was not as difficult as the public had been led to believe.

The Ambassador knew about the guarding of High children, and he wavered. "They did speak of bribes and extortion . . ." It was a terrible breach of courtesy, even to mention it, but he was too deeply involved to deny his knowledge.

The Undersecretary bit out a laugh. "What man of Sub-council Hariv's stature would have such servants around him? He would never tolerate so low a status to enter his House. How do high status servants behave? Bribes are out of the question." That much, at least, was correct.

"I hadn't considered . . ."

Navbe remembered how very long it had taken for him to find his accomplice, one who shared his need to use the young bodies for cruel pleasure. How delicate the maneuvering had been, and how quickly the problem had been solved when he had discovered the night handservant to be addicted to Unjy. Then it had been easy. All the careful searching, the obtuse questioning, the days of painstaking effort had been worth it. He could recall the tearing of the flesh when his antlers touched it, the smell of the soft inner tissues when he fingered them . . .

"Yes, I had not thought of that. With such talk rife in the lower strata, the honor of high status servants would be impugned. It is no wonder you chose to disassociate yourself from such improper conduct."

"So you see," Navbe said expansively if vaguely.

The Ambassador was painfully relieved. He settled back in the soft cushions and offered the Undersecretary another dish of Merui. Navbe accepted it with a skilled blend of humility and contempt.

All the Papi that waited at the gates looked uniformly young to Navbe. They all had the serene, child-like faces and downy antlers that marked Janif children, made more attractive by huge violet eyes. Their clothes were a soft, clinging fabric that Navbe longed to fondle.

"We bring you the morning, you who are new among us," the Papi said in chorus. "We have come to welcome the new Janif visitor and to beg him to visit us in our houses."

The Ambassador stole a warning look at the Undersecretary, but Navbe was far too careful to be so carelessly trapped. "It will give me much honor to walk with you one sundown," he said with a slight bow in the proper ritual intonation.

The soft garments moved in the wind, and the Papi were outlined in their clothes, naked to Navbe. His thumb sensors stirred urgently. "It is close to the First Meal, and I wish you nourishment."

The Papi were obviously happy with him. They rustled among themselves, whispering in their chantlike speech.

Then a Papi, whom Ambassador Lesh had identified as the local leader, came forward with his offering of three finely wrought platters. Each was covered with squares of the fascinating cloth. "A gift for you," he said to the Janif with an acceptable show of respect. "It is our delight to bring these few things to you, in the hopes they might please you."

Navbe had studied this part of the ritual the night before, and was able to respond without noticeable hesitation. "Here are three rare things; but the light in the valley and the mist ensnared in a tree are rarer." He touched each of the platters without removing the cloths. "I will value the gifts as they are valued by the givers."

The Papi and Ambassador Lesh regarded him with approval, although Lesh's look was tinged with relief. "You will be welcome among us at any sundown," said the Papi spokesman. "I am known as Nara-Lim. This one is Tsu-Lim and this one is Ser-Tas." He did not introduce the others, to Navbe's delight. Apparently only the platter-bearers had that distinction. Navbe approved of that, the recognition of status. Ambassador Lesh had told him that Lim and Tas were thought to be titles, which revealed the extent to which he had deluded himself about the Papi's intelligence potential. Titles among those who lived as the Papi did would be ludicrous.

The platter-bearers put their offerings on the steps, then went ceremoniously to the rear of the group. Nara-Lim touched each of the platters and then he, too, went to the rear of the group.

"I am honored by Nara-Lim and his generous companions." And Navbe turned, walking slowly up the steps at the gateway.

Behind him, the gentle, fragile Papi waited until the gates were closed before they left the Ambassador's estates.

"That was well done," Lesh said, forgetting himself.

"I wish to make my stay as pleasant as possible," Navbe informed his host with a sarcastic laugh. As he spoke he was thinking of ways to obtain a Papi for his own use. Seeing those lovely animals at the gates that day had awakened his need again and had strengthened his resolve to have one. He knew that his position was an advantage, but could not find the best means of using it.

"Make no doubt, Undersecretary; they will want you to visit them." Ambassador Lesh stopped at the terrace. "Will you take your meal now?"

"It is customary," Navbe said witheringly.

"Must this be with the Janif meats, or will the local ones do? We have the Janif available, but during the day I have tried to run this establishment on native foodstuffs . . ."

"Your economy is no doubt admired. Serve what you wish. If I am to go to their homes, I should learn what to expect." He saw Lesh's embarrassment and was pleased.

Nara-Lim looked expectantly at his guest, hesitating as

he held the door to his house open to the Janif. "Undersecretary? What am I to have the pleasure of doing for you?" He bowed low.

Klin Navbe opened both sets of hands in obsequious display, hoping to disarm the Papi with this extraordinary courtesy. "I have come as a student, Nara-Lim. I desire to learn more of the life of your people." He knew that these natives were stupid and trusting. This approach would be the most likely to succeed. Any species of low technology that flattered itself with the illusion of intelligence was easy to convince of your interest.

"We are delighted," Nara-Lim opened the door wider.

"I wish also to thank you for the cloth, the stone work, and the herbs you presented to me. I am impressed."

"It is enough that you value them. If you enjoy our poor offerings, they are made rich."

Navbe moved closer. "You must tell me how to proceed, since your ways are not the ways of the Janif." Cynically Navbe watched the approval in the old Papi's eyes. These little people were incapable of understanding insults.

"Certainly. It will be an honor to this house." He stepped aside to let the Janif Undersecretary enter.

After a long and boring afternoon, Navbe was allowed to leave, promising to return when he could, thanking his host in the most effusive terms.

Then, when he stood in the door, he turned back, as if suddenly aware of a new question. "I have just thought ... But it would be too great a favor. I must not ask it."

"What were you thinking of?" Nara-Lim asked eagerly, his wide Papi eyes alight, and his soft clothes quivering. "The Janif have not shown so much curiosity about us until now. We are certainly ready to fulfil any reasonable request."

With this encouragement Navbe put on a display of reluctance, sneering privately at the naiveté of the creatures. As if any Janif could be so concerned with Papi.

"You told me of the ... did you call them companions? ... Yes? Companions."

"Yes?"

"They are adapted for the pleasure of the owner, is that not correct? Do I chose the words badly?" Navbe paused as if uncertain as to how to continue. "I thought that I might arrange to buy one, if that is the usual transaction ... You see, I would then have one of you with me, to instruct me and tell me what I need to know of your world and your ways. I am right that the companion is always with its ... master?"

Nara-Lim looked chagrined. "I should have suggested it to you. You must forgive my manners. It would naturally have been offered to you if I had thought your interest was so great."

Realizing that his boredom had shown, Navbe made a show of confusions. "I will confess that when I first asked you, it was idle speculation bit your talk has shown me that Papill has much to offer those of us from Jan." It was the first honest statement he had made, and it pleased him to think that Nara-Lim would hear it as a compliment. Such foolish creatures deserved to be prostituted.

"Then I will arrange for a companion for you. Perhaps you will be kind enough to call here one day soon."

"In three days, then?" Here Navbe held his breath.

"Of course," was the answer as Nara-Lim bowed. "I will select a companion for you, one known for grace and docility and boasting much beauty." He paused, looking up to the sky. "There will be heavy mists tonight. You will want to return to the Ambassador's estates quickly. It is dangerous to be abroad in the mists. Even Papi have been lost quite hopelessly in them."

"Your concern flatters me," Navbe said, touching the homing device that would guide him unfailingly back to the estates. "I will leave you now."

"Your interest in Papill is a great honor to our people. Your companion will be here in three days." He kept his deep bow even as he closed the door against the approaching night.

As he strode back along the mountain path in the steadily thickening fog, Klin Navbe gloated to himself. Success was so easy with fools, and the Papi were certainly fools. They thought themselves possessed of tradition when all they had was a stagnated culture of decaying blood lines. What an opportunity this presented to him! It would be ridiculous to waste it.

Ambassador Lesh met him by the terrace. "You were out?" he asked shrilly. "Where were you?" In his fear he forgot to use Navbe's title.

"I went to see Nara-Lim. For what little concern it is of yours." He paused for this to sink in, then: "I will require room to accommodate a Papi servant. Nara-Lim is providing me with a companion."

"A companion," Lesh repeated blankly. He had a sudden picture of those most special Papi with Undersecretary Navbe and was afraid.

"It will arrive here in three days. I assume you can be ready."

Lesh's primary arms twitched. "I can." He thought for a moment. "We can move you and your companion into the Terrace House." Ordinarily such a thing would be unthinkable, but Lesh no longer wanted to be involved in the affairs of the Undersecretary any more than protocol made necessary.

"That should be satisfactory. I rely on you to arrange it for me in time for my companion's arrival." And with that he went past the Ambassador into the house, his robes hissing derisively.

The companion looked up at Navbe with huge, adoring eyes. It was specially dressed for the occasion, wrapped in innumerable layers of tissue-fine cloth. It regarded Navbe with awe and a little ill-concealed fear.

"This is most kind of you, Nara-Lim," Navbe said with-

out looking at him. "I will treasure this, you may be sure."
He reached out to touch the slender sprouting antlers.
"Remarkable."

Nara-Lim looked pleased and murmured some words
that Navbe didn't hear.

"Yes, I will certainly treasure this." Inwardly he was
still reeling from the first sight of the companion. Of all
the Papi he had seen, this was the most childlike; a small
figure without any of the grosser features of most of the
natives. He had been told that they were made so, but did
not realize until now that the change would be so impressive. Formed like a Janif child, with limpid eyes and soft
antlers that were downy to the touch. He would have to
be careful at first, make no moves to reveal his intent.

"You are pleased, then. This is satisfactory?" Nara-Lim
asked quietly.

"Are you pleased?" The companion asked with a becoming urgency.

"Yes. Yes, I am pleased." He dragged his eyes from the
companion and turned to Nara-Lim. "You have done me
great honor, and I am beholden."

The old Papi turned almost double. "It is we who are
honored. No Janif has ever before been so generous of his
interest, no Janif has even bothered to learn from us. You
have been most kind."

"Really," he said. "What more is there for me to do?
Are there rituals, or documents . . . ?"

"A brief ritual," Nara-Lim said diffidently. "It is to assure your care of your companion, since it is wholly dependent on you. They are made for one individual and
may not be changed. We feel it is essential to have a ceremony to establish this."

"Commendable," Navbe said, hoping that the ritual
would be short. He was anxious to return to the Terrace
House. The companion would be his then, for whatever
purposes he chose. His auxiliary arms drew his robes more

closely about him so that the Papi could not see the agitation he was feeling.

"Then, if you will come this way?" Nara-Lim held open the door to the garden. "I arranged for the proper setting earlier. I hope this does not distress you. Ordinarily it would be for you to do, but I thought that you would forgive me this liberty."

"Your behavior is excellent, Nara-Lim." How he hated exchanging these useless formalities with this race of precocious animals. Only the promise that was held in the companion's body kept him reasonable and accepting of the ridiculous wishes of the Papi. "I am unfamiliar with your ways and find your tact most rewarding."

They went into the small garden where Nara-Lim had lit a number of ornamental fires in braziers. Then he threw scented water on the companion. He next gave each a plant to hold while he recited some unfamiliar words. When the plants had been burned in the braziers, it was over.

"Very pretty," Navbe remarked, thinking it all very stupid. The companion clung to his auxiliary arm.

"In five days there will be a ceremonial visit paid to you, as assurance that you are taking proper care of the companion. But you must not let this concern you. It is merely our way." He made an elaborate gesture to signify the perfunctory nature of the visit.

"I thank you for telling me." This was genuine thanks, for Navbe realized that he must be careful to leave no mark that might arouse suspicion as to his use of the companion. There must be no sign of abuse, at least, not for the first five days.

The Papi elder bowed. "Go then. And learn of each other."

Navbe led the companion away from Nara-Lim's garden with unseemly haste, smiling ferociously.

Although Ambassador Lesh suspected why Navbe had

taken the companion, he was careful not to show this in his manner. He greeted Navbe as he returned and directed his servants to show them to the Terrace House.

"I know you will understand that this is the best of the separate houses I have," he said uneasily.

"Of course. This had to be expected." The patronizing sound of his voice grated and Ambassador Lesh had to force himself to ignore it.

"You should find it adequate," he responded at last, when he was sure he would not overstep his status.

"Adequate," Navbe agreed. He turned to the companion, glowing fragile and childlike beside him. "It will do for you," he told the companion with a sound curiously like a snort.

"Wherever you are, that is truly the best place to be," murmured the companion in a sweet, trilling voice.

Navbe was surprised. He hadn't expected quite so much ability in the companion and was not sure he wanted it. But devotion would be something new and he thought it would amuse him.

"Do you hear, Lesh? It's quite alarmingly faithful." The cruel eyes mocked the rigid control of the Ambassador. "Were you about to warn me of the natives? Your little Nara-Lim has done so already. Charmingly. We went through a ceremony designed to overwhelm me with the honor of the occasion." He turned again to the companion. "He wanted me to understand what I was being given. As if I needed him to tell me." He laughed. It was not a pleasant laugh.

"They are meant to be faithful, Undersecretary. I understand that they cannot be altered to suit another once they have been given to ... someone ..." he ended awkwardly.

"Are you suggesting that I take this with me when I leave? With all that's being said about me?" He had taken the precaution of speaking Janif rather than his approximation of Papi. "Really, Lesh. This is an animal, no more. I have it to amuse me and stave off the unutterable boredom of this place. When I leave, it will return to its people. You're wrong, you know, to think that creatures like this one really care about their masters. It's sham, Lesh. Just cunning and sham."

"You're not to harm it," Ambassador Lesh cried recklessly.

"Would it make your position here embarrassing?" Navbe looked at Lesh until the Ambassador was forced to look away. "I can't adapt my wants merely to suit you, Lesh. You know that, don't you?" He put his primary arm under the status badge on the front of his robe. "You do know that."

"If Nara-Lim were to discover—"

"Discover what?"

"Certain things," Lesh said petulantly.

"Lesh, you forget who you are." This was harshly said and to emphasize the harshness Navbe put both auxiliary arms outside of his robe, thumbs twitching.

"You will do as you wish," Ambassador Lesh allowed, in a defeated tone. "You will be shown to your Terrace House."

"Oh, you may lead the way," Navbe said maliciously. It pleased him to take vengeance on Lesh by making him do servant's work, lower status servant's work.

"As you say," Lesh said tightly.

"I have not pleased you?" the companion asked anxiously.

"Does it matter?"

"I have tried to do as you wish. What more do you want of me?" The great sad eyes hovered over him.

"What are you doing off your mat?" Navbe asked, entirely out of patience.

"You are not pleased with me. What must I do?" Even the downy antlers quivered with emotion.

"Do not fret. You were all compliance. Return to your

mat." But even as he said it he was annoyed afresh. The children had not wanted him; they had fought him with their hands and new antlers as well as struggling and crying out when he assaulted them. This creature had accepted him, making no more than a whimper at the worst of it, and looking with dumb reproachful eyes as it was ravished.

"I must please you."

"Then go to your mat!" With this he turned away and had the satisfaction of hearing the soft sounds as the companion curled on the mat at the foot of his bed. There was vulnerability after all.

"Companion," he said without turning or rising.

"Yes," answered the eager voice in the gloom.

"You will learn to please me. It is that we are different in our ways. In time we will grow accustomed to one another."

There was relief in the little voice as it answered. "Oh, yes. There is plenty of time. I will learn. It is a promise. I will be as you want me."

As Navbe fell into sleep he knew that the companion would learn. He would see to it.

Nara-Lim and the visitors were disturbed when they made the prefunctory five day visit. There was a lingering pain in the eyes of the companion, an elusive sorrow that they could not understand. Questioned in private, the companion said: "We are different. That is the trouble. It will take time."

"You are well, then?" Nara-Lim asked, uneasy without knowing why. He felt something he had not felt before, an oppressive air, a touch of hidden fury. He did not have a name for it, but he was afraid that the companion did.

"I am well." The companion turned its eyes away, looking toward Navbe across the terrace.

"Is there some trouble?" pursued Nara-Lim.

"Just that we are strange to one another. I am learning

to ... please him." The trouble in the deep eyes faded. "He has promised to teach me and keep me by him forever. He promised."

Nara-Lim nodded, and felt that he ought to be satisfied: "It is probably as you say. They are not as we are."

The companion came near to Nara-Lim. It gestured formally, a pale imitation of Navbe. "He is my master, Nara-Lim, and I am his companion. I must be his way now."

"Yes," said Nara-Lim with equal formality. "That is the way of companions." But he was still unsure.

"Come, you will talk with him. You will see how much he cares for me, and how great is his esteem for me. I am fortunate indeed in this master." So saying, the companion led Nara-Lim across the terrace to where Navbe stood, surrounded by Papi, a gargoyle surrounded by fauns.

When the visit was concluded, Nara-Lim went away with the rest, fearing that his gift had been a betrayal to his people. He had seen the look in the Janif's eyes, the contempt of his manner, and had heard him say fleetingly to Lesh that it would be welcome to him to be among civilized beings again. He had issued the binding orders himself, and felt no doubt at the time, but seeing the companion with the Janif now, he feared.

"Another postponement!" Navbe snarled, hurling the directive to the floor. His sensors writhed on his hands and his tongue flicked uneasily over his outer lips.

"What delay?" asked the companion meekly. It had seen fury in Navbe's stride when he had left Ambassador Lesh, and could feel the rage that consumed its master.

"I am not summoned back ..." He broke off, realizing who he was answering. "It is not important to you."

The companion came to Navbe's side, its soft clothes whispering as it moved. "This thing has disturbed you. Let me bind your brow, or bathe you."

Navbe tore the delicate primary hands from his forehead. "No!" He stormed across the room. "I do not want you sniveling around me!"

The companion was shocked. "But I am here . . ."

"I don't want you here!" Navbe punctuated this with a blow, and was rewarded with a moan. "Go away. Go bother someone else."

"But I can't," the companion said softly. "I was made to be your companion and I serve no other. I cannot leave you."

Navbe turned murderously on it. "Then keep out of my way."

"As you wish," the companion whispered unhappily.

"And be silent!"

Then he sat on the reclining cushions and thought. The delaying order was not entirely unexpected, but it angered him. There was not reason enough to refuse him the right to return to Jan. To be left on this outpost world with talkative pets was driving him distracted. He pulled at the directive with all four hands. The children could not have betrayed him. They were too frightened and too badly hurt. And for that they would have ordered him exterminated, not exiled. He feared that they might delay him forever, shifting him from remote world to remote world until his name had no power and his status was reduced to nothing. He scuffed at the tattered directive. That some low status clerk had sent it only made matters worse.

"Would you want food, my master?" came the question from the far corner of the room.

"No." There had to be something he could do to force the issue. He would protest to Secretary Vlelt. It was a risky business but he was not without status, and the Secretary might listen to him if he were careful in his phrasing. He made up his mind to work out a plea that very evening.

"May I help you?" the companion asked, the ghost of a voice in the gathering dusk.

"Come here," Navbe commanded, and when the companion was beside him, he sank all his hands into the young flesh.

It was Ambassador Lesh who gave him the news that the Secretary had called him back to Jan.

"When?" the Undersecretary demanded urgently.

"As soon as possible." There was an expression on the Ambassador's face that might almost be disgust. "He needs your services, it would seem."

"How many days before I must depart?" Navbe had unwittingly shown his interest in the order and felt that he had to brazen it out.

"Four days, Undersecretary. I think you can be ready in that time."

Navbe scowled. It was more than he was willing to tolerate, this superior attitude from an inferior. He would have something to say about it when he got back to Jan.

"The Terrace House is yours until you leave, Undersecretary." Lesh started to move away.

"I will expect you to prepare my belongings for departure," Navbe said smoothly. "All things suitably crated for the journey. That will include the bolts of cloth given me by the Papi, and that worked stone." It had been in the back of his mind to bring these products to the attention of the Merchant Council. That Ambassador Lesh had not done so would be a mark against his record.

"And the companion."

Navbe was getting out of patience with Lesh. "Send it back to its people. What good is it to me?"

"I can't do that." Ambassador Lesh turned on the Undersecretary. "It has been made for you, and it is yours. If you abandon it, it will die. It cannot go back to its people." The heat in his words alarmed Navbe. He had been aware that Lesh was too wrapped up in the Papi, but had not thought it was this far gone. He would have to recommend treatment when he saw the Representative Master.

"Calm yourself, Ambassador. You make too much of these creatures. Certainly they are pleasing to look at, and they have their uses, but like all domestic livestock, they will transfer their allegiance in time." He put the directive in his sleeve. "Well, you will be busy the next few days, preparing to send me off." There was a quiet threat in his next words. "I don't imagine you will mention the companion to the Secretary. For the same reason I will not mention the unwillingness you have shown in the exploitation of the crafts of the Papi. They are worth a lot. Were you saving them for yourself?" Then he stood back.

The Ambassador's auxiliary hands grew livid, but he controlled himself enough to say: "I will say nothing." It was only when Navbe had walked away from him that he dared to ask: "How *did* you get to those children?"

Klin Navbe only laughed.

All his things were packed. Navbe surveyed the mound of crates in front of the door to the Terrace House and was satisfied. At last he was going back to Jan, where he would be with intelligent beings once again. He felt cleaner, better than he had since his arrival on Papill. It would be so little time now. He would be with real people.

Ambassador Lesh was not there, nor had Navbe seen him at any time the past two days. Such was the way of those of low status: when challenged, they hid. It was part of the natural cowardice of the stratum.

Behind him, Navbe sensed the companion, standing helplessly amid the desolation of the rooms. For the last day or so it had wandered disconsolately from room to room as the contents were crated and put outside the door. Now it stood, bewildered, looking at Navbe.

"Don't worry," Navbe said without turning to it. "I'll leave you a present."

"Leave me?" asked the Papi, uncomprehendingly.

"You'll need something to live on. All right. I'll arrange it with Lesh." His mouth puckered at the thought.

"No." It was a little word, barely said, as the companion sank to the floor, its huge eyes glazed as with a fever.

Navbe twisted in impatience. It was always this way with house animals. "You'll be fine," he told the companion, joviality in his manner to conceal his impatience. "You knew I was going away. Don't let it bother you so much." He nudged the huddled figure at his feet with his boot.

Four eager hands grabbed his leg through the folds of his robe. "Take me. Take me. Don't leave me here. You can't leave me here."

Disgusted, Navbe shook the foot free of the desperate fingers. "Don't be foolish," he snapped, striding back to the door.

"I belong to you," the companion said. "I was made to be part of you. You must take me with you." There was anguish in the little face now, and foreboding.

"I am tired of this," Navbe announced. "If you want to see me off, you may follow me to the landing place. If not . . ." He shrugged elegantly.

"There is nowhere I can go," murmured the companion to itself.

"Nara-Lim will take care of you. Lesh will see to it. Now, I want no more of this. You served me adequately and you'll be paid. Nara-Lim can manage the fee, if you like." He rang a bell for the servants, knowing they would be slow.

"It doesn't matter," the companion said blankly, looking away from the Undersecretary. "If you go, it doesn't matter."

*Why is it these animals take everything so personally?* Navbe asked himself as the servants came along the terrace. "Here, you," he called to them. "These are to go to the landing place. Nothing is to be dropped or broken, do you understand?"

The crates were loaded into the boxlike rolling platforms and dragged away from the Ambassador's house to the landing field.

"Come along," Navbe said to his companion. "Walk out with me, why don't you?"

Numbly the companion stood and numbly it followed Navbe across Ambassador Lesh's estate.

The squat craft waited, a mushroom ready to assault the sky. Around it Papi and Janif workers were loading and pampering the machine, readying it for the surge upward, away from the soft mists of Papill for the bright scraps of light that were stars.

Ambassador Lesh was not there.

A low status officer examined the directive Navbe held out to him and made him welcome with becoming deference, concealing his hands and moving his mouth as little as possible. This was much more to Navbe's liking.

"I will board soon," he informed the officer and was pleased to see the officer rigid. As he turned back to his companion, he felt the first tuggings of civilization on him, and found the sensation a warm delight.

"Well, companion, here is what I've promised you," he said, handing the creature a voucher and the border from one of his sleeves. The companion took the sleeve and pressed it to its face. The voucher slid away on the wind, unheeded.

"I forbid you to behave in this way," Nabve said to the companion as it looked at the ship with hopeless eyes. He found the manner attractive, even stimulating, but it was a feeling he could not afford now.

"Don't go," whispered the companion. "Or take me with you. I will die without you."

That was truly too much for Navbe. He wrinkled his face in frustration, and then, with a half-smile he said: "But I'll be back, of course. I'll want you here when I get back."

Joy transformed the delicate face. "When? When? I

cannot live long without you, but if you are coming back, I will try . . ."

It was remarkable how easily the creature was fobbed off. Navbe chided himself for not thinking of it sooner. "I will be here in the season of the Amber Rivers." That was sufficiently far in the future that the companion would have time to forget him.

"I will try to live until then," the companion said eagerly. "I will try. It is long, but you will be back." It clutched the sleeve border fiercely. "I promise I will wait for you. I will live until you come back."

"Good," said Navbe absently as he watched the last of his crates moved on board.

"Until the time of the Amber Rivers. It will be hard but I will live."

"Fine, fine." The Undersecretary put his badge of office in place and went to the boarding ramp. The young officer stood waiting for him. Without a backward look he went aboard and the door swung closed behind him.

The companion waited in the landing place where Navbe had left it, the sleeve border in its hand, thinking of the reunion that would come in the season of Amber Rivers. Somehow it would have to live that long, for the joy of its master, for the better part of itself.

When the craft rose into the air, it covered the companion with dust.

# KISS OF FIRE

## Harlan Ellison

Had **Harlan Ellison** not existed, it would have been necessary to invent him—if for no other reason than to provide
a topic of conversation when science fiction writers get
together. Small in stature, alternately grim and wildly
elated in mood, possessed of a driving enthusiasm that
consumes at least a thousand calories an hour, he has been
the subject of more anecdotes (real and apocryphal) than
any other writer in the field. He lives alone on a hill in
Sherman Oaks, California, in a movie-set house christened
"Ellison Wonderland," and writes incessantly for the magazines, the Los Angeles Weekly News, television, and on
occasion the movies. He was an associate editor of
**Rogue** magazine in the late fifties and later editor of
Regency books, in which capacity he bought Scortia's first
novel.

He is noted for his anthology and short-story-collection
introductions that approach novel length and press-agent
hyperbole. No author introduced by Harlan in print is
ever again quite convinced of his own mortality. His own

work has received repeated accolades from colleagues and
fans in the form of Nebula and Hugo awards.

He is addicted to non-stop conversations, faddish new
clothes, and the tireless promotion of new writers, many
of whom he helped develop in the famous Clarion work-
shops. He is (in the words used by August Derleth to describe H. P. Lovecraft) his own most fantastic creation.

•

He drank ice crystals laced with midnight and watched
their world burn. A greenperson floated up beside him,
and touched his sleeve. There was static electricity in the
compartment; a tiny spark. "Mister Redditch, when you
have a moment, the Designer would like to disturb air
with you."

Redditch looked down. The greenperson's eye was water-
ing. "Tell him I'll be along." The greenperson's flaccid
skin went to an ivory-gray hue, capturing the disquiet and
weariness in Redditch's voice. He floated away, adjusting
his hue exactly, so the message could be transmitted without the slightest semantic misinterpretation.

Redditch turned back to the teleidoscope, the tanger,
the sensu, the catcheye, and the straight black tunnel that
showed him their world burning. The solar prominences
had died away to self-satisfied blandness; unctuous. There
was little out there now but smoldering ash, although the
sensu was still getting a reading high into the nines and the
teleidoscope was turning it, turning it, combining colors
and sending them back in some new spectral spectrum. He
raised the drink to his lips, but he could not taste it. The
tanger overrode, even in the control compartment. It was
the smack of salt-rising bread and salamanders.

A rolling checker came out of its bay and made its way
through the coils of readout sheets littering the deck. Red-

ditch had designed and combined and set up the nova with great care, and the sheets had endlessly tongued out of the aesthetikon and he had let them lie. The checker got through the tangle and palmed open the hookup compartment and re-attached the feed to stateroom 611. But it hardly mattered: the clients in 611 had played gin rummy straight through the program. The checker returned to its bay.

Redditch downed the last of his drink, ran his tongue around the rim of the hollow crystal, and set it down on the console. He sighed and rubbed his weary, itching eyes. He was tired from the inside-out to the very tips of his fingers. And now, the Designer . . .

When he emerged from the dropshaft and walked through the theater lounge, a blustery purple-class voyager and a fat duchess with sausage fingers and noisy rings greeted him, congratulated him on the performance, offered him social congress. The man was probably a salesman of myth-sticks, and the woman was clearly a remittance relative. He smiled and thanked them and hurried on through the theater. A clique still plugged into their tunnel applauded him, and he acknowledged their appreciation with a vague gesture of his sensor hand. It sparkled with reflected light from the overhead inkys.

Whores were busily trying to drum up business, to catch a few voyagers who had absorbed the empathy of the programmed death and who were, at least for the moment, "alive."

They were having a rough time of it. One lithe creature with a charged ring through the lips of her vagina was trying with all the powers at her command to get a thin, salivating messenger to buy her favors. She was bent over him, her hand inside his chiton, massaging his privates. But his eyes were rolled up in their sockets and Redditch would have taken odds her till and her ring would go empty.

A tag-team, two black-and-ochre Sedalians, had a suety

emissary trapped deep in his formfit. One of them had pulled off his embassy pouch and sash, and had lowered herself onto his body. It seemed unlikely she would be able to get him erect enough for insertion, and her sister was tonguing one of the several underarm vaginas the man had had surgically added to his grotesque bulk. While they worked over him, Redditch passed and heard the man mumbling, "Don't be ridiculous, this is ridiculous, my sperm brings a thousand a decaliter, I'm certainly not going to give it away and *pay* you for the privilege." Redditch quite agreed. He wondered why the ship's comptrollers continued to hire on whores; they were virtually an anachronism, holdovers from centuries before. They certainly couldn't be doing enough business to warrant their continued employment.

He kept walking. Once, after a long programming, he had passed through the theater and one of the new whores, a lanky young man with pustules, had propositioned him. Redditch had laughed and there'd been some repercussions with the guild, until the Designer had straightened out the matter.

He saw her sitting alone, and when she looked up at him as he approached, the singular beauty contained in her face, particularly her slanted eyes, made him slow his pace. Her right arm was lying along the rest, and she bent it at the elbow, raising the slim-fingered hand. It was enough to stop him.

"You programmed the death?" she said, with no rising inflection. He nodded, smiling in a sudden rush of anticipation of her congratulations. She looked away.

He felt as though something had been stolen from him.

The Designer was lying out in a leaf chair that moved idly in its free-fall nimbus. Every eye in his forehead row was closed, but Redditch could tell he was perceiving his surroundings by the fibrillation of root threads that spiked his cheek-pouches. Crystals of ergonovine sparkled amid the threads. The Designer's backers were seated around the observatory suite.

"Come in," the Designer said. The leaf chair moved.

"I'm in." He slumped into a composeat and punched out tranquilizers and an antacid. He wanted to stay calm through it all. Outside the observatory cycle ports the nova phased through from yellow ochre to gold as he watched. "Something on your mind, Keltin?"

The Designer opened three yes eyes.

"Where must your mind be?" He said it with carefully chilled contempt. A greenperson hovered just beyond the nimbus, unnecessarily translating the tone in colors.

Redditch yawned. *"Madison Square Garden*, a 1932 Paramount Pictures release starring Jack Oakie, Marian Nixon, Zasu Pitts, William Boyd, and Lew Cody. 'A romantic, dramatic story of three men and two girls fighting desperately to rout the mechanism of unseen forces.' Running time, seventy-six minutes."

One of the backers threw his drink at the bulkhead. He started to shout something, but a checker emerged from its bay and caught the crystal before it hit, sucking up every drop of fluid before it could stain the grass. The backer turned away in frustration.

The Designer opened a no eye. "There are clauses in your contract, Redditch."

Redditch nodded. "But you won't use them."

He only wished Keltin *would* relieve him. Fat chance.

Another of the backers, a florid man with a thrilled and dyed topknot, hunched forward. "You can't possibly call that death viable? Sparks, man, there were actually paying guests *sleeping* through it. I saw a monitor estimate that it had thirty-two percent, that's *thirty-two* percent of the audience into the sevens with boredom! How the hell do you expect us to drain off enough empathy to syndicate this . . . this abort you call a death?"

Redditch sighed. "Stop inviting your relatives to the premieres and perhaps we'll get a few guests onboard who can still feel something."

"I don't have to take this!" the backer shouted.

"That's true," Redditch said. The tranquilizers were holding.

"That's true," said the Designer, meaning something else entirely. "Let me handle this, Mr. Nym. If you please."

"Stars!" Mr. Nym said. He turned away. Now there were two looking out the cycle ports.

"Redditch, this isn't the first inadequate job you've programmed. The *Faraway Forever* program. The *Rightful Loss* program. Others."

"Maybe I'm bored."

"We're *all* bored, dammit," said a third backer. He had his hands clasped in his lap.

"I spend considerable time designing these deaths," the Designer continued, "and I cannot permit my work to be underdone this way. These gentlemen have very legitimate complaints. Their audiences are waiting for the syndication of what we mount out here; their business is providing their audiences with top-grade empathy material. When it goes to you from my workshop, it's right. When it's actualized it lacks verve, pace, timing. There are clauses in your contract. I won't tell you again."

Redditch rose. "Don't. Refer it to my Guild." He turned and left.

Behind him, all three backers were staring out the cycle ports as the nova pushed to deep purple. His soul was quiet.

He strode through the theater lounge quickly, no glance left, no glance right. If he was going to sedate and blot, he would do it alone.

She wasn't in her seat. The formfit still held the shape of her body. Glance right.

He floated lazily in the nimbus, his spine like water, his

thoughts relaxed. He was talking to the memory box that contained his wife, dead these last sixty-three years—since his most recent anti-agathic rejuvenation.

"It's the end of summer, Annie."

"How did the children take it, Rai?"

They had had no children. It was an old memory box, the synthesizing channels were worn: the responses were frequently imprecise or non sequitur. The bead in which her voice had been cored had become microscopically crusted; Annie now spoke with a slur and sometimes-drawl.

"I look about thirty now. They even fixed the prostate. I'm taller, and they lengthened the fingers on my sensor hand. I'm much faster at the console now, wider reach. But the work isn't any better."

"Why don't you speak to the Designer about it, darling?"

"That sententious lemming. I may be undertalented, but at least I don't try to sustain a miserable existence by deluding myself I'm creating great works of art."

He turned onto his stomach, staring out the port. It was dark out there. "And while we float here talking, outside this great space-going vessel cut in the shape of a moonstone the universe whirls past at millions of light-years an hour, doo-wah-diddy mop-mop."

"Isn't that parsecs, dear?"

"How should I know? I'm a sensu programmer, not an astrophysicist."

"Is it chilly in here, Rai?"

"Oh, Annie, forget it. Say something I haven't heard. I'm dying, Annie, dying of ennui and the stupids. I don't want, I don't need, I haven't anything, don't care!"

"What do you want me to say, dear? I miss you, I'm sorry you're lonely—"

"It's not even that I'm lonely. Annie, you went through three rejuvenations with me. You were the lucky one."

"Lucky? Lucky that I died during the fourth? How do you get lucky out of that, Rai?"

"Because I've had to live sixty-three more years, and in another ten or fifteen I'm scheduled for a fifth, long-dead baby wife of mine, and I tell you three times—one two three—it's the end of summer, love. Gone. Done. All the birds has flowed south for the final flutter. I'm going to give it a pass when rejuve comes around. I'm going to settle into dust. Summer ends, goodbye, Mother of Mercy, is this the end of Rico?"

"What sensu is that from, Rai?"

"Not sensu, Annie. Movie. Movie film. All-singing, all-dancing, all-talking. I've told you a million times, by direct count. Movie. *Little Caesar*, Edward G. Robinson, Warner Brothers. Oh to hell with it, there was a woman in the lounge tonight, Annie . . ."

"That's nice, sweetheart . . . was she attractive?"

"God help me, Annie, I *wanted* her! Do you know what that means to me? To *want* a woman again? I don't know what it was about her . . . I think she hated me . . . I could *feel* it, something deep and ugly when she stopped me—"

"That's nice, sweetheart . . . was she attractive?"

"She was bloody gorgeous, you ghost of Christmas Past. She was so unbelievably unreal I wanted to crawl inside her and live there. Annie . . . Annie . . . I'm going crazy with it all, with what I do, with the novae, with programming death for indolent swine who need their cheap death thrills to make it through the day just to make it through a day . . . God, Annie, speak to me, come out of that awful square coffin and save me, Annie! I want night, my baby, I want night and sleep and an end to summer . . ."

The suite door hummed and a holograph of the one seeking entrance appeared in the tank. It was the woman from the theater lounge.

"That's nice, sweetheart . . . was she attractive?"

He swam out of the nimbus and whistled the door open. She came in and smiled at him.

"You were always like that when I was alive, Rai; you simply never talked to me; you never listened . . ."

He lurched sidewise and palmed the memory box to silence.

"Yes?" She stared at him with curiosity and he said it again, "Yes?"

"A little conversation, Mr. Redditch."

"I was just talking about you."

"To your little black box?"

"To what's left of my wife."

"I didn't mean to be flippant. It's very personal and dear to many people, I know."

"Not to me. Annie's gone. I'm still here . . . and it's getting to be the end of summer."

He motioned to the nimbus, and she walked to it with her eyes still on his face. "You're a very attractive human," she said, removing her clothes and sliding into the free-fall glow.

"Can I get you something? A crystal? Something to eat?"

"Perhaps some water."

He whistled up the dispenser. It rose from the grass-rugged deck, and revolved. "Fresh water, three sparkles of seed in it," he said. The checker in the dispenser mixed up the drink and set it out for him to remove.

He carried it to her and she took it, giving him a faint look of amusement. "I seem to entertain you."

She drank from the crystal, barely moving her lips. "You do."

"You aren't from the Near Colony."

"I'm not a Terrestrial."

"I didn't want to say that; I thought it might offend."

"We needn't circle each other, Mr. Redditch. Clearly, I sought you out, I want something from you, we can be straightline with one another."

"Apart from sex, what do you want from me?"

"My, you're taking the initiative."

"If you don't care for me, you can move out now. I'm frankly not up to badinage." He turned sharply and went back to the dispenser. "It's the end of summer," he said, softly.

She sipped at the cool water in the crystal. He turned back to her, a melt in its helical container warm against his hand, and caught her unguarded expression: there was so much amusement in her face, in every line of her languid body, he felt like an adolescent again. "Oh, Mr. Redditch!" Her chiding was as deep and meaningful as that of a mommy's suitor, feigning concern for the offspring of the ex-husband. He turned back a second time, feeling violence in him for the first time in years; furious at her for playing him like a puppet; furious at himself for being furious.

"That's all . . . get out."

"The end of summer, Mr. Redditch?" She made no move to go. "What do you mean by the end of summer?"

"I said out. I mean out."

"You're going to ignore the rejuvenation next time? You must want something on the other side very badly."

"Who the hell *are* you? What do you want from me? It's been a bad day, a bad week, a rotten year and a stinking cycle, so why don't you just put an egg in your shoe and beat it?"

"My name is Jeen."

He shook his head, totally bewildered. "What?"

"If we're going to touch, you *should* at least know my name," she said, and held out the crystal for him to take it away. But when he reached out, she laid her other hand on his wrist and drew him into the nimbus. It had been a very long time since he had wanted a woman this way, but his body betrayed him the moment her lips touched his naked chest. He lay back and closed his eyes and she made it all silk.

"Talk to me," she said.

The things he said were not love matters.

He spoke of what it was to live as something like a man for over two hundred years, and to grow weary of it because its infinite variety *did* grow stale. He spoke of what he did to send emotion and dreams of conflict to a race that ruled whole galaxies, entire nations of planets, great sectors of space. He was a programmer of death. A practitioner of one of the last occupations left to humans. And he spoke of ennui, of jaded appetites, of nights and days aboard a moonstone vessel as large as a city. Roaming through emptiness till worlds were pinpointed. And then they were surveyed with sophisticated equipment that told them the peoples who had lived there were gone, but their racial memories were still preserved in the stones and soil and silted river bottoms of the planet. Like ghosts of alien dreams, the remembrances of all times past were still there, contained forever, immolated in the soulskins of worlds, like haunted houses that had soaked up the terrible events that had transpired within and retained them as ambience. He spoke of Designers and their special talents—those peculiar alien empaths—and how they designed the demise of whole solar systems.

How the endless sleeping memories of the peoples who had lived there were gathered up as the sun went nova; how they streamed into the sensu and the tanger and the other empathy machines, to be codified and stored and then taken back to the human worlds, to the New Colony, to sustain the weary existences of those who had no fresh dreams of their own.

And he closed with words about how he hated it.

"But the worlds are empty, aren't they?" she asked, and then put her face once more to his tensing flesh.

He could not speak. Not then.

But later he said, yes, they were empty.

Always empty, she asked.

Yes, always empty.

You're a very humane race.

I don't think there's anything left of humanity to us. We

do it because it's for a greater good. And he laughed at the words, greater good. His fingers roamed over her body. He grew excited once more. It had been so long ago.

"On my world," she said, "we live much warmer than you. In times past, my race had the power of flight. We have a heritage of sky. Closed in like this makes me uneasy." He held her in the circle of his arms, his thigh between her long legs, and he drew his fingers down through her thick, deep blue hair.

"I know words and songs from four hundred years of myself and *my* race," he said, "and I wish to God I could think of something more potent to use, but 'I love you' and 'Thank you' are the only ones that come to mind . . . those, and 'The Earth moved,' but I'd better not use it, or I'll start to laugh, and I don't want to laugh."

He slid his hand down to her stomach. She had no navel. Very small breasts. Extra ribs. She was very beautiful.

"I'm happy."

"When we care, we have a way of making it last much longer. Would you?"

He nodded and her head lay at his shoulder and she felt him move. She sat up, kneeling before him in the nimbus. Her earring was hollow, and from it she took a tiny jewel that pulsed with pale light. She crushed it under his nose and leaned forward so she could inhale the pale light mist that sprang up from the dead jewel. Then she lay down again, precisely fitting in to the waiting space.

And in a moment they began again . . .

. . . as she took him with her to her world.

A warm world, all sky, with a single sun that held the same pale light as the jewel she had used to drug him. They flew, and he saw her people as they had been ten thousand years before. Lovely with wings, bright with the expectation of a thousand years of life.

Then she let him see how they died. In the night.

They fell from the sky like tracers of light, brilliant,

burning. Onto the great dust deserts already filled with the ashes of their ancestors.

Her voice was warm and soft in his mind. "My people live with the sky for a thousand years; when their time comes, they go to rest with all those who came before them.

"The deserts of dust are the resting places of my race, generation upon generation, returned to their primal dust ... waiting for the ten thousand years to pass until they are reborn."

The world of sky and dust swam in his mind and as though it were captured in the catcheye it faded back and back; he was looking down on the world of the phoenix creatures from deep space, and he knew why she had drugged him, why she had taken him into her mind's memory, why she had come to him.

The death he had programmed had been the death of her sun, her world. Her people.

They came back to the nimbus within the suite in the moonstone vessel. He could not move, but she turned him so he could stare out through the cycle port at the emptiness where her world had been. Only dust remained. And she let him hear one last trailing scream from that world, at the moment of its death; the wail of her race, a nation that would never rise from its own dust and ashes.

The ten thousand years might pass, but the phoenix people would never again soar through their skies.

"Can you hear me? Can you speak? I want you to know why."

His mouth was thick and his speech was clumsy, but he heard her and he could speak and he said he understood. She bent to him and took his face in her cool hands. "Centuries ago, my ancestors were sent away. They were ..." Her hesitation was filled with pain and loneliness. "... imperfect." She turned away for a moment and he saw high on her back two knots of atrophied muscle, and the vision of winged men and women came to him as it had in the vision she'd let him see, and he understood that, too. Then she turned back, stronger. "There were a few like them in every generation, and they gave birth to others who gave birth to us. But no more. Now we are so few, so very few. Now almost all the people are gone."

"It was a mistake," he said. She could not tell what he had said through the drug, and he repeated it. She looked at him and nodded gently; but she was stronger.

"You said there was very little left of humanity in your race. That is the truest thing you could have said. What I do is what will be done to all of you. There are a few more of my race, and when they are gone there will be others, of other races. And they will finish the job. You may not be the first, but you will certainly not be the last. Your time is past. You had your chance and turned it against every race you ever met. And now that your time is done, you think you'll take everyone with you."

He could not regret dying, as he knew he would die. She was right. The time for men had come and gone, and what they did now was useless, but more than useless . . . it was senseless.

Unlike her people, men did not have the good grace to go off alone and die. They tried, in their deranged way, to drag the universe into the grave with them. Not just the leaching out of preserved memories for the momentary amusement of the jaded and corrupt, but *everything* men did, now that they owned the universe. It was better that the human race be aided in its slovenly demise than to be allowed to leave nothing but ashes when it vanished at last.

He had killed her race, lying sleeping, waiting to be reborn in flames. So he could not hate her. Nor did she need to know that she brought him the dearest gift he had ever received. It was the end of summer and he was content knowing he would not have to wait for the chill of winter to descend on his race.

"I'm happy," he said.

She may have known what he meant. He thought she knew: her eyes were moist as she bent to him for the final time, and kissed him. It was the longest kiss he had ever known.

There were flames and heat as great as a nova and then there was nothing but ash that floated freely in the nimbus.

When they came to the suite of the sensu programmer, none of them knew they were looking at the last days of the race of men. Only Keltin, the Designer, seemed to understand, in some deep racial way, and he said nothing.

But he smiled in expectation as the moonstone ship sailed away into the eternal night.

# WILLO DAVIS ROBERTS
## and
# THOMAS N. SCORTIA

# A PERSONAGE OF ROYAL BLOOD

## Willo Davis Roberts

**Willo Davis Roberts** ventures far too rarely into the world of science fiction, spending most of her writing time in building a library of gothics second to none in that field. She is amazingly prolific, turning out an average of eight novels a year as well as doing short stories, such as the one in this collection.

She has also written mainstream novels, particularly on themes associated with the medical profession, and, as is true of all her writing, these have the tight plotting and strong characters that are her trademark.

Willo lives in Humbolt County, far in the north of California, between the redwoods and the Pacific Ocean, with her husband and family. She is a long way from the usual haunts of the West Coast writer, but has certainly proved that geography has nothing to do with talent and professionalism.

●

They hated him, the crew of the *Arvella*. He'd known it from the first, from the way they looked at him, from the way conversations ceased when he entered a compartment, from the fact that he was never invited to join any of their activities.

Not that there were any activities to intrigue anyone of intelligence. He wasn't used to crummy little explorer ships ... not enough room in this one to turn around without bumping into something. Two of the ship's officers had doubled up to provide the quarters for Erak, which no doubt accounted for their hostility. But it wasn't his fault his father had sent him on their ratty little vessel, and they certainly couldn't expect a Prince of the Realm to share quarters with a half-breed engineer, could they?

There was something wrong with the airconditioning and it was always too warm and smelled strongly of human beings. Erak had never been subjected to such strong odors before in his entire twenty-four years, and there were times when he was actually nauseated.

Thinking of the mission ahead on Llargos didn't help his sense of humor, either. It seemed straightforward enough: deliver the papers to Emperor Horad, convey the best wishes of his father, King Ipod, present the young princess with the necklace, and withdraw. But he knew his father ...

"Why me?" he had protested. "Why not send someone from the regular diplomatic service? You know I'm preparing for the Games Competition early in the year ..."

King Ipod did not allow himself to be diverted by trivialities. "Plenty of time for that when you return. This could be very important to us. It will be good practice for you, to represent me in a minor court. Don't argue, my son."

Well, he had packed, and he was here, hurtling toward Llargos and the unknown and undoubtedly hideous princess ... *Great Richos*. Erak sat up abruptly, striking his head on the bulkhead. Was that it? The princess? Had they cooked up something to do with the princess? But what could they have arranged, other than a political marriage, and his father wouldn't do that to him.

Would he?

Erak was a handsome young man, slim and graceful and attractive of face, but this twisted now into a scowl. Surely not. He was letting this impossible ship and its intolerable crew affect his brain. King Ipod wouldn't marry him off to some provincial clod simply to gain ... whatever it was he wanted.

He sank back onto the bunk, shaken and unconvinced. King Ipod was an indulgent father, a benevolent ruler ... but he would not countenance opposition in any form. Erak had reason to know this.

He tried to remember what he knew about Llargos, which wasn't much. A planet only a little smaller than his home world of Iphos, it had less than a twentieth of the population. That wasn't a crucial factor, however, because Iphos had been colonized less than two hundred years and the space and natural resources were ample for many years to come.

Was that it, though? The natural resources? For the first time it occurred to Erak that there might be some value in listening to the conversations at state dinners. Wasn't Llargos richly endowed with minerals?

Certainly there would be a way to get them, if minerals were what Ipod desired, without sacrificing his number three son to a meaningless political mating.

The explosion and the resulting lurch threw him onto the deck with such force that he lost consciousness, putting an end to his speculations.

"Hell of a note ... the first interesting thing that's happened during the entire voyage, and I have to be knocked out." Erak winced as the sealing plaster was applied to his head, wondering why they didn't devise a way to handle it at lower temperatures.

Forgast, the medical officer, surveyed his handiwork with grim satisfaction. "There. You'll heal. You consider it unlucky to have been safely tucked away when the ship's been hit by a meteor and other men are dying?"

Erak twisted to look up at the man. "Men were killed?"

"Two. There are other injuries, as well."

"Captain Radja?"

"The captain is uninjured. But we must make repairs that cannot be done in space; the captain will have his problems."

"We'll be delayed, then, in getting to Llargos." Erak felt a creeping sensation of unease. He hadn't wanted to go to Llargos, but he didn't want to end his life prematurely out here in this black void, either.

"They're selecting a place to put us down." There was a glint of malicious amusement in the medical officer's eyes, as if he'd felt that gut-twinge of alarm. "Don't worry, Prince Erak. The captain is aware of his valuable passenger; he will do everything possible to see that you are delivered safely to Llargos."

Erak didn't ordinarily mingle with the others in the common room, but now he couldn't resist. He wanted to know what was happening. He brushed past Forgast into the narrow corridor.

For once they didn't stop talking when he entered. In fact, he wasn't sure anyone was aware of his presence. He saw a few minor wounds, no worse than his own. Who was missing? There were only fifteen members of the crew; he ticked them off mentally, feeling a burst of gratification to realize that one of the fatalities must be Storn, who had been particularly insolent.

"Putting down . . . at 4000 hours. Place called Capron II." Erak slid, unnoticed, into a seat and listened. The name meant nothing to him. No doubt there would be breatheable air on the planet, which was more than could be said for the *Arvella*. Had the meteorite further damaged the purifying system? he wondered. It seemed closer, warmer, than ever.

"Capron II. Never heard of it." The speaker was Advers, the chief engineer. "But if it's charted, I'm for it. Air's getting so damned thick you can chew it."

Not his imagination, then. Panic pricked him, then eased. These men were experienced space travelers, for all their grossness, and they didn't seem unduly alarmed. It wouldn't do for him to show fear.

"Capron II. Here it is." Janis, a half-breed with a darker skin than most, fed them the information. Erak didn't pay particular attention; he wasn't interested in mass and gravity and velocity and position. The important thing was, how close were they to it? He glanced at the crystal embedded in his wrist. Not more than half an hour. He hoped to Richos the air held out that long.

"Get to the interesting part," someone prodded. "Is it colonized? Humanoids?"

"One landing party led by Klas Blavvak, a molecular biologist, a native of Urth." There was a murmur of interest, not shared by the young prince. For all that some considered Urth to be the cradle of civilization, Erak knew it for a small, crowded, dying planet. Nobody who was anybody continued to live there. "Left Urth with a party of fifty to colonize Capron II, which had previously been explored by—"

"A society founded by malcontents is rarely a stable one," Erak interjected. "In a study at the Universal Institute on Regas it was proved beyond any doubt that colonies such as this one are—"

A rude voice interrupted, so loud that Erak had no choice but to shout above it or cease to speak at all; he subsided, reddening with anger.

"Come on, get to the point! Fifty people, how long ago, for Richos sake? Do we have to hunt one leaf in the forest, or have they had time to multiply?"

"Two hundred thirty-seven years ago." Janis snorted.

"Who knows? It doesn't say how many of his colonists were women, and there hasn't been so much as a supply ship passed within voice range of them since they landed."

"Women! By Richos, that would be a bonus!"

Erak swiveled his head to find with an unpleasant shock that Storn, whom he had presumed dead, stood behind him. Not dead, but filling in on the bridge for someone else . . . It must be Thaves who had died.

The conversation degenerated into an explicit discussion of women and the uses to which they could be put. Erak stood up, surveying his companions with disgust. "The level of intelligence in any group is easily determined, according to the Pregos study," he observed in a carrying tone, "when women are mentioned. Roughly translated, they opined that swine are unable to conceal their gluttonous appetites."

There was a moment of silence, into which Storn commented with a laugh, "Any adolescents may withdraw from the company of men if the talk grows too strong for their delicate ears. Eh?"

In the chorus of raucous and ribald remarks, Erak retreated to his own quarters; he wished with intense emotion that he could have them all on Iphos for a day or two.

He wondered if there was any way to find out his father's real intent in sending him to Llargos. Had there, for instance, been additional orders given to Captain Radja?

*I am more than a pawn in my father's master-chess game,* Erak thought angrily. *He cannot strand me forever on some misbegotten provincial planet, away from my friends, my equals, my customary divertisements.*

He flung himself onto the bunk, glowering at the blank bulkheads, imagining the crudeness of the court of Emperor Horad, the revolting countenance of his long-toothed daughter. *Marry an inferior princess to gain mineral wealth for Iphos?*

It was too much to ask. His mind darted this way and that, seeking a way out of the suspected trap.

Capron II proved a welcome respite from space travel aboard the *Arvella*. It was a small planet, less than a third the size of Iphos, and bucolic in the extreme. But the air was sweet and fresh, and there were women.

Erak saw her the first evening in the town. Radja had given them the customary warning, of course, before they left the ship. Fraternization was up to the natives; if they were friendly, the crew could mingle at will. However, they were on no account to intrude where they were not invited, and most particularly they were to make no attempt to accost or seduce the females.

"Being what the females are on most of these little planets," Storn joked, "they'll be covered with either fur or scales."

"They were brought here by Blavvak," someone reminded him. "He was apparently a crusty old goat, but he was rich enough to buy and supply a ship big enough to carry fifty people through half a galaxy . . . the rich have impeccable taste in women, I understand."

Storn sought Erak's eyes. "Is that true, Your Excellency?"

Erak's mouth tightened. He returned the gaze haughtily—as imperious and as regal as his father. "The cultures of this level are generally promiscuous, which is no doubt fitting and appropriate for a crew of scurvy space vagabonds. It is to be hoped that neither crew nor natives will lower the mental or moral level of the other." It was long seconds before Storn laughed and turned away.

The city . . . how in the name of Richos could they call it a city? Erak thought, longing for his own home of pink-spired castles and crystal towers. The streets here weren't even paved, although the houses were decent enough in a peasanty fashion.

The crew moved in groups of twos and threes, searching out the drinking places (none of them had ever been anywhere throughout the galaxy that didn't boast a drinking place) and looking over the girls.

There was an abundance of females, most of them young, and such swarms of children as he had never seen elsewhere. Yet it was the girls who drew his eyes.

Erak surveyed them with mild interest. They were poorly dressed, by the standards of Iphos, but comely at that. Their garments were simple and revealing, and they wore assorted pale colors with matching ribbons in their hair.

The girl in white stood out from the others, both in purity of dress and the beauty of her face and hair. The hair was long and richly dark. Under the thin material her breasts were full and lovely, though curiously low; Erak wasn't the only one who stared. But it was her face that really held him, held him so that he forgot the others.

He had never seen such a face, not even on Iphos. His breath quickened as his eyes clung to that delicately lovely visage. The eyes were widely spaced and of an unusual coloring, a light, bright blue with an oddly shaped iris.

She walked as if unaware of the newcomers, head carried high, her stride as light and confident as that of one of his mother's proud Urth pets. It was the way a princess should walk, Erak thought, mesmerized. If he could be sure the Llargosian princess looked like this, perhaps he'd go along with what his father had in mind . . .

"By Richos, that one's a beauty!"

The coarse voice cut through Erak's near-hypnotic state. Storn . . . how had he managed to get drunk so quickly? But of course the man was a swine, drunk or sober . . . Erak felt the rush of blood in his ears as his resentment rose. A man like Storn . . . and the beautiful young girl . . . That he should dare . . .

Storn reached the girl in long strides, putting out a

rough hand to her shoulder, swinging her around. "Ah, there, what's your name, girl?"

She stared up at him, the unusual eyes widening, the soft blunt hands folding in on themselves, and the curious, almost melodic thrumming she had been making—Erak realized for the first time—stopped.

"You speak a civilized tongue, don't you?" He turned to show his companions his progress with the girl, his body swinging suggestively. "On the other hand, what difference does it make? A man and a woman don't need words"— here he leered openly—"to communicate, do they?"

Erak caught a glimpse of her face with its beginnings of alarm before Storn's head came between them ... Storn's mouth fastening on those innocent lips ...

Almost before the girl could struggle Storn found himself jerked around; he released his captive and the girl fell back.

"By Richos, I thought I'd have to kill a man for touching me ... but it's only His Highness, the little prince! I'll forgive you this time, boy, but once you've reached your full growth you'd better think twice before you put a hand on Adros Storn!"

Erak's mouth was dry. "Leave the girl alone."

The *Arvella* crew drifted toward them. Storn gave a shout of laughter; he always played well to an audience.

"The little peacock makes threats! Don't tempt me, Your Highness, into letting your blood! I've a lifelong curiosity about the color of royal blood!"

Erak had no weapon, nor did any member of the crew. Weapons were forbidden on civilized planets. But there was something leaning against a wall of one of the primitive cottages. Its use was uncertain, perhaps an agricultural tool of some sort, but it came readily to hand and Erak found with a fierce satisfaction that it was nearly the weight of the sword so regrettably at home on Iphos.

Storn's mouth went flat, the amusement draining from his face.

"You want to fight?" The question was incredulous. "A boy? A child? I'm to fight a child?"

He looked around at his comrades, and Erak had time to do the same. There was no sympathy for Erak anywhere; he knew they'd like nothing better than to see their fellow crewman stomp him into this alien soil.

Not that Storn would kill him, of course, but it was clear that the man had no qualms about drawing blood, whatever color it might turn out to be.

"He's going to hit me with his stick!" Storn taunted. He'd forgotten the girl. She watched wide-eyed; Erak caught the briefest glimpse of her face and then concentrated on his enemy.

The "stick" shot out and dealt Storn a quick blow alongside the head, and Storn was moving toward him with deadly intent, the large hands ready to tear him to pieces.

The stick went out again, this time in a vicious jab to the shoulder. Storn was powerful, but he wasn't particularly quick, either mentally or physically, Erak decided. He wasn't adept enough either to avoid the blow or to grab the improvised weapon; on the other hand, while the blow hurt, it didn't slow the man down.

With a snarled obscenity, Storn flung himself forward, only to find that Erak was no longer where he had been seconds earlier.

"Here! Fight him on his own terms!" someone shouted, and another of the implements was thrust toward Erak's opponent.

From that point on, Erak had only to follow his instincts, to allow his reflexes to take over. He was a champion in the ancient sport of fencing, which had been revived until it had become a leading sport among the young men of Iphos.

In a match of physical strength Storn would have murdered him, but he hadn't a chance with these improvised weapons. Erak was fast on his feet, he moved without having to think or plan ... and while the "sticks" were a far cry from the sword he was accustomed to, it did have some sort of metal tip (it was so primitive it could scarcely be called a blade) that made it reasonably formidable.

Erak proceeded, methodically and cold-bloodedly, to cut the other man down. He knew the crew were shouting encouragement to Storn, but he closed his ears, concentrating entirely on putting an end to this man. A slash here, a thrust there ... so far he himself had endured only a few moderately painful blows, but it was easy to see the color of Storn's blood. It oozed from a gash on one cheek and from the laceration on his shoulder.

Rage rumbled out of Storn's massive chest; he was outmatched with these simple weapons, and he knew it.

"Get rid of the bloody stick, and kill him!" someone shouted.

Storn had come to the same conclusion on his own; the stick was cast aside and the man lunged forward in a rush of fury so great that caution was forgotten. He knew if he could once get his hands on the impudent young bastard he could tear him to shreds ...

Erak made one final thrust, putting all his muscle and weight into it, into the most vulnerable part of Storn's anatomy; he had a second to think that his fencing master would have chastised him most severely for such a move, and he saw Storn's eyes widen as he realized what was coming, then darken and glaze with agony as the blow connected.

Storn went down in silence, the pain too great to allow him to draw the breath necessary for speech or moan, folding forward into the dust.

The men fell silent and fell back as Erak moved toward the girl. He didn't look back at Storn, he didn't care if the misbegotten wretch were dying ...

"Come. I'll take you home," he said to the girl. For a moment she only stared, her sweet face pale, her breasts rising and falling rapidly and intriguingly under the thin white material.

She swallowed and seemed to recover control of her limbs. She let him take her arm and guide her around the silent onlookers and on down the pathway that served as a street.

He felt a tremor in the arm he held, but he didn't want to pause until they were out of sight of the men from the *Arvella.*

"Are you all right? He didn't hurt you?" They halted in the shadow of the unfamiliar trees. He didn't take his hand from her arm; he liked the feel of the soft, warm flesh, the fragile bones, the leaping pulses.

"I am unhurt." The eyes *were* wide and beautiful and of an uncanny blue, almost too large for her face. The delicate nose and pointed jaw gave her face an upturned look that was even more enchanting now that he saw it up close. Her voice was the most entrancing he had ever heard and now that they were alone he heard again the sound she had made before. "I have never seen men fight this way . . . to kill . . . It was to kill?" She looked at him.

"I wanted to kill him but I didn't. He won't be able to walk for a few days, but after that he'll be all right." Erak didn't want to talk about Storn. He didn't want to let her go, either. They were jostled by a band of laughing youngsters who came running through the trees, chasing each other and themselves. It gave him an excuse to touch her again, to steady her. "So many children . . ." And then, fearing she might take that as a criticism, "I've never seen such beautiful children."

"Yes. Our children are our future; our laws require that we produce many of them. It is most essential." She shook off her intense look. "Please, who are you?"

"I am Erak, Prince of Iphos. And you are . . . ?"

"Tahni." The name was velvet on her lips, where a smile had begun to form. It gave a secretive light to her blue, blue eyes and made the thrumming noise all the more fascinating. "Please, come to my home. We will have a cup of *svelge* and you will feel better, I think."

The smile grew, and Erak's matched it.

"What's *svelge*?"

"Very good to drink. You will come?"

"I will come," Erak agreed.

Captain Radja was so angry that it was possible to see the muscles pulsing in his jaw as Erak faced him with insolent disinterest.

"Please get on with it, Captain. I have other matters to attend to." He examined the toe of his boot for scratches.

A dull red suffused the man's face. "You have crippled a member of my crew, Your Highness. The man will be unable to fulfill his duties for days."

"He was molesting a young girl. Intergalactic law clearly states—"

"The others report that he merely spoke to her."

"He did more than that," snapped Erak.

The Captain took a deep breath, prepared to deal with Erak once and for all.

"He was insulting her," Erak said.

"That's not what the others say," the Captain spat.

"Then they are lying."

Erak waited for the next blast, and was not disappointed.

"Drawing a weapon on your own kind on a planet like this one is very dangerous, Your Highness," he managed to make the title an insult. "The natives don't always understand—"

"This one did."

The Captain went on doggedly. "And there are other methods of stopping a drunken man than by injuring him so that he can't function as a ship's officer."

"I didn't have a stunner available. Are you finished, Captain?"

Erak was well aware that had he been a member of the

crew of this miserable ship he would have been subject to arrest. He was equally aware that the captain, for any crime short of murder, would not dare to punish him in any physical way.

Radja's mouth was flat and hard. "We will be underway in one hour. I will expect you to confine yourself to your quarters during the remainder of the journey."

"As you like. A young lady will be sharing those quarters . . . the Princess Tahni has consented to be my wife."

The red in Radja's face deepened until Erak wondered if the man might suffer a stroke. "You will take no one, Your Highness. No one."

The captain wasn't the only one who could put steel into his voice. "I shall be accompanied by the Princess Tahni, Captain, or I will not go."

For a moment it seemed that Radja experienced indecision; then he turned abruptly and reached into a compartment for a packet. Erak recognized it at once; it bore the Royal Seal of Iphos. So. There *were* additional orders from his father.

"These were to be presented to you after we had reached Llargos. Under the circumstances, I believe I am justified in presenting them to you now." Radja thrust them at him with a violence only barely controlled.

And there it was. In black and white, his father's impossible order: a marriage of convenience with the Princess of Llargos, the object the unlimited mineral wealth of a fifth-rate planet.

While here on Capron II was Tahni, the daughter of their ruler. She didn't call herself a princess, but the daughter of a chief; however, she was a royal personage if Erak had ever seen one. And he meant to have her as his wife.

He tossed the papers toward the captain and watched them slither about on the floor of the compartment.

"Well, you'll just have to inform my father that I had other plans, I'm afraid. If Tahni doesn't go, I don't go."

Radja's teeth closed with an audible crunch. "You will go, Your Highness, if you have to be taken in irons. Believe it or not, we still have such a medieval device aboard."

For a matter of seconds the two men stared at one another; then Erak strode off.

It was a simple matter to assure that the *Arvella* would explode within minutes of take-off. For the first time Erak was glad his father had insisted on sending him to the Academy with the other young nobles; he had learned something of practical value, after all.

It gave him a grim sense of satisfaction to know that they would all die . . . Storn, the captain, the others who hated him. They deserved to die like the swine they were . . .

There was the problem of how to make himself unavailable until the ship had departed. Using his head, Erak called upon a native of the planet to help him. Tahni was only too happy to oblige.

"No one will find you in the Place of the Old Ones," she assured him. "Come, and I will tell you more of our ways."

It was a long walk, up into the hills; they were tired when they arrived at the cavern. From the heights they could look down on the city and see the hulk of the *Arvella*. It worried him, a little, because it ought to have left an hour ago, but of course the captain would have instituted a search; he would, after all, have to face King Ipod when he returned from his mission.

Except, Erak thought with wry humor, that he would never return to Iphos. And King Ipod, damn his eyes, would think his son had vanished with the ship. They would never look for him here, on this isolated and little-known planet. Erak would one day be king here, in his own right, and when he was he'd show them a few things . . .

"How long must we stay here?" Tahni asked.

"Until the ship has gone. They won't waste much more time, I think. They're already behind schedule, and my father will be angry about that." Erak's mouth twisted in amusement.

"Is your father a very stern person?" Tahni inquired.

"Stern. Yes, that would describe him. Yours is, too." But the old chieftain would not live much longer, Erak thought. It was easy to see that he was ill. And when he was gone, Tahni would be the ruler ... He had no doubts of his ability to control Tahni, to rule Capron II. So what if they were a provincial planet? They would learn to build pink castles with crystal spires, such as he was accustomed to, and he would teach them a thing or two about taxes. Incredibly, they didn't even know the word, let alone its meaning.

Tahni stood looking down over the valley. "Yes. My father will expect great things of us. Heirs ... grandsons. These things are important to him."

"Sons are important to any man ... sons and grandsons."

"Father Klas Blavvak taught us this, as he taught us everything. We must multiply, we must populate our world," Tahni said earnestly. "So it became a law, that we multiply."

"A law?" A frown creased his forehead as he sought to make out if there was any activity around the *Arvella*, but it was too far away. "The law says you must have children?"

"Oh, yes. Those who do not reproduce are put to death."

Startled, he turned toward his intended bride. "To death? Great Richos, that seems a bit strong!"

"But it is necessary, you see. To insure the population of our planet, so that one day it will be as great as Father Blavvak's home planet, Urth. Our society shall not support those who do not do their share."

He laughed a little uneasily. "It's a good thing you're a princess, Tahni. And I a prince."

"That will not matter, my Erak. The law applies to everyone."

His frown returned more deeply. "The laws apply the same to king as to peasant?"

"But of course. We all come from the same stock, you understand."

His eyes strayed to the entrance of the cave behind them. "Oh, yes. Blavvak and the others. This is their burying place? Where all your ancestors lie?"

"All the Old Ones. Look, Erak! The ship is lifting!" Tahni extended a finger, pointing, and he saw with relief that it was true. The *Arvella* was leaving without him, and they'd never find him . . . or by the time they did, he'd be King Erak.

The explosion was so brilliant that they felt their eyes seared by its heat, although they could not actually feel it. Tahni turned to him stunned.

"They are all gone! They have been killed, all of them! What a waste of men!"

"We can go back, now," Erak told her, reaching for one of the pliable hands. But Tahni pulled him toward the cave. "Now that we are here, you must come to Father Blavvak, our Beginner. He gave us our rules, our laws, and we obey them forever."

Erak stared down at her. She was, indeed, beautiful, but he was beginning to find her to be childishly simple. He was used to ladies of the court, who knew how to please a man and avoid annoying him. Still, she *was* a princess, of sorts; by the time civlization again touched upon Capron II, he would have formed her into the real thing, and no one need ever know that he'd married beneath himself. There was, too, the possibility of other women . . . there seemed to be plenty of unattached females.

A princess, to make him king, and he would teach the others the pleasures of diversions, all those lovely maidens.

Erak smiled, giving in for the moment to his bride-to-be, allowing himself to be led into the cave.

There was a fire burning in a niche in the stone wall; Tahni selected a taper and lit it from the flame, then led him into the vault itself.

"The Old Ones," she said in a reverent whisper. "All of them, and in the center is the tomb of Father Blavvak, who gave life to our entire nation."

He wasn't really interested in their ancestors; it was their future that promised, not their past. Still, if they worshipped these Old Ones, he might be able to put the information to some good use.

His fingers obediently traced the date cut into the stone of the crypt. "He lived to be an old man."

"Yes. A very lonely old man, he was, but happy that he lived long enough to succeed in his life's work."

Erak moved on around the circle of tombs, absently noting the dates until it began to dawn on him that, with the exception of Blavvak's, they were all identical. As this fomented in his mind, not yet culminating in a clear thought, he asked, "And what was that, his life's work?"

"Why, my people, of course. So that he should not be alone, he must create a people to cover this world."

He felt a strong sense of chill. Perhaps it was only the dampness of the cave, but his eye fell yet again on a date ... the same as the others, eighty years preceding the date of the death of Blavvak.

"Tahni ... what is this? Why did all the Old Ones die at the same time?"

"Why, they were killed in the crash, of course. When their ship landed it was out of control ... everyone was killed, except for Father Blavvak."

"Everyone?" He swung dark eyes toward her, alarm glimmering although he didn't know why. "But how could that be? You're here, your people fill the valleys ... someone besides Father Blavvak must have lived."

Tahni shook her head. "No. All died, everyone. And

this is why he had to create us, or go mad ... the only man on an entire planet. He was a very clever man, you know, almost a god ... some say he *was* a god."

They had moved to the entrance to the cave, and Tahni put out her torch.

"Our blood will be strengthened by the addition of one of Father Blavvak's own kind." She looked with great earnestness up into his face. "I hope that it will be possible for our blood to mingle, my Erak. It would be very painful to me, to see you put to death."

The pale yellow sun overhead ought to have warmed him, but he was cold. Cold. "What are you saying? Why should our blood not mingle? Do not joke, my princess."

"Joke?" Her face was blank, as if she didn't comprehend his meaning. "He never knew about that, poor Father Blavvak ... whether or not our races could intermingle. It was not possible for him, but he hoped ..."

His jaws closed with a violence that was painful, as were his fingers gripping her shoulders. "What are you saying? Explain to me, what is this gibberish you spout? Your ancestors, all of them in there"—he flung out a wild hand toward the cave—"they were human beings, they came from the planet Urth, the same as my own ancestors ..."

"But no, my Erak. The Old Ones, I told you, they all died in the crash. All but Father Blavvak."

Panic screamed through his veins and he shook her until her head wobbled.

"But that's impossible! You're a princess, you're a human being ... !"

"Ah, no! You hurt me, let me go ... !"

"Tell me!" His heart was a pounding piston, out of control. "Tell me what you mean! Blavvak, he couldn't have made you out of *nothing* ..."

"No, of course not. Let me go, your hands are painful." Only when he had released her did she speak. "He used the only thing he had, the pets he had brought ... he was a . . ." —she formed the words carefully, as if they were seldom spoken—" . . . a molecular biologist, and he was very nearly God, to create a new race."

Erak stared at her through a red haze. His voice was hoarse.

"Out of . . . what? How did he . . . create you?"

"From his cats, of course. You did not know? We are cats, and you are a human being. And now shall we go down into the village and prepare for the ceremony? My father will be very happy, and very soon we will know. All we need do, my Erak, is produce a fine litter and my father will die happy, knowing we will carry on."

A litter. *Of kittens* . . .

He said the words aloud, dully, as the blood drained from his face. "A litter. . ."

"The usual number is four to six. Any more than that is truly a royal production. Of course, Father Blavvak didn't know what might happen, in cross-breeding our race and his own. He would be so happy, if he were here to learn, now."

Down in the valley below the city lay in the summer sunshine. There was no sign of the *Arvella* or its crew. Nothing to show they had ever been there.

"Come, my Erak," Tahni said, and numbly he accepted her hand as they began the descent into the town.

# THOU GOOD AND FAITHFUL

## Thomas N. Scortia

Saying that **Thomas N. Scortia** is prolific and energetic is like saying that the Kremlin is a neat little fort: basically true, but missing the point by several orders of magnitude. Always knee-deep in writing projects, this former biochemist maintains a literary output unusually high even in this field of rapid production.

But he does not stop with science fiction. He is equally at home in mystery writing ("Goddess of the Cats" in Doubleday's **Men and Malice**), in article writing ("Our Unemployed—and Disillusioned—Top-Secret Scientists," **Gallery**, February 1973), in editing (**Strange Bedfellows** from Random House, and this volume), and in technical writing (**Selection and Characterization of Solid Propellants for Space Vehicles**, NASA, 1972).

He is presently at work with Frank M. Robinson, erstwhile **Playboy** associate editor, on a big non-SF novel for Doubleday which has been purchased by Twentieth-Century Fox for Irwin Allen of **Poseidon Adventure** fame.

Tom Scortia is also a superb cook, an enthusiastic host, a tireless promoter of young writers, and an art collector with Picasso and Chagall prints lining his walls. When you combine all that with his imposing six feet two inches and the smile of a well-fed vampire, the whole effect is as amazing as his farthest-out story.

•

On the second night of planetfall on Berrigan's World, Lieutenant Royce met Meer on the Street of Reeds. In the half light of the ochre moon, her face was delicate and only slightly alien. The fine down that covered her face and hands shone like a faint aura. She smiled when she saw him and hurried to meet him.

"It is good to see you," she said. The greeting was ritual but he sensed something more than that in the tone.

"It is good to see you," he replied and then explained, "I was restless; so I decided to take a walk."

"Past your guards and your screens and all that into the night of an alien planet. Is that not dangerous?" she teased.

"I suppose it's against regulations," he admitted, "but the party commander does have certain prerogatives."

"Come walk me to the square," she said, touching his arm. He felt a flush of pleasure at her touch. Watch yourself, he told himself. It's only a pretty girl and you've been on space duty a long time. Still it's a pleasant night and . . .

"I'd be delighted," he said, extending his arm.

They walked to the edge of the square which was almost a thousand meters across. Actually it was an ellipse dominated in its cobblestoned center by a featureless monolithic structure that towered into the yellow-streaked night sky. It seemed strangely brooding and manacing.

"It is my turn to watch in the Archives over the sacred Vessels tonight," she said. "I'm late and my sister will be impatient."

"What are these Vessels?" he asked. "I would like to see them."

She shook her head. "You know it isn't possible. My father explained that. Of all the things you might ask, this one only we cannot allow. Berrigan in the ancient times made the rule and only the daughters of the Senior and those who are joining their lives may ever see the Vessels."

"But what are they?" he asked.

"Really nothing," she said. "A few plastic cases of records, ancient histories, several pieces of apparatus we do not understand, nothing really."

"I've seen odder things form the basis of a religion," he admitted.

She laughed in the half-darkness. "No, it is not a religion with us. Still, Berrigan made the rules long ago and we keep the rules."

She turned and he watched her delicate form move across the great square, treading a flattened parabolic path that was traced by deeper colored stones into the pavement. The reason for the path eluded him but he supposed that Berrigan, that ancient recluse who had settled this world, had some odd symbolic reason for structuring the square in this manner.

He waited until he could barely make out her form against the darker shadows of the building they called the Archives. Peculiar. Why not temple or some similar word? No, she had said that there was nothing of a religious nature about the building. There wouldn't be, of course; all the old records showed that Berrigan had been a militant atheist.

He returned to the shuttle encampment by the way of the Street of Willows, thinking that it was a shame they would be on this lovely world for such a short time. The *Deneb* was his first starship post as executive officer and this was the first extended planetfall of their extended duty. He was grateful for the respite. It was the only time in a year he had allowed himself to relax from the heavy demands of his new assignment. The *Deneb* orbited invisibly high overhead under the command of Captain Grek and Royce supposed he should shuttle back within the next two days to report their progress. At the moment he was too concerned, however, with seeing the first fermenting batches of keelgrass run successfully through the extraction process.

Besides there was Windom. Mr. Windom, he corrected himself with faint irony. It was the custom of the military to refer to civilians, even civil servants of Windom's rank, simply by their last names, reserving the "mister" for someone of military rank. Not so with Windom, who insisted from the start on being addressed as Mr. Windom. It was bothersome, Royce thought, but you didn't lock horns with a man of Mr. Windom's rank on trivial matters of etiquette.

He reached the edge of the encampment which sprawled on the north border of the city, its temporary metalar building ordered in ranks like the points of a star around the *Deneb*'s shuttle. The sentry challenged him and then saluted when he returned the challenge. His ring chronometer told him that it was already into the second watch, much later than he had thought. He was surprised as he approached his quarters to find Mr. Windom standing by the officer's mess, staring silently into a burning rjiehlstick. He did not identify the man immediately, but the faint coal glowing in the darkness told him who it was. No one on the crew indulged in this particular mild vice, indeed few of the officers or men could afford it.

"Mr. Royce," the man began without preliminary, "I've been waiting for your return. There's something we must discuss." Windom's voice was cold and mechanical in the dark, its accents just faintly slurred from the influence of the rjiehl.

"Tonight, Mr. Windom? I'm rather tired."

"Tonight, Mr. Royce," the man insisted.

"Come on in," Royce said, gesturing toward his quarters.

They entered the outer wardroom and he keyed the light with a modulated whistle and then toned it to a soft blue that rested the eyes. Windom entered behind him and noting Royce's pointed gaze at the rjiehlstick, discarded it in the corner dispenser. The stimulus of the smoke was the last thing Royce wanted in his system before bedtime.

"Mr. Royce," Windom said, "I'll come right to the point. We are already thirty hours behind in the assembly of the towers and we may expect the first of the keelgrass to be out of the fermenters by second watch tomorrow afternoon."

"We've gone ahead as fast as we can," Royce said.

"The designs I brought you when I came aboard were detailed and highly simplified. Your engineers should have been able to assemble the towers and run their first tests by this afternoon."

"I'm sure Mr. Gerhardt has done his best . . ."

"Which is certainly not good enough," Windom interrupted coldly.

Royces's first impulse was to snap at the man but he contained his temper with difficulty. "The difference between a computer model study of an assembly and the reality on foreign terrain is something we should all appreciate," he said. He found his dislike of the man with his supercilious manner coloring his speech. It was an unfortunate reaction, he told himself. Like many humans, Windom came from a planet where genetic manipulation had made changes in the basic stock. The changes about the nostrils with the heavy filter membranes flaring the nares, coupled with a pronounced mongoloid fold, gave Windom a look that on Royce's world was associated with an expression of disdain. The cast to Windom's features was subtle and Royce knew that he was operating under an unreasonable prejudice. Still he could not but think the man was sneering at him as he spoke.

"Mr. Royce," Windom said in a more conciliatory voice, "I understand the problems of command. This is why I was assigned to this project from Prime. Nevertheless, every day we delay means the death of thousands of highly civilized beings and the slow collapse of a hard-built society on Aldebaran II. The biological we were sent to procure can halt the plague and little else that we know can help."

"You'll have your five thousand kilos in the ninety days," Royce promised.

"The ninety days was the estimate Prime gave us. We must better that if we can," Windom said.

"Yes," Royce said, "it would look better on our efficiency reports." He emphasized the "our" and then wished he hadn't. Windom's gaze was cold.

"It's not a question of our efficiency reports," Windom said. "I grant you this is important to us personally, but even more important is that every day shaved from the estimate represents several thousand lives."

"Of course," Royce said. "I'll meet with Mr. Gerhardt first thing tomorrow."

"Good," Windom said rising. At the door, he paused and looked back. "Mr. Royce," he said somewhat hesitantly.

"Yes, Mr. Windom."

"It isn't too wise to become too close to the natives."

"I quite agree, Mr. Windom," Royce said angrily. "Now, if you don't mind . . ."

"Good night," Windom said and the hatch irised behind his lean back.

For a long time Royce sat, staring at the discarded rjiehlstick. His anger was unreasonable, of course. Windom had conducted himself in every way in the most correct of fashions. There *was* a severe pressure on them to complete the mission. The DEA, the complex nucleic acid—dipinacolamine adinolic acid—could not be synthesized in Prime laboratories and only an extensive search of the old archives had shown that the keelgrass on Berrigan's World produced the material in small quantities. The medicocomputer models had predicted that this was the specific for the Aldebaran II plague, and fortunately the one report filed by Berrigan before he broke off all communication with Prime included a sample of the grass.

He must have been a remarkably odd man, Berrigan, Royce thought. One of the leading molecular biologists of his age—indeed the man who had been primarily responsible for inventing the genetic manipulation techniques that opened so many inhospitable worlds to human beings. Yet he had been a recluse and a profound misanthrope. (There was reason enough for that, Royce thought, considering the history of old Earth during that period.) He had assembled a group of colonists, set out for a perimeter of the galaxy and, except for the one robot probe that returned basic information on the world, he had simply disappeared from human society. And during that period human society was too much occupied with its own troubles to worry about him. Until now when only Berrigan's World could yield the specific biological for the Aldebaran II plague.

Royce turned to the day's reports on his desk. He had to admit that Windom was right. That was the trouble with the man; he seemed always to be right. They were behind schedule and the reason for that was largely poor planning by Gerhardt's men. He would have to push him harder and, of course, they would have to push the natives harder for the keelgrass. God knows, they got little enough of the DEA out of the stuff. Scarcely ten micrograms from a kilo of the stuff and that meant a great deal to process before they reached their target. He closed the folder and decided to call it a night. Time enough tomorrow to talk with Gerhardt. He was not disturbed as he drifted off to sleep to find that his thoughts were pleasantly and somewhat erotically occupied with Meer.

The next morning Royce found the *Deneb*'s chief engineer, Mr. Gerhardt, climbing over the huge distribution towers, a radiation counter in his hands as he sampled effluents from various plates and tested them. Finally he dropped to the ground, a look of triumph on his face, and approached Royce. "Dammit," he announced in a rumbling gleeful voice, "I knew we could improve on the design."

"What do you mean?" Royce demanded.

"We changed the angles and the distribution of the plates from the original design."

"You should have consulted with me," Royce said hotly.

"Come on, Mr. Royce, you wouldn't have allowed it. You're too much at odds with Windom. Anyway it worked; I've just run a complete tracer analysis on the columns and the separation has been increased by some thirty percent in efficiency."

Royce's anger evaporated in an instant. He chuckled and said, "Come with me. I want to see Windom's face when he hears this."

They walked across the processing area to where Windom was speaking with Couton, Meer's father and Senior of the loose Berrigan's World government.

"Couton has promised a fifty percent increase in keelgrass delivery by four days from now," Windom said.

"Really," Royce said feeling smug. "How will he do that?"

"Some of their less desirable agrarian areas will be converted to growing the grass. It's a weed, you know, and matures in about a week."

"Good, we can certainly handle it." Then he told Windom of what Gerhardt had done.

"That was rash, of course," Windom said slowly.

"We are faced with a *fait accompli*," Royce said innocently. Windom looked at him closely and then at Gerhardt whose face bore an expression of quiet triumph.

"I don't think you understand me, Mr. Royce," Windom said. "I said it was rash but obviously Mr. Gerhardt had his reasons for the gamble. I never challenge the results of a man who shows he knows how to do a job."

Royce's face fell. He had been expecting some sort of diatribe about exceeding authority and jumping channels. Instead . . .

"Well done, Mr. Gerhardt," Mr. Windom said. "We can now use your extra capacity."

"Thank you, Mr. Windom," Gerhardt said. Royce was annoyed at the obvious signs of Gerhardt's pleasure. He realized that in some fashion Windom had snatched a clear moral victory out of defeat.

"I will go about the arrangements for greater deliveries," Couton said. "You may require a better transportation system than your animal carts," Windom said.

"We have anticipated that. I have alloted a crew of five thousand to build a gravity monorail from the fields that are a hundred kilometers or more distant." He secured a map that Windom was holding and pointed out the extent of the operation.

"But that's your most productive farm land," Royce objected.

"Is this not more important?" Couton asked. "Besides we can make do."

Royce nodded doubtfully and the old man left. "That will probably disrupt the local economy," Royce said slowly.

"That's true," Windom said.

"Do we want to do that?"

"We are in the process of saving lives. If the Berrigan people are inconvenienced, Mr. Royce, let me remind you how much more inconvenient it is being dead."

He whirled on his heel and walked away.

That afternoon Captain Grek videoed from the bridge of the *Deneb*, his bluish face severe and unsmiling. The only sign that betrayed his concern was his tendency to flick the nictitating membranes rapidly across his eyes.

"Mr. Royce," he said, "there is something quite odd

happening in the northern part of the major continent a thousand kilometers north of you."

"What's that, Captain?" Royce asked.

"As you know, that area is covered with heavy virgin forests. It appears that a very large work force has descended on this area and in a matter of a day has already deforested almost a quarter of the area. They appear to be about to make a complete job of it."

"I would imagine they are gathering materials for the monorail they promised," Royce said.

"The point is, Mr. Royce," Grek said slowly, "these forests are essential to the control of ground water during the rainy season. The removal of them will result in disastrous floods later this year and probably a large loss of life."

Royce considered this and said, "I'll look into it, Captain."

The monorail was needed, of course, to fulfill their mission and the Berrigan natives for some reason were content to menace their own ecology to help fulfill the *Deneb*'s mission. Should he interfere? After all, after the mission was complete they could send other missions to help reforest the area. Still . . .

Still, he thought, it presents a difficult moral problem. He thought of taking it up with Windom but he was quite sure already what that man's reaction would be. Still, the whole problem bothered him. He promised himself he would speak with Meer at the first opportunity about it.

By the next day the first of the fermented keelgrass was well into the processing cycle. "It's quite apparent," Windom said, "that our capacity is quite a bit greater than what we had hoped."

"We have a great deal of the weed maturing in the north and central provinces," Couton said. "It's normal cycle is six to seven days which means that we can increase our deliveries severalfold later this week."

"I thought you'd practically eliminated the keelgrass except for the central plains," Royce asked.

"That is true," Couton shrugged, "but we have diverted more land to its cultivation. The yield of the material you need is so low that we must grow a great deal of the grass to meet your needs."

True to his promise the deliveries of the grass to the fermenting racks increased by more than twice in the next four days. Gerhardt one evening triumphantly entered Royce's quarters, where he was in conference with Windom, with a small vial. "Well, there's the beastie," he announced, holding out the vial.

Nestled inside were several small opalescent crystals. "The product of three days' extraction," Gerhardt said.

"And we need five thousand kilos," Royce said. "We'll never get it at this rate."

"Not at all," Windom said, before Gerhardt could speak. "The solutions of the extractors had to reach saturation first. From this point on we should expect nearly a hundred kilos a day."

"That's right," Gerhardt said, eyeing Windom oddly. "How did you know that?"

Windom smiled distantly. "I have always made it my business to know as much about the details of an operation as possible."

"That's very good," Royce said, feeling vaguely put down.

He was still a little disturbed at this new evidence of Windom's competence when he went for his walk that evening. Like many military men, he had been brought up to believe that bureaucrats were largely generators of red-tape and road blocks, people who interposed masses of paper between the doers and the task. It must have occurred to him at one time or another that the complex workings of Galactic Prime could not be carried out by incompetents, but this was his first exposure to a high-ranking civil service rating. The man, he finally decided, was working overtime to impress him.

His path inevitably took him down the Street of Reeds and he realized that he had timed his arrival to that hour when he knew Meer would be relieved by her sister at the Archives. Consciously he had not intended this, but he realized that a deeper motivation was working. The girl had been on his mind for some time with her fey beauty and her special winning grace. He had never found a woman before who seemed somehow to mesh so completely with his own inner image of maleness. He supposed that it was a matter of being personally flattered, coupled with a basic animal lust.

Only he wondered if it were not more than that. He would have to be careful, he warned himself. It would be so easy under the watchful eye of Windom to compromise his career at this time.

He was standing against the adobe wall of a two-story building when he saw her wending her way across the square, following the devious elliptical pattern. She came abreast of him and started.

"Oh, I didn't expect you," she said.

"Didn't you?" he asked.

"Well, that's not true," she said. "I hoped you would be here. I've expected you the past three nights."

"Can I walk with you?" he asked.

"Of course," she said. "Come to my home. My father would be pleased to share keelwine with you."

They took up a pace side by side. Royce felt awkward, almost as if he were a teenager on his first date. He had never felt so with women before, but the women he had known were knowledgeable and adept at the little civilized games the sexes play on the humanoid planets. Meer was completely innocent. Yes, he thought, that was exactly the word. Innocent.

After several blocks, she turned down a side street and

stopped at an unimposing single-story sprawling structure. "This is my home," she said. "Won't you come in?"

Couton met them in the single common room. Royce noted sleeping pallets laid in the far corner and several low tables designed obviously for squatting rather than sitting.

"You honor my house," Couton said.

Royce made polite noises. They spoke of the day's happenings for some moments while Meer busied herself in the corner. She returned with a tray of earthenware mugs and a large earthenware bottle.

"We have little to offer in hospitality," she said. "The supplies of food and wine are growing increasingly scarce."

"I didn't know that," Royce said.

"It's of no matter," Couton said. He poured the wine into two mugs and they squatted and drank. Meer squatted beside Royce and after his first sip, she took the mug and sipped herself. He wondered at the gesture until it was repeated each time he drank. Couton looked on with approval.

"I must leave," Royce said at last.

"You would not care to spend the night?" Couton asked.

"I'm afraid I would cramp you," Royce said, noting that there were only two pallets.

"You would be with Meer, of course," Couton said matter-of-factly.

Royce fidgeted uncomfortably. Was this a part of the local custom? Would he commit some grievous offense by refusing? He eyed Meer, who looked at him with great brown eyes that were moist and very willing. For a moment he felt a tense excitement well up in him and he thought, who would know? Then common sense asserted itself and he knew he would have to take the chance of offending.

"I'm sorry," he said, rising. "It's not possible this evening."

Couton's face fell while Meer turned hers aside. "Did something displease you? Is there any way that I can make amends?" the father asked.

"No, no," Royce assured him. "Your daughter is a delight and certainly the most desirable woman I have ever met. It's just that it's impossible now."

"An injunction?" Couton said, nodding. "We understand that. We have been obeying Berrigan's injunctions for centuries. Perhaps the situation will change?"

"Perhaps?" Meer asked, her voice low and hopeful.

He patted her hand self-consciously, suddenly painfully aware of the odd articulation and the soft, almost invisible coating of down. "Perhaps," he said, feeling completely defeated by the situation.

He finally took his leave, pausing to talk with Meer at the door, and returned to the encampment. He fell asleep, feeling vaguely disturbed and more . . . vaguely disappointed.

The noon staff meeting the next day proved disturbing. "One of the problems," Gerhardt said, "is that in spite of our greater purification capacity, yields of EDA are off by about eighteen per cent."

"Have you run an analysis of the keelgrass we're getting?" Windom asked.

"Of course. That seems to be the problem. The natives rely heavily on phosphate and inorganic nitrate fertilizers they get from mines to the west. Now that they have been diverting a good portion of their farm land to the grass, they're forced to use land that's been heavily fertilized grass for centuries."

"That stuff is a weed," Royce objected.

"That's true," Gerhardt said, "and weeds are highly adaptive. The keelgrass adapts to a high nitrogen soil by producing a diamino analogue of EDA which cuts down on the available EDA itself."

"Then we'll simply have to increase production," Windom said.

"I don't think you realize what that means," Royce said. "We've already in the past three weeks diverted a large part of their labor force and a good portion of their arable land to our purposes. To increase that demand might be dangerous to them."

"We will not have to make the demand," Windom said somewhat smugly. "They'll do it willingly."

"Dammit, I won't have you jeopardize the lives of hundreds of innocent natives to carry out this mission."

"Mr. Gerhardt," Windom said, "will you leave us?"

As soon as the Chief Engineer had departed, Windom whirled on Royce. "Mister Royce, I respect your humanitarian concerns but the fact remains that I will willingly sacrifice the lives of thousands of backward natives to save an advanced culture such as the one we have planted on Aldebaran II. You can call that cynical or inhuman or what have you, but the choice is simple enough. It is a choice that I'm empowered to make."

"You bastard, Windom," Royce said; "you're a devil." He rose to leave.

"All effective men at times are devils," Windom said wryly, "and it's Mr. Windom, if you don't mind, Mr. Royce."

Royce stalked out in disgust.

The crude wooden monorail brought in fresh keelgrass from the north and west each day. Some of the outlying dairy islands were now involved in the effort and as the weeks wore on into the second month, the racks of fermenting keelgrass mounted around the extractors and countercurrent towers. Royce shuttled back to the ship the fifth week to report and confer with Captain Grek. The man's lidded eyes were cold and emotionless but Royce noted an undercurrent of concern about him.

"Mr. Royce," Grek said at last, "as you know, my own race has quite a history of exploitation at the hands of the parent stock."

"Yes," Royce said.

"A most shameful history, if I may say so?"

"I agree," Royce said.

"What I see happening below is very much the same kind of exploitation. Whole cities to the north have now been abandoned and are deteriorating as the inhabitants moved to the harvesting work camps."

"This is not something we requested," Royce said.

"Nevertheless, this is what is happening."

Royce returned troubled and mentioned it to Windom. Windom said, "No, I didn't expect that, but I'm not surprised."

"Surely you can put a stop to it," Royce said.

"And miss our goal?" Windom demanded. "I think not."

Royce first heard of the famine in the north from Meer in the seventh week. On impulse he had again met her on the Street of Reeds after her vigil at the Archives. "I would invite you to late feeding," she said, "but we have little enough these days."

"You always seemed to be self-sufficient on your world," he said, dreading the answer.

"Still we are better off than the north people, many of whom have died in the past two weeks."

"But why?" he demanded.

"You arrived at the start of the harvest," she said. "Naturally when we heard of your need, we destroyed the crops and turned the land to the grass."

"You destroyed your food?" he asked.

"Naturally. It was necessary."

"I'm sorry," he said, touching her. "I'm terribly sorry."

She looked up at him and said, "It is what we wanted to do. We wanted to please you." She paused and looked at the ground. "Only I seem not to please you."

"No, that's not true," he said, feeling the tense stirring in his being.

She shook her head without speaking and suddenly quite on impulse he leaned over and kissed her. She responded in a complete fashion, pressing into him, passive and yet somehow aggressive. He felt his hands reach out, follow the primordial route, and then . . .

"My father is gone tonight," she said. "Come . . ."

He let himself be drawn silently through the dark streets to the door of her home and inside and then he was engulfed in quite the most intense sensation he had ever experienced in his life.

When early morning came, he left her just at the first touch of light on the horizon. All the way back, he walked in a dazed inner contemplation of what had happened. Over and over in his mind the same phrase recurred. That's the way it should be. That's the way it was meant to be.

He saw her regularly in the next two weeks but the intensity of his involvement with her was tainted with the knowledge of what their coming had now done to her people. He had never seen anything quite like the natives of Berrigan's World and their almost monomaniacal efforts to please the foreigners. New fields were destroyed for the keelgrass and the fermenting racks proliferated across the plain. To make room for them some of the nearer buildings of the city were destroyed.

And all around, day by day, he saw the effects of their wanton disregard for their own wellbeing. The men who brought the great carts of grass were now gaunt and hollow-eyed and moved with increasing slowness. The news of growing famines in the north and now the west came to him. The *Deneb*'s officer reported that some of the workers were now showing definite signs of malnutrition. The speed with which the famine and other associated diseases developed in the ninth week surprised him. The medical officer assured him that this was quite in line with the accelerated metabolism of the natives, however.

Finally he sought out Windom again in protest. "We can't go on this way," Royce said. "We're destroying their whole society."

"We can remedy the damage," Windom said. "The important thing is that we must have our five thousand kilos within the next two weeks."

"The whole social structure of the planet could collapse by then. Don't you realize what is happening?"

Windom turned on him with a look of anger. It was the first time, Royce realized, that he had seen him show the emotion. "Yes, Mr. Royce, I know what is happening and it's no more pleasant to me than it is to you. The fact remains that you and I have a duty that transcends what is happening here."

"I'll protest to Prime," Royce threatened. "What we're embarked on now amounts to genocide."

"Look, Mister," Windom said slowly. "Don't confuse your personal emotions with your duties. Oh, yes, I know all about your little dalliance. If you want to endanger your career . . . well, that's your business, but you will not endanger my mission."

"Or your efficiency report at Prime," Royce sneered.

"If that's what you believe," Windom said. "It doesn't matter. The only thing that matters is that we will have our supply of biologicals in time to save millions. Then we will do what is necessary to repair the damage we have done here."

"I'm sure the Captain will have something to say about this," Royce snapped.

"I have already briefed the Captain on the realities of our situation," Windom said. "I thought it necessary as you became more deeply involved here."

"He can't allow this to happen, not a man with the Captain's background."

"He is fully in agreement with my actions," Windom said.

Royce made his way as quickly as he could to the communications hut and videoed the Captain. Grek's blue face was pained but he shook his head sadly. "Mr. Royce, there are certain data just made available to me that alter the whole complexion of the operation. However, I promise you that you and your party will leave within two weeks."

"After how much damage?" Royce demanded.

"I have already contacted Prime," Captain Grek said. "Three ships are on the way with supplies and equipment for quickly restoring the status quo."

"While a great many people will die."

"It is necessary, I'm sorry to say," Grek said sadly.

He spent that night with Meer and told her of what had happened. "I don't understand your people," he said. "Why do they do this?"

"There is no other way. It has to be that way," she said. "You know there is nothing I would not do to please you."

"Will you leave with me when we go?" he asked.

"Berrigan's injunction says—"

"Damn Berrigan's injunction," he snapped. "There's precedent for this sort of thing. I can get Prime's permission."

"I can't leave unless it is recorded in the Archives," she said.

"What does that mean?"

"We go and join our names in the Archives. It is the only time any one other than the Senior's family is ever allowed there."

"We would have to wait on my world to be married," he said.

"In our eyes we would already be so," she said. She sank her head softly on his shoulders and sighed. "It would be what I want most."

"Then I'll prepare a request for Prime's permission," he said. "First thing tomorrow," he added dreamily.

Yet it was almost a week before he could bring himself to do so. He knew that the request would probably be granted. Yet he preferred a direct request which would take days longer rather than going through channels and the captain. Somehow he found himself very reluctant to take this route, especially since it would probably come to Mr. Windom's attention.

By now the effects of the northern famine were all too apparent in their area. News of the plagues and widespread disease in the west came to his morning briefing and Royce grew progressively more angry. Along with this was the insistent feeling of guilt. He argued with himself that this was the reason why he had not pursued the petition to Prime.

He had one final confrontation with Windom. "Dammit," he said, "we have almost all of the five thousand kilos now. Where are your relief ships?"

"They'll be here," Windom assured him.

"With all of your vaunted skill in planning, they should have been here weeks ago."

"Mr. Royce," Windom said slowly with an unexpected gentleness in his voice, "I understand all of your concern, probably more than you realize. Grant me that I am not an evil man. Do that at least. I came here as you did with a limited knowledge of the society we were asking to help us. It's been only in the last few weeks that Prime has finally acquainted me with the complete profile of these people. So much has been buried in the old records."

"I fail to see how this excuses your genocidic tactics," Royce said.

"I would have done what I did regardless," Windom said. "I would have prepared to repair the damage sooner, had I known how profound the effect of our visit would be."

"Knowing you, I find this hard to believe," Royce said.

"It doesn't matter," Windom said. "What does matter is that you are a young officer with an unusual second-in-command for one of your age and the beginning of a promising career that may well lead you to the very top. You've shown considerable ability and intelligence and you're now prepared to discard much of this for a transitory emotion."

"Spare me your deep concern," Royce said, scarcely bothering that his full contempt was showing.

"We need men who have wide command abilities," Windom said slowly. "They're few enough considering the sprawling multiples of worlds we must police and administer. You're just that to me, Mr. Royce: good material about to be destroyed."

"Thank you for placing me in proper perspective," Royce snapped. "I seem to fit well into the pragmatic scheme you've ordered for the Berringers and the rest of the galaxy."

Before Windom could say more, he left. It was growing dark as he left the encampment and made his way angrily to Meer's home. Couton met him at the door and offered the ritual gestures of hospitality. The man looked drawn and weak. God, Royce thought, doesn't even the Senior get food?

"Meer," he said to her, "can it be tonight?"

She came up to him and he held her close, alarmed at the way the flesh now seemed to hug her oddly-shaped ribcase. He could feel every bone; yet there was still something sensual and overwhelming about her.

"Yes," she said. "Now, if you wish."

"Now," he said.

"I must come also, of course," Couton said. "It is the only time I am allowed in the Archives." Royce nodded and waited while Couton and his daughter found wraps against the early night chill. They made their way through the Street of Reeds and finally to the square.

"You must follow the path," Meer said, and led the way. They walked the deep parabolic path set in the stones toward the brooding monolith that was the Archives.

At the broad steps ascending into the black maw of the building, Royce felt a sudden sense of panic. "It's very dark," he said.

"There are always lamps burning inside," Meer said, and led the way up the stairs.

They entered and he found himself in a single large room that stretched the full height of the building. There were several shrouded alcoves on either side. It was much like entering a darkened cathedral with dim flickering tallow lamps stationed along the walls. They moved past glassed cases of instruments whose intent Royce could not define. All of them had an air of the antique about them. Finally they stopped before a dais and Meer ascended to a large sprawling platform where a single manuscript book lay open. Behind the platform, half shrouded in shadows, Royce saw rank on rank of similar books; enough, he thought, to trace the bloodlines of the planet back through the centuries to the original colonists.

"I had already selected the appropriate Archive," Meer said. She motioned him forward and as he stood by her side, she took a simple reed pen and began to inscribe her name on a separate page. At her instructions he did the same and in the far left margin Couton finally added a witnessing notation.

"Is that all there is to it?" he asked.

"That is all," she said.

"No ceremony?"

"I told you that the Archives were not religious," she said.

He felt distinctly relieved.

"We will make one final formality to the founder," Couton said.

"To Berrigan?" he asked.

"To Berrigan and the founder," she said and led the way down the dais. They walked back the way they came and at a juncture turned. In an alcove the full height of the building they stopped while Couton came forward and began to light torches on each side of the passageway.

He waited as the flames leaped and defined the great statue occupying the alcove. It was the massive idealized figure of an earthman ... Berrigan, Royce supposed, standing heroic and stern, looking down at a group of figures that assumed the attitude of children.

There were a whole series, culminating in two heroic figures smaller than Berrigan, but clearly human. A woman of remarkable beauty linked hand in hand to a man of similar beauty. The sculpture was quite remarkable, a labor of years, only ...

Only it was the lesser figures that occupied his gaze. The smaller figures growing larger, changing definition until they merged with the heroic couple and then ...

The knowledge was like a physical blow. He turned and moved rapidly away, feeling suddenly the panic, the fear that he had not felt for years.

Behind him Meer called, "Wait, wait," but he could not stop.

The party from the *Deneb* must have entered silently. Quite against regulations they were suddenly there, three senior officers including the Medical Officer and Mr. Windom.

"I had to stop this," Windom said.

"Let me alone," he said, half in hysteria and tried to push past them. In the next instant the Medical Officer had touched his arm with an impulse syringe and he was sinking into Mr. Gerhardt's arms. From a great distance he heard Mr. Windom say, "What a damn waste. What a damn terrible waste."

His first impression when he awoke aboard the *Deneb* was of the bluish face of Captain Grek, leaning close. "I think he is awake, Doctor," Grek said and he felt gentle fingers touching his forehead. His consciousness seemed to clear quickly at that point.

"I'm glad you're well again," Captain Grek said. "These indigenous diseases can be pretty bad after several centuries of isolation."

"Disease?" he asked.

"Apparently viral," the *Deneb*'s medical officer said in a lofty manner and moved away.

"I think that must have been the problem, don't you think?" Mr. Windom said, coming into view. When Royce said nothing Windom continued, "You'll be glad to know that three ships are landing emergency forces at this moment. They will take perhaps two months to restore the social and ecological balance of Berrigan's World. The probe with our five thousand kilos of EDA has been dispatched at ten light speed to Aldebaran II and we are on our way back to base."

"That's fine," Royce said quietly. "Will Berrigan's World ever be the same?"

"As near as we can make it," Windom said. "After that, of course, it will be forever quarantined against human contact."

"Quarantined?"

"It's the only moral solution Prime will accept."

"That's an odd morality," he said, remembering Meer and the feeling of loss.

"What other solution do you have? A race of natural slaves? Any human may command them and they will destroy themselves carrying out a human's wishes."

"I suppose so," he said. "It's probably the only way."

He felt Windom's hand on his shoulder. "I haven't saved you from your foolishness for yourself. We need bright young men and in spite of all this you're worth saving."

"Thank you," he said. "I don't suppose that there'll ever be a chance that. . . ."

"Would you really want such a wife?" Windom asked.

"No, not really. It was a pretty fantasy, but not really."

"Besides, the quarantine. We only realized with what we were dealing in the last weeks, as I told you. Berrigan was truly a remarkable man, a bitter warped man, but a remarkable one."

"Yes," Royce said sadly, "more bitter than anyone

knew. Who would have thought that he would set out alone with such a remarkable plan?"

"For him it made sense," Captain Grek said. "He had grown to loathe his own race."

"Yes," Windom said. "It seemed perfectly logical. Why not populate the new world with the one race he loved and admired. Why not people a whole new world with mutated dogs?"

"Yes," Royce said, feeling lost and somehow cheated. "I suppose it makes a great deal of sense."

# THEMES

(1) After watching the televised torture-murder of his/her lover, the protagonist must devise a communication system for the revolutionary underground in a society tyrannized by complete electronic surveillance.

(2) The protagonist is the manager of a vast megalopolis that is breaking down because of transportation failure. Protagonist has commissioned a research group to solve the problem. The group comes up with the answer, a form of instantaneous matter transmission. The manager is aware of the decaying quality of life in the city. Shall the protagonist use the invention to prolong the existence and growth of the impractical city or, knowing that the proper use of the invention will render cities unnecessary, can he/she devise a scheme for using the invention to reverse the whole social trend?

(3) The protagonist, a biochemist, is faced with the problem of releasing a newly discovered serum that confers near-immortality. The only problem is that it does not stop the normal aging process.

(4)   In a society critically overpopulated, all citizens suffering from chronic, debilitating, or terminal diseases are subject to euthanasia. The protagonist, involved in a love-hate triangle, discovers that one of the other two members has successfully concealed a chronic disease.

(5)   Through a destructive act, the protagonist becomes involved with an alien, unaware that because of their different natures, their relationship will destroy one or the other of them.

(6)   The protagonist is part of a starship party rediscovering a planet settled years ago by a misanthropic molecular biologist and party. Protagonist falls in love with a native only to discover that all inhabitants of the planet are not human but rather mutated domestic animals.

*BALLANTINE BOOKS BRINGS YOU*

# STAR TREK

——◆——

## THE MAKING OF STAR TREK
### Stephen E. Whitfield • Gene Roddenberry

The book on how to write for TV! The complete story on how the *U.S.S. Enterprise* was designed, the original concept behind the show, backgrounds of the characters—the whole authentic history.

## THE WORLD OF STAR TREK
### David Gerrold

Here are the worlds of Star Trek: Gene Roddenberry's brilliant conception; the show itself and the people who created it —the writers, the stars, the technicians; the fans—the world the show created.

## THE TROUBLE WITH TRIBBLES
### David Gerrold

The full story of one of Star Trek's most popular episodes from first draft to final shooting of the script.

*Each book contains photos!*

To order by mail, send $1.50 per book plus 25¢ per order for handling to Ballantine Cash Sales, P.O. Box 505, Westminster, Maryland 21157. Please allow three weeks for delivery.

# SELECTIONS FROM THE PUBLISHER
## OF THE BEST SCIENCE FICTION
## IN THE WORLD

———◆———